Praise for *Good Sam*

"Meserve's narrative has a . . . dry wit and well-conceived dialogue throughout. Kate's relatable qualities of self-reliance tinged with vulnerability drive this gratifying mystery-romance about finding the good guys—and knowing when to recognize them."

—*Publishers Weekly*

"In her debut novel, Meserve writes a . . . solid feel-good romance sparked with mystery."

—*Kirkus Reviews*

"If you are a Nicholas Sparks or Richard Paul Evans fan, I'm betting you will like author Meserve's book *Good Sam*. Uplifting, heart wrenching, and a two-hankie read, this story is a winner."

—Cheryl Stout, Amazon Top 1000 reviewer and Vine Voice

"This story has everything from suspense to drama. And the heartfelt ending had us smiling for days."

—*First for Women* magazine

Praise for *Perfectly Good Crime*

"A first-rate and undaunted protagonist easily carries this brisk tale. Kate is intuitive and professional, but it's her steadfast compassion that makes her truly remarkable."

—*Kirkus Reviews*

"Dete Meserve delivers a novel that is simultaneously mysterious, fascinating, and inspiring."

—Buzzfeed.com

"A feel-good mystery . . . an enjoyable escape."

—BookLife Prize in Fiction

"In a novel saturated with unexpected twists and shocking motives, Kate Bradley follows clues—and her heart—to discover that some crimes have powerfully good intentions."

—*Sunset* magazine

Praise for *The Space Between*

"Chiseled prose gleefully weaves the protagonist through bombshells . . . a labyrinth of plot and character motivations makes for a thoroughly enjoyable novel."

—*Kirkus Reviews*

"*The Space Between* is a fast-paced novel that combines the best elements of suspense and romance. In this story of a broken marriage, Dete Meserve uses the mysteries of the universe to keep you on the edge of your seat as she weaves a tale that winds its way through the past and present to bring about a truly satisfying conclusion. Highly recommended."

—*USA Today* bestselling author Bette Lee Crosby

"From tragedy to triumph, Dete Meserve's new novel took me on a roller-coaster ride I'll not soon forget. Coupling the mysteries of the night sky with an unthinkable domestic situation, this tale is stunning and unlike any I've read. *The Space Between* is a must must must read!"

—Heather Burch, bestselling author of *In the Light of the Garden*

"As captivating and complex as the night skies that feature in *The Space Between*, this is a thrilling read. A precipitous shift in perceived reality causes everything past and present to be suspect. Meserve skillfully crafts all the elements of a superbly suspenseful page-turner."

—Patricia Sands, bestselling author of the Love in Provence series

"Dete Meserve's *The Space Between* has it all. It is a story written with a knowledge of space, realistic characters you want to root for, romance, and a mystery with a satisfying ending. I predict that after you read the book, you'll gaze at the stars and think of them in a new way."

—Judith Keim, bestselling author of the Fat Fridays series

"Woven with the stars, this is an incredible story of love, betrayal, and the infinite power of hope. Suspenseful to almost the last page; I couldn't put it down."

—Andrea Hurst, author of *Always with You*

"Dete Meserve's *The Space Between* hits all of the sweet spots: a smart and engaging female lead, an intriguing mystery, and elements of danger and suspense sure to keep readers turning pages long past bedtime. If you're a fan of Nicholas Sparks or Kerry Lonsdale, grab this book!"

—Kes Trester, author of *A Dangerous Year*

"With the starry heavens as a backdrop, Meserve spins a fast-paced story about astronomer Sarah Mayfield as she questions everything she believes to be true in the space between the heartache of her rocky marriage and the mystery surrounding her husband's disappearance. This is Meserve's best work yet, a romance wrapped in suspense that will keep readers guessing until the very end."

—Christine Nolfi, bestselling author of *Sweet Lake* and *The Comfort of Secrets*

THE
GOOD
STRANGER

ALSO BY DETE MESERVE

Good Sam

Perfectly Good Crime

The Space Between

Random Acts of Kindness (with Rachel Greco)

THE GOOD STRANGER

A KATE BRADLEY MYSTERY

DETE MESERVE

LAKE UNION
PUBLISHING

Published by Lake Union Publishing, Seattle
www.apub.com

Amazon, the Amazon logo, and Lake Union Publishing are trademarks of Amazon.com, Inc., or its affiliates.

ISBN-13: 9781542004701
ISBN-10: 1542004705

Cover design by Caroline Teagle Johnson

Printed in the United States of America

For my father

CHAPTER ONE

The high-pitched alarm pierced my sleep, jolting me awake. Five more alarms screeched, squeezed on me from all sides, scrambling my thoughts.

I grabbed my phone. Groped in the blackness for my shoes and shoved my feet into them.

A baby was crying.

Voices shouted in the hall, but I couldn't make out what they were saying. Someone banged on my door, insistent.

My body suddenly felt heavy, weighed down by a wave of foreboding.

I raced into the hallway, where the alarms wailed, louder now, slamming into my eardrums.

Empty.

My heart jackhammered. I yanked open the heavy front door and hurried outside into a downpour. Sharp needles of rain pelted my skin, drenching my flimsy pajamas in seconds. Water swirled around my feet, soaking through my shoes.

A pudgy man in a black T-shirt shouted at me from the bottom of the stairs, "You waiting on an invitation? Get out of there!"

I scurried down the steps and sprinted past a heap of black garbage bags on the sidewalk, then ran across the street to join a group huddled under a skinny tree.

"Did anyone see Artie?" a woman in faded plaid pajamas was saying, eyes darting. "I didn't see him come out."

"My cat is still inside," the blonde woman next to me whispered, her face wet with tears.

My pulse pounded. "Has anyone called 911?"

A large guy in a shabby gray bathrobe raced out of the building. "It's a false alarm!" he shouted. "I checked every floor. No smoke. No fire."

The pajama woman crossed her arms. "I'm not going back in until the fire department says it's okay."

"Suit yourself," the bathrobe guy said. Up close, he looked older than I had originally thought, forty maybe, with dark-olive skin and a week's worth of black stubble. He glanced at me. "You the new neighbor?"

"Kate Bradley," I answered, sweeping damp hair from my face.

"Raymond Cruz." He grasped my hand in a death grip. "Heard you're from LA and—"

His words were drowned out by the loud blast of a horn and the scream of sirens as an FDNY fire engine barreled up the narrow street.

He popped a stick of gum in his mouth. "Welcome to Manhattan, Kate."

∽

I was ready for battle.

My leather tote was loaded with electronics: a laptop, a digital voice recorder—even though I had a recording app on my phone—and noise-canceling headphones. Gear: running shoes, an umbrella, a small makeup case. And a journalist's armor: pens, notebooks, a cell phone. A cup of coffee buzzed through my veins, and I clutched another one in my hand. I'd already scrolled through the morning's headlines, checked Twitter, and texted my boss, the EVP of news at American News Channel, about a story I hoped to cover on my first day as a national news correspondent.

Squeezed on a Fifth Avenue sidewalk packed with a sea of people and with my earbuds at full volume, I was immersed in a rapid run-down of the day's lead stories.

That's when I saw them.

The little girl with a blonde ponytail giggled as she bounced up and down on her dad's shoulders, high above the throng. Clutching a balloon in her chubby hand, she pointed at the glittering window displays.

My eyes met hers, and I flashed her a smile.

This was how I'd always imagined the idyllic wonderland known as Manhattan. Glorious blue skies and puffy white clouds on a summer morning. Smartly dressed people heading to do important work after grabbing breakfast on an outdoor patio bustling with waiters bringing trays of inspired dishes.

Then a sudden whoosh of movement and the scrape of tumbling metal. The next thing I knew I was flat on my stomach, hit by a force so hard it knocked the wind out of me. My bag followed me, spilling its contents across the sidewalk. My coffee cup tumbled a second later, hitting the pavement, then bouncing into the gutter.

I watched a guy on a green bike whiz ahead and snake his way through the crowd, but it took me two full seconds to register that he was the one who had knocked me over.

"Hey!" I tried shouting, but it sounded thin. Weak.

A canvas bag brushed the back of my head. A still-smoldering ciga-rette landed beside me. The crush of commuters and tourists journeying the avenue that morning kept going, stepping around me as though I were simply an obstacle on the busy sidewalk, not a person who might need help.

I tried gathering the lipstick, pens, and keys that had spilled from my bag, dodging the feet of passersby—and two massive dogs—to grab at them. But as I knelt on the sidewalk stuffing everything back into my bag, I was engulfed by the foul smell of the sewer just a few feet away. Putrid, the odor was so potent I felt a wave of nausea.

I should have . . .

I should have what? Had eyes in the back of my head? I should have focused on the people and cart-pushing vendors around me, not the girl with the balloon?

I should have worn something with more padding.

"Hey, are you all right?" a man asked.

I looked up, but he was backlit by sunlight, so I couldn't see his face. He extended a hand and helped lift me to my feet.

He eyed something on the ground and then disappeared from my view before returning seconds later clutching a set of keys.

"These yours?"

It took me a moment to recognize them. The simple key ring, graced with an enamel palm tree and surfboard charms, was a gift from my friend Teri so that I would always remember Southern California, where I had lived up until two days ago. And although the keys dangling from the chain were tired brass, they were new to me: one for the new apartment and a smaller one for the mailbox.

"Thank you." I took the key from him, my hands still stinging from where they'd slammed against the pavement.

He shifted his position on the sidewalk to make way for a guy in a suit yelling into his phone, and I got a good look at him. Yankees ball cap. Blue eyes beneath dark eyebrows. Muscular arms under a black T-shirt. Serious running shoes. For a moment, I thought his face looked familiar, but I blamed that effect on the fall.

"Can I get you a cab?"

"I'm good." I pointed up the street. "Just a few more blocks to go . . ."

4

A woman pushing a double stroller barreled toward us, so I moved aside to let her pass.

He handed me an unopened bottle of water. "Want me to walk with you?"

"I'm fine. Really. But thank you."

"Okay then." His eyes took me in. For the brief moment he studied my face, I thought he might have recognized me. That happened a lot in Los Angeles, where I'd been on TV as a Channel Eleven reporter for seven years. But I hadn't even filed my first report on ANC.

"Glad I could help," he said, then watched me go.

ANC's newsroom was filled with a steady hum, a murmur of electronics coming from row upon row of computers on every desk and an array of TV monitors that lined the walls throughout the cavern of a room. Mixed in with the thrum were hurried discussions and the soft scuff of producers and reporters rushing across the vast carpeted landscape.

I drew in a deep breath, trying to steady my jittery nerves. After years covering breaking local news—violence, disasters, and tragedy— in Los Angeles, I'd dreamed of working at a national news network. And here I was, recruited by ANC's executive vice president, Andrew Wright.

"Only the elite survive there," my former boss, David Dyal, had warned me. "You're fearless, but you're not ready for the kind of politics and competition a place like that serves up every day."

I was planning to prove him wrong.

Still rattled by the fall on Fifth Avenue, I felt nervous energy churn in the pit of my stomach as I wound my way through the aisles in search of my assignment editor, Mark Galvin. At least fifty reporters were seated in the open area, but unlike in the Channel Eleven newsroom in LA, no one turned to greet me. And the few who even glanced in my direction went on with their work without even a nod, as though I were just another cog in the vast ANC machine.

An intern had told me I'd find Mark at the "Hornet's Nest," also known as the assignment desk, and it didn't take me long to spot it. The iconic blue letters—ANC Headquarters—loomed large at the front of the room. Positioned below the sign, beneath banks of monitors and fortressed behind a low wall of signature royal blue, was a line of stressed-looking assignment editors. Even from a distance, I could feel the tension and frustration as they tried to direct and appease the news directors, producers, reporters, and cameramen gathered around them.

"You're Kate Bradley, aren't you?"

I whirled around.

"Jeremy Whitfield." Dressed in a midnight-blue suit and matching tie, Jeremy had thick black hair combed tightly to his head and a carefully groomed beard. "White House reporter—I've interviewed your father a few times. With all the battles about the budget and possible shutdown, he's on everyone's interview list these days."

"I have a hard time getting on his call list too," I said with a laugh.

"What brings you to ANC?"

"I work here. Today's my first day."

He shot me a look of surprise. "Our lucky day then. Let me take you to lunch while I'm in town. Let's team up together on a few stories. You probably have some good insight and connections on the Homeland Security bill that's stuck in Congress. And it'd be fascinating to hear what it's like to be a senator's daughter."

I drew a deep breath. "I'm not here covering politics."

"You're not?" He raised his voice. "Then what are you covering?"

"Crime and justice."

He looked at me as if I'd grown two heads. "You're not covering politics?"

"It was nice meeting you, Jeremy."

As I started to walk away, he called out to me, "So, is that yes to lunch?"

I glanced at him over my shoulder. "It's a no. But thanks for the invite."

I found Mark Galvin in the Hornet's Nest a few minutes later, but unlike Jeremy, he didn't seem happy to meet me. In fact, he looked a bit unhinged, his bristly gray hair tufted oddly on one side as though he'd just gotten out of bed.

"You're late," he said without looking up from his iPad.

"Andrew Wright said I should come in at nine instead of—"

"Andrew may be the head of this division, but he doesn't set the hours for my reporters."

"Got it. But Andrew did say I should—"

"Name-dropping may get you something with other folks here, but not with me."

"I was just trying to say that—"

"I know," he said, his tone sharpening. "You and my boss are old pals. Your father's a US senator. But when you're working here, you're going to be treated like every other reporter on my team."

He looked up then, fixing a pair of steely-gray eyes on me. Their downward slope made him look like he was perpetually disappointed.

"Got it."

"Your desk is by Stephanie over there." He pointed off to a wide swath of desks to the right, but I decided against asking for more specifics. "I need you to work up a story on the Homeland Security bill that's at an impasse in Congress."

"Homeland Security."

"Yeah, you are up on that, aren't you?"

For a minute, I thought he might be joking, but his thin lips were fixed in a tight, flat line.

"Of course."

"Maybe you can call your dad and ask him what it's going to take to get the sixty votes they need." He drew a big *X* through whatever he had been reading on his iPad. "Welcome to ANC."

⁓

"Sixteen people shot in under seven hours yesterday," Stephanie said as I laid my bag on my desk, in a surprisingly spacious cubicle not far from the Hornet's Nest. "All over the city: Bronx, Queens, Brooklyn. Insanity." She rose from her chair. "Stephanie Nakamura."

"Kate Bradley." I extended my hand.

Stephanie was a classic network-news beauty: chin-length dark hair, high cheekbones, and flawless skin. This morning she was dressed for off-camera work: skinny jeans, a long-sleeved white cotton top, and black boots, Prada maybe.

"I'm on deadline for a piece on the uptick in violence in New York and other major cities. Guessing they put you on the political hamster wheel?"

"Apparently. Even though that's not what Andrew promised me."

"I wouldn't bank on whatever promises he made," she said, frowning. "The news always comes first in Andrew's world. What we reporters want is . . . well, let's just say it's further down the list of priorities."

"I didn't cover politics when I was in LA, and I don't plan to be covering it here . . ."

She flashed me a wry smile. "You think that, with the ten to fifteen White House and congressional story lines happening every day, they're going to assign Senator Bradley's daughter something else besides political stories?"

I felt the heat rise to my face. "Most of my experience has been in breaking news. I broke the Good Sam story a while back. And then the Robin Hood story—"

"That's why you made it this far. But you know who had that desk of yours? Bryan Griggs. He covered major stories like the Las Vegas shooting, Weinstein, OJ's release from prison. One of the best. Pressured Andrew and Mark for more freedom on the stories he covered, and now . . ." She lowered her voice. "He's not working here anymore."

I swallowed hard. "I can handle anything these guys throw my way. I had a tough assignment editor and hard-ass news bosses in LA."

In the blue-white light of the newsroom, Stephanie's face had an almost ghostly glow. "Not like this, you haven't."

CHAPTER TWO

Sirens blared as I walked back from the ANC studios that day, plodding three blocks on packed sidewalks to the subway. The ambulances' earsplitting wails were only part of the aural assault—backhoes digging up a foundation on a new apartment building, a deafening rat-a-tat of jackhammers at another building site a block away, and a rhythmic banging, metal on metal, that ricocheted off the brick and echoed in the streets.

After a face-melting, hair-frizzing ride on the cramped subway, I stepped out into the fading sunlight and headed into the crosswalk. A taxi driver honked and screamed at me in a language I didn't understand. But its meaning was clear: *Hurry up. Move. Idiot.*

Impatience rode on air thick with car fumes. A red-faced man with a thick beard barreled out of an electronics store shouting into his cell phone. Maybe a business deal that had gone sour. A bad breakup. Hard to tell. I stepped out of his way and nearly fell against a bus waiting at the stoplight. It wheezed loudly, spewing warm exhaust in my face.

When I finally reached the apartment, sweaty and tired, I sighed. But not with relief. Instead of taking the corporate suite ANC had offered me, I'd agreed to sublet this apartment for two months as a favor to my best friend from college, Janet, so she could move to Denver with her boyfriend. Our arrangement would save them $3,000 a month in unused rent and give me a chance to figure out where in NYC I wanted to live. Besides, Janet had assured me, it was near an all-night newsstand, a block away from the most heavenly tapas, and down the street from the "best cheese and beer shop in America."

No good deed goes unpunished.

The 645-square-foot apartment in the heart of Chelsea was newly renovated but hardly deluxe. Perhaps the landlords hoped the floors looked like hardwood, but anyone with eyesight could see they were cheap vinyl. And the cabinets and shelves were made of flimsy pressboard, the kind that should've had a two-month expiration date. The apartment's only redeeming feature was two big windows that let in a lot of natural light, even if the view wasn't great—a close-up of the apartment building across the street.

Raymond, my friend from the night before, had plopped his hulking frame in the center of the concrete front steps and was wearing an orange T-shirt that read, "Safety First."

"Tell him to stop leaving the gate open, damn it!" he yelled into his phone.

He nodded at me but didn't move. "And he better not take the brand-new Black & Deckers off-site either!"

I squeezed past him, then unlocked the building's front door and was immediately overpowered by a strong odor in the hallway. A rotten-egg stench I recognized as steamed broccoli, but intense, like someone was cooking an entire field of it.

I turned the key in the lock to my apartment, but the wooden door, swollen by the humidity, wouldn't open. I slammed a shoulder on the door a couple of times until it finally budged. At this rate, by the time I moved out of this apartment in two months, my shoulders would be strong enough to earn me a place on the New York Jets.

I slumped into the couch. Instead of the familiar trio of palm trees that swayed outside my window in LA, my new view consisted of a brown brick apartment building. One particular window—framed in sagging yet colorful Christmas lights, even though it was August—caught my eye. A woman sat by the window, eating noodles in a hazy pool of light from a small lamp. Alone.

My cell chimed. I smiled when I saw Eric's photo flash up on the screen.

"Hey," I murmured. "I miss you."

His voice was warm, thick with emotion. "Me too. It feels like forever since you left. I don't sleep well without you."

"Same." I heard engines idling in the background. Voices shouting. "Where are you?"

"I'm up at the Warner fire."

"The one near Sacramento?" Anxiety crept into my veins. That massive fire was so destructive it had been all over the national news today.

"Yeah. They called in our search-rescue team yesterday for what we thought would be a couple of days, but this fire is deadly. It's like a war zone here."

I padded across the room to turn on the AC unit. It whined, then groaned to life. "ANC reported that the fire has already destroyed three thousand homes. You okay?"

"I'm surviving on beef jerky and one-hour naps."

"But you're safe?"

I could feel his smile through the phone. "I'm safe." His voice cracked. "But it looks like we're gonna be here awhile. Ten days. Maybe longer."

I didn't hide my disappointment. "Ten days. How did your talk with FDNY go yesterday?"

"Not good. The fire chief put in a good word for me high up in the chain of command, but it's still gonna take years to get trained and certified in search-rescue there. And the work they had hoped to give me training their fire teams in swift-water rescue hasn't been approved. The chief says it's stuck in a bunch of red tape and could be a year or more before it gets authorized."

"A year," I said softly. "But could you start some kind of work at FDNY before that? Once you get here?"

"Doesn't look like it."

I heard something steal into his voice. Something I'd been hearing ever since he'd promised to join me in New York: sadness.

"All I've ever wanted, everything I dreamed about, only matters if you're with me," he had said when I'd told him about the ANC offer. Then, on a starlit night, he agreed to come with me to Manhattan. "This is me starting an adventure. With you."

But the words we say don't always mirror what we end up doing. Even if we are certain we mean them. The world shifts in ways we can't predict. Dreams collide and break us apart.

Love is not always enough.

∽

The impending government shutdown was keeping my dad so busy that all my calls to his cell went to voice mail. Even the call I placed at close to midnight a few nights ago went unanswered until the next morning. Eventually, he responded by texting me that he'd call me later in the day. Then he didn't.

At least I didn't have to worry that something had happened to him. I saw his image flash up periodically on the monitors in the ANC newsroom as he issued an occasional sound bite as the Senate majority leader or, earlier in the week, in a meeting with the president.

I didn't keep tabs on my dad's whereabouts otherwise, but apparently Stephanie did.

"Looks like you missed the dinner for the British prime minister at the White House last night?" she asked when I arrived at my desk the next morning.

I laughed. "Yep. Instead, I was here in Manhattan, being blasted by a playlist of Dean Martin's greatest hits from the world's largest speakers."

"Loud neighbors, huh?" She turned her laptop around and pointed at the screen. "Is that your sister?"

I didn't have a sister. And the woman standing next to my father didn't look anything like me. But she was at least a decade younger than my sixty-two-year-old dad, with breezy golden hair that fell in tousled layers just below her shoulders. "Not sure who she is," I said flatly, masking my curiosity.

In the decades my father had spent as a US senator from California, I'd never seen him take a date to a formal government event. My mother died nearly twenty-five years ago, and while I knew he had gone out with several women since then, none of them ever had staying power beyond a few dates.

"Rumor is that the defense secretary just resigned," Mark interrupted, suddenly appearing at my side. "Kate, you got contacts with White House officials who could give us confirmation or detail?"

"I didn't come here to cover—"

He raised his hands, signaling a time-out. "Anyone you can call?"

I frowned. Mark knew I'd covered breaking news in Los Angeles, which would hardly prepare me to have contacts at the White House. Maybe he thought I'd have them because of my dad's political position. More likely, he was trying to make me look bad. "Not off the top of my head."

He stared at me, and although no more words came out of his mouth, his eyes said it all.

What good are you then?

⁓

14

I tried to turn Manhattan into an adventure. I memorized the subway lines. Made lists of all the iconic places I would visit and Broadway shows I'd see when I wasn't working or speed-reading the news or figuring out where to buy groceries or trying to troubleshoot my snail-like Wi-Fi. I'd even tried my hand at a game of chess in Union Square—and lost to a nine-year-old.

Still, being here didn't feel like the adventure I'd imagined.

Thousands of people intersected and intertwined on the streets of Manhattan, yet it felt as though we lived our lives in parallel. On the subway, no one made eye contact. Instead, their glowing faces were consumed with unrequited love for their phones. And when they did look at me, watch out. A woman's bag had its own seat during the packed rush hour, and when I asked if she would move it, she lifted baleful eyes from her phone and said, "Yeah, no."

"Here we go," the guy behind her muttered.

Everywhere I went I was pressured to buy things. Leon the Vietnam Vet—or so his signature T-shirt proclaimed—hawked his "mojo" hot dogs a block from my apartment, shouting at me, "The secret's in the char." A teen wearing long red basketball shorts and a white T-shirt blocked my passage at the top of the subway stairs, imploring me to buy designer sunglasses. But it was a frail Latina with mournful eyes who managed to sell me a snow cone from a pushcart the size of a minifridge, even though I didn't like sweets.

On the subway ride home from work, I made the mistake of scrolling through Instagram. Teri had posted photos from our friend Mayi's thirtieth birthday, a party on Dockweiler Beach. As I scanned the photos of a half dozen of my closest friends, their smiling faces lit by the glow of the bonfire with a fierce orange sun setting over the Pacific Ocean behind them, I felt the ache of loneliness.

I messaged Teri: *Miss all of you.*

CHAPTER THREE

"I've been doing a lot of thinking," Eric was saying on the phone that night.

My stomach lurched. Something in the way he said those words, a tone that was probably undetectable to anyone else, made me think that whatever he was going to say next would be painful to hear.

Anxiety sped through my veins. I wanted to ask him point-blank: *Are you coming to New York?* But I was afraid of the answer. And as long as I didn't ask the question, I could keep pretending. Hoping.

I heard a raspy edge in his voice, as if the words he was saying were causing him physical pain. "People are counting on me here. As much as I might want to, I can't leave."

Might want to. The tiny word had slipped into that sentence, changing everything. But maybe I'd misunderstood. "Maybe in a few weeks then? A month?"

He was silent for a long moment. "This isn't something I wanted to say on the phone. But I think . . . I think it's better to be honest rather than waiting for the right time for us to be together to talk about it. I can't come to New York."

His words sounded final.

"That's not what I was hoping you'd say," I said, mournful, defeated.

I wanted him to fight for me. To tell me all the reasons we had to be together. To propose the sacrifices we'd both make. But even as I wanted that from him, I knew this wasn't his fault. It was mine. I was the one who'd left LA to take a job on the other side of the country. "I'll come back to LA."

His breath was heavy. "Would you really move back?"

And then it was my turn to be honest, and I didn't know how to answer. As frustrating and difficult as Manhattan was, I couldn't see running back to LA after less than a week here. Even though words were the tools of my trade, I suddenly didn't know what to say. Maybe because I was discovering a hidden truth. A realization that loving someone didn't always mean you could build a life with them.

"No, I can't," I said tentatively, then felt tears sting my eyes.

"I get it." His voice broke. "People spend their whole lives searching, hoping to find work they'll love. You've found it."

I swallowed my tears. I knew where this was headed. "Let's not make any decisions right now."

"We can't keep pretending that things are as they used to be, when we both know they aren't."

The silence on the phone was deafening, and my stomach gripped as it continued. Three seconds. Then four. I sat down on the couch, shaking. The room closed in on me.

"It sounds like you've already made up your mind," I said.

"I'm only saying . . ."

I should've accepted the uncertainty of his words. I should have been patient. Instead, I rushed in. "Are you breaking up with me?"

He didn't speak for a long while. And when he did, his voice shook. "I'm sorry . . ."

I let his words hang there. Then I felt my heart crumble, remembering all that I'd loved about him.

My lips suddenly felt thick, too heavy to form words. I imagined the future, and all I could see was black. "How did it come to this?" I asked, wiping tears from my eyes.

His voice sounded far away. "Kate, I'm so sorry . . ."

✹

My whole body was numb.

Although the last place I wanted to be was the newsroom, the next day I threw myself into covering the last-ditch negotiations to avert a government shutdown. For a few moments throughout the day, the story offered a distraction from the breakup. But most of the time, I felt like all the oxygen had been sucked out of the room. A memory of us together would float up, and then my head was spinning. Stringing words together into a story seemed like a hopeless effort.

My reports throughout the day focused on a couple of senators who had stepped into a cloakroom on the Senate floor, frantically trying to map out a strategy on the phone with the White House chief of staff and the vice president.

The "national crime and justice" beat Andrew promised me was thrown on the back burner in favor of a story that could have been on *House of Cards*: quotes from anonymous insiders, dour assessments of odds, the drama and spectacle of procedural bickering, and the play-by-play of the rituals of political negotiation. If aliens had watched the last hour of ANC, they might have assumed that the entire human race was a shouting, arguing circus of anger and hate.

As I trudged back home in the stifling, muggy heat, the city amplified my agitated mood. A block from my apartment, a guy was sitting on a milk crate throwing crumbs at pigeons while a barrel-chested man in a wrinkled white T-shirt yelled at him, something about a taxi. The pigeon feeder kept rambling on about baseball. Meanwhile, everyone around them just kept walking, ignoring them.

At least Leon the Vietnam Vet was in a good mood. "Our mustard's homemade," he tried with a wide grin.

"No thanks. Dumplings tonight."

I held up the still-warm bag from Bao Dumpling House, the place Stephanie swore was New York's most hallowed haven for dumplings and dim sum.

"Good choice."

When I got to my apartment, Raymond had taken over the steps again, this time smoking a cigar. If the sound of a crying baby could be converted to a scent, that was what his stogie smelled like. "No, you're wrong about that," he shouted into the phone. "Louis is gonna take care of it. Tomorrow."

I shuffled around him, only to be stopped by my neighbor from across the hall.

"You have drinking problem?" she said in a thick eastern European accent.

She was barely five feet tall—either forty or seventy, I couldn't tell—with wispy brown hair and thick, doughlike skin and bright-red lips. "What did you say?"

From a bag by her door, she withdrew two empty wine bottles. "I found these in your trash."

"You've been going through my trash?"

"Not on purpose," she said, her accent thickening. "I lost a receipt and went to the dumpster to look for it—"

My voice rose a notch. "You went through my trash."

"If you're drinking two bottles of wine by yourself, you have problem."

"I didn't drink two bottles by—wait. What I do is none of your business."

"Neighbor upstairs has drinking problem. Years I put up with him being awake at all hours. Banging, stomping all night long. Vomit on the stairs." She looked away. "I can't take it."

"What makes you think the wine bottles are mine?"

"Aren't they?"

I stifled the urge to shout, even though shouting was what I had been hearing all day. "No. They were open bottles of wine in my friend's fridge. I dumped them out and tossed the bottles. I can't believe you went through my trash."

She turned on her heel. "You'll get over it," she said, then disappeared into her apartment.

⌒⊙

I sank into the couch and dove into the dumplings. Soggy. Pasty. Bland. Wasn't New York supposed to be the "greatest food city in America," and possibly on Earth?

I set down my fork and tried to make sense of the numbness, the sensation of being adrift in a vast and endless ocean that had engulfed me ever since Eric broke up with me. Sometimes I was relieved for him, knowing that he didn't have to leave the team he captained and the work he loved to be in this hellhole with me. Other times, my thoughts burned with anger. Our love was not enough—I was not enough—for him to choose me.

It wasn't hard to see my own fault in this. Why had I left behind everything I loved, everything I cared about, for this frustrating job? Why hadn't I been content to stay where I was, doing what I knew how to do? I couldn't see that I had gained anything by coming here. Only soul-crushing loss.

A text from Josh, my former cameraman at Channel Eleven in Los Angeles, swooped across my phone.

Hope you are living it up in the great metropolis.

I frowned and then replied, *Hardly.*

Probably already forgotten us at Channel Eleven . . .

I cracked a smile. I missed covering the news in Los Angeles. Not just because I knew practically every street and neighborhood in the city and was on a first-name basis with hundreds of contacts, from the head of the sanitation department to the chief of police, but also because I understood where I fit in. Here, I felt like I was balancing on a high wire, desperately trying to decode how things worked, knowing that it was a scary, lonely ride down if I fell.

Never. Miss you.

Admit it. You just miss my stash of Snickerdoodles

Upstairs, the neighbors were in the midst of a Sinatra marathon, and the familiar strains of "New York, New York" began to play at unimaginable volume. I set the soggy dumplings aside and gazed out the window and into the apartment window framed by Christmas lights across the street. The blinds were lifted again tonight, and the woman with a cloud of black hair sat at a table illuminated only by a small lamp. Silky red fabric draped around her small frame, her fingers fluttering like moths in the light. It took me a moment to realize what she was doing: sewing.

I watched her for a few minutes, haunted. Her loneliness mirroring my own.

Upstairs, Sinatra crooned about New York, wanting to be a part of it. But as I looked out at the sea of apartments across the way, thinking about how many people were cloistered in them with the rumble and screech of the city as a dizzying backdrop, I wondered why anyone would want to be a part of this.

I was about to close the vinyl shades when a huge boom split the air.

The lights flickered, then blinked off. In the darkness, the air conditioner did a slow groan and stalled.

I glanced out the window to see a pulsing orb of blue in the sky, casting the skyline in an eerie silhouette. Then suddenly the whole eastern side of the sky lit up and changed colors from pink to red, then eerie electric blue.

I heard shouting in the streets. Dogs barking.

My heart pounding, I flung open my apartment door and ran into the hallway, now plunged into darkness.

A bright light swept across my face, blinding me. "Who's there?" a woman's raspy voice called out.

"Kate Bradley. 1B."

The woman lowered her flashlight, but the bright light had left spots in my eyes.

"Your neighbor. Cora," she said, her voice sounding hollow in the dark. "We met . . . earlier. You think it's terrorists?"

"Let's go see what's going on."

Her voice shook. "It's not safe walking around in the dark like this."

"Let me help you." I reached for her hand and found it, bony and trembling. As I walked with her to the door, I felt oddly protective of her, when less than an hour earlier I had been angry at her for her nosy assumptions about wine bottles in the trash.

Outside, the aqua glow lingered in the sky, and I smelled electricity in the air. The neighborhood, the entire city—except for the sky—was pitch black and blanketed by a low-frequency hum. A giant plume of smoke filled part of the skyline. Was it over Queens?

People surged into the streets shouting. Panicking. Traffic was snarled, and the din of honking cars only added to the chaos.

"What's happening?" someone shouted.

"What do you think it is?" Cora whispered.

"Aliens!" a man shouted in the streets. "Call 911!"

At the busy intersection, a couple of drivers tried directing traffic themselves using flashlights but only added to the confusion.

"Cell phones aren't working!" someone in the apartment across the street yelled.

"It's terrorists!" a woman screamed as she sprinted down the street, hauling a large duffel bag.

Then, from behind me, I heard Raymond's familiar voice boom, "It's like every alien-invasion movie ever."

I ran back inside, grabbed my phone and my running shoes, and went to work.

CHAPTER FOUR

Kenny Chang owned an electronics store a few blocks away that was looted as the power remained off. "They kicked out the window, then ran out of here with TVs. Computers," he told me, visibly shaken, as I recorded him on my phone. "They were shouting 'Christmastime.' Like it was some kind of game."

A few doors down from him, a young woman cried as she told me about the robbers who threw a rock through her first-floor apartment window—even though it was fortressed by steel bars—then reached through the bars and stole her son's laptop from a table by the window. "Makes me lose faith in humanity."

Just six streets over, a fire raged through the top of a six-story apartment building, sending up billowing black smoke before firefighters could get there, delayed by clogged city intersections and stoplights that weren't working. "One minute we're having a party. The next minute . . . this," a woman named Angie said, her voice choked with tears.

As I watched FDNY firefighters battling the blaze, my mind drifted to Eric. Wondering if there would ever be a time when I'd see a firefighter or pass by a fire truck and I wouldn't think of him. Miss him. But I had to keep moving.

About a half mile from the ANC studios, I interviewed a woman and her daughter who had just been trapped alone in an elevator on the thirty-ninth floor for nearly an hour.

"We had no cell phone. No water. And it was so hot in there. Only thing I had was TUMS. We started to panic because no one answered the emergency alarm. And my daughter's in a wheelchair. Seemed like forever before the generators kicked in and a maintenance worker helped us out."

Although cell phones didn't work, many people shared information they'd heard on car radios or TVs operating on backup generators. LaGuardia Airport had shut down, with flights rerouted to nearby airports. Subway service was disrupted, and thousands were trapped in tunnels throughout the city. Aliens and terrorists were ruled out. An explosion at a generator in Queens was the likely culprit.

Thousands of people were gathered in the streets, escaping the stifling heat of their apartment buildings. Some were laughing and drinking as though it were some kind of late-night block party, while others clustered together, sometimes clutching small children, worried expressions on their faces.

On the off chance power was restored quickly, I gave out my cell phone number to everyone I met, urging them to text me if they saw anything or had a news tip about the power outage.

Ninety hectic minutes later, I ran the last few blocks to ANC, using the flashlight on my phone to find my way in the dark. A meaty security guard I hadn't seen before stood inside the glass doors of the ANC building, his face lit by the harsh glare of the emergency lights in the lobby.

"I'm Kate Bradley," I said, out of breath. "I work here."

"You got ID?"

In the rush, I'd left my ID at home. And I was too new at ANC for him to recognize me. "I left it back at my apartment."

He shook his head. "Can't let you in without ID."

I noticed the firearm on his belt. "I work with Mark Galvin. Call him. He'll confirm."

He didn't budge. "Phones are down. I need ID."

I zipped through the photos on my phone, found one, and pressed the phone to the glass door.

He peered at it to get a closer look. It was a photo of me reporting from a massive mudslide on the iconic Pacific Coast Highway in Malibu with my former station Channel Eleven's news banner on screen.

"This is my ID."

∽

Mark Galvin was happy.

Okay, not happy. Not even cheerful.

But his gray eyes lit up for a brief moment as I played the footage I'd captured.

"You got all this since the power went out?" he asked. Before I could answer, he was waving his hands at a nearby producer who was racing through the newsroom, dimly lit now because we were operating on backup generators. "Isabelle, get this to the editors. Justin, specifically. I want it ready in ten."

Isabelle looked exhausted, her red hair clipped in a messy bun and her hands juggling a coffee mug, a tablet, and a sheaf of papers, but she took my phone with crisp efficiency. "Back in a minute."

"You're surprising me," Mark said, turning to look at me for the first time. He stood. "You're sturdier than I expected."

Sturdier. Was that supposed to be a compliment?

"I'll take that to mean you like it."

He glanced through a list on his iPad. "We're short on reporters tonight, so I need you to get out there and cover the counterterror security precautions NYPD is taking at city landmarks."

"Terrorism has been ruled out."

"True. But I covered the Northeast blackout in 2003. When the power went off, it was a free-for-all. People are at their worst in times like this."

∽

I set out that night armed for battle in a city without power. A city in crisis.

But unlike my first day at ANC, when I'd calmly assembled a tote bag full of a reporter's essentials, a production coordinator and I had thrown together a backpack with flashlights, phone chargers, a GoPro camera, and several bottles of water in under a minute. She'd even tossed in a loaner phone from ANC, in case the cell service came back on and my phone didn't work.

"You can never be too careful," she said with wide eyes, clipping a 130-decibel personal alarm to my bag. Then she reached into a cabinet, pulled out a bright-pink canister of pepper spray, and slapped it in my hand. "Be safe."

My nerves hummed as I left the busy newsroom and headed into the streets, where the wail of sirens assaulted me from every direction.

It turns out that New York City is very dark without the street-lights, the glare of taxi headlights, or the floodlights that shone on the facades of some buildings. And without the interior apartment lights or the fluorescent-lit grocers and stores, those streets without heavy traffic were so dark I couldn't see more than five feet in front of me without a flashlight.

Above our heads in the inky-blue sky, I could make out hundreds of newly visible stars, a sight that seemed to baffle many, including a group who gestured wildly at the sky. I stopped to watch with them. On a night with only a sliver of a moon and no clouds, I was amazed at the glittering map of constellations unfurled above us. I'd seen the stars stretch from horizon to horizon once deep in the Anza-Borrego desert, but in the sprawling sky glow of LA, I was lucky if I could spot the Big Dipper.

"Wow," I whispered.

"Exactly," the woman next to me answered.

After that, making my way in the dark illuminated only by flashlight was unsettling. I had no way to tell the difference between, say, a woman clutching a baby and a man with a gun. "Hello," I said as people passed by. Some responded with a quick remark about the power outage, but plenty didn't respond at all, as though the darkness had somehow taken away their voices.

I headed first to city hall, the landmark nearest ANC. I'd been there once with my father when I was in grade school and remembered gazing up at its soaring rotunda and feeling dizzy. My nerves were on high alert now because Mark had told me to expect "heavily armed teams of special counterterror officers," but as I passed the fountain in City Hall Park, I saw no signs of law enforcement.

Instead, I saw . . . balloons.

Hundreds of them. No, thousands. Purple and white balloons tied to every column and balcony of the iconic white limestone building and every flagpole, lamppost, and fence in the square. Thousands more were tied to the trees that flanked the building. Lit by the silver light from the emergency lamps in the square, they had an almost mystical glow to them. As I watched them sway and bob in the gentle breeze, tingling goose bumps raced through my body, and I was overcome by a feeling simple and pure: awe.

I'd had a similar feeling when my dad took me to see the Grand Canyon when I was eight. And I remembered experiencing something like it when I watched gold and red leaves pirouette in the light wind one fall day in DC. But I always thought the feeling was reserved for majestic things we saw in nature. Yet here it was, sparked by the sight of balloons.

The hundreds of people milling around the square seemed mesmerized as well, snapping selfies with the balloons as a backdrop. I found Melanie McComb from the Office of Management and Budget on the city hall steps, easily identifiable as a city official by her charcoal-gray suit and heels on a hot night during a power outage. She denied the City was behind the balloon displays. "The New York City government is not wasting money on thousands of balloons when we have a power crisis," she said curtly.

"Then who did?" I asked.

She had no answer.

Purple and white balloons floated from lampposts and fences on the way back to the ANC studios. Hundreds of them. They seemed to be everywhere. But in the narrow beam of my flashlight, I noticed something else. Bouquets of purple and white flowers graced countless stairs and doorways to apartment buildings. They were simple arrangements—purple coneflowers and a kind of daisylike white flower tied together with brown twine—but during the blackout they seemed especially vivid and radiant.

"I don't know who they're from, but I love them," a very pregnant Chinese woman told me. She brought the bouquet to her nose and breathed deeply. "I found them here on the steps. Gave one to my neighbor. Keeping this one for me."

I pulled together footage and a few more quick sound bites, then zipped back to ANC to show my report to Mark.

His eyes were cold, unsentimental, as he watched the images on the screen. Then he was silent. The kind of long moment that made me think he was either having a stroke or very angry.

"People are getting looted. A guy in the Bronx went missing. Food shortages are coming if power doesn't come on soon. And you want me to run a story about balloons and flowers?"

"Aren't you curious what it's all about?" I pointed at the monitor as images of balloons and flowers floated by. "And why?"

I met his eyes and saw something mocking in them. "Balloons and flowers. That's a story for children. Not a news network."

I shook my head. "It's part of the story."

His eyes suddenly seemed smaller. Darker. "It is if you're looking for a very short career at ANC."

Was he threatening to fire me? Or seeing how far he could push me?

"Maybe more good things are happening out there, if we're willing to look for them."

He crossed his arms. "Tell that to Jim Hollister, who just had his clothing store looted in SoHo. They broke down the door and stole armfuls of T-shirts and sweatshirts. Go interview him, take a look at the broken glass and massive loss, and then tell me about 'good' things happening."

CHAPTER FIVE

By early morning, power was restored throughout the city, and Manhattan went back to business as usual. Kids trudged off to school, the trains were running mostly on schedule again, people commuted into work, the emergency generators were moved off the streets, and workers were back to fixing potholes and sewer lines.

But something had changed. When I got into work, the first text I got was from one of the women I interviewed who'd found flowers on the doorstep to her apartment.

Felicia here. You interviewed me last night. I work at the DMV in Lower Manhattan. Someone left flowers on every single person's desk here this morning.

Anyone see who did it? I typed back.

Boss thinks they must have snuck in with the early morning cleaning crew.

Moments later, Stephanie rushed in and tossed her bag on her desk. "This is a first. I had breakfast with Ashley Clark at Le Pain Quotidien on Broad Street. She's the executive producer of *ANC Investigates*. You'll never guess what happened."

"Dead rat?"

She frowned.

"Homeless guy dropping his pants?"

She flashed me a wry smile. "Seriously?"

"What? Both those stories were on the NYC news rundown this week."

"True. But get this, before we finished eating, the waiter came over and said our bill had already been paid. We looked around, figuring maybe someone had seen us on ANC or something. But whoever it was paid cash for everyone's meals, not just ours."

"The whole restaurant?"

"There had to be forty, maybe fifty people there. No one could believe it. We all started talking to each other because of it. I ended up meeting a guy I'd seen in there lots of times but never talked to until today. Turns out he lives in my building."

"Any idea who paid for all the meals?"

"Our waiter told us a girl came in when they first opened up, dropped two thousand dollars cash on the counter, and told them to use it for everyone's breakfasts that morning."

"Did he say what she looked like?"

She applied a quick coat of gloss to her lips. "All they remember is that she had blonde hair. Maybe a teenager."

"A teenage girl paid for everyone's breakfasts?"

"Crazy, right?"

I tried to focus on my report about the government shutdown, but my mind kept wandering, thinking about the events happening around Manhattan. Maybe because they gave me a glimmer of hope that the unbearable city I'd been trying to survive wasn't as heartless as it seemed. Or maybe I just needed a distraction from the maneuvering and negotiating and posturing that was happening on Capitol Hill.

Politics was never supposed to be my beat. I'd made that clear when Andrew had recruited me. Andrew had assumed I avoided political coverage because my father was a senator, but I told him that I didn't like sifting through a rising churn of spins and lies and closed-door meetings to get at the truth. But Andrew was still out of town, and until he got back, I had no doubt Mark was going to confine me to this miserable beat.

As I started a call with someone in the justice department about the furloughed employees, my cell phone chimed. Unknown number.

The text read: *I started a Facebook group. NYCMiracles. Check it out.*

My phone didn't recognize the number, so I figured it was spam. Until:

This is Corinne. You interviewed me after I was trapped in the elevator last night. I started the group because I just found a car key dangling from a purple ribbon on the door handle to my apartment.

Blue dots flickered on the screen, indicating she was still typing.

With a note saying to take it to the Chevy Dealer in Hell's Kitchen. Did you?

Key is to a van. With wheelchair lift for my daughter. Free.

From who?

They don't know. A woman paid cash. And told them to give the van to me.

⌢⌢

"I know what you're thinking," Mark was saying. "But the answer's still no."

"You're saying no before I ask the question?" I pressed, trying to keep pace with his fast clip through the newsroom. I'd heard Mark thought sit-down meetings were a waste of time, so if you wanted to talk to him, you had to do a "walk and talk," pitching your ideas as he paced through the newsroom checking in with other reporters and producers.

He cracked his lower jaw like he was trying to clear his ears. "You're thinking that since you had big success with the Good Sam and Robin

Hood stories in LA, that maybe you should chase this story about a couple of good things happening after the blackout."

"More like an avalanche of good things," I said, feeling the heat rise in my cheeks. My tone must have been sharp because the producer whose desk we were standing by looked at us and quickly slipped on her headphones.

"It's not a national news story when some people do a few kind things."

"But it *is* a national news story when people are looting and stealing?"

A vein bulged in his forehead. "I'm not having this debate with you."

I steadied my voice. "This isn't all that different from the crime wave story Stephanie's been covering. Instead of killings and assaults, we've just got a wave of people helping others."

He heaved a disappointed sigh. "From where you sit, it may be hard for you to see it, but people are scared, the economy's bad, and we're more divided than ever. That's what we cover here."

"From where I sit?"

"We can't pretend the world isn't in chaos by chasing after a story about a woman who received keys to a new van—"

"From a stranger. While thousands and thousands of purple and white balloons and flowers mysteriously appear around Manhattan."

"And what about the gift cards that someone's leaving on windshields all over?" a man said from behind me.

I turned to face him. He was in his midthirties, dressed in a tailored dark-blue suit and holding up a gift card wrapped in purple ribbon. "Found one of these on my windshield this morning. They're all over town. Hundreds of them."

Mark looked intrigued. Or maybe his interest was just for appearances because the man speaking was Scott Jameson, star of the very popular ANC series *Wonders of the World*, where Scott explored the most wild and beautiful locations in the world. Mark took the gift card from him and turned it over in his hands.

"Something's going on," Scott said. "Worth looking into."

Mark frowned. I could feel a no bubbling up. "All right," he sighed. "Give it a shot, Kate. But make it brief."

Before I could reply, he walked away.

I blew out a breath. "Thank you. He was putting the kibosh on that story before you got here." I held out my hand. "I'm Kate Bradley."

"Scott Jameson." He shook my hand with a firm grip. "We've met."

Scott was tall, over six feet, with the kind of piercing blue eyes that look great on camera. But although I had seen practically every episode of his show, I knew I'd never met him. I would've remembered.

"I don't think—"

"Fifth Avenue. Your collision with a bike," he added.

"That was you?"

"Not the one on the bike. The one who helped you up."

"Sorry, I didn't recognize you—"

"You had a lot going on that morning. Besides, I was in disguise. I was wearing a Yankees ball cap. And I'm a Cubs fan."

I laughed. "The disguise worked. Thanks for your help. It wasn't one of my better mornings in Manhattan."

"Some days here are actually tests of your survival skills."

"And thank you for helping convince Mark to give me this story."

He flashed me a smile. "That's three thank-yous in less than thirty seconds. Obviously, you're not a real New Yorker."

"Guess my Los Angeles stripes are showing."

"They are," he said in a conspiratorial tone. "But if you don't want everyone else to know that you're not from here, you'll drop all the thank-yous."

"Manhattan rule number seventy-two." I pretended to write in my notebook. "No thank-yous."

"Besides, you don't need to thank me. You had already convinced Mark before I got here. He just likes for his reporters to claw and fight for the stories they want to do."

"I heard that can get you fired around here."

"Sometimes it does," he agreed. "Mostly it makes for stronger reporting. But glad you're taking on this story. The city has a kind of weird and wonderful feel to it right now." His eyes met mine as he handed me the gift card. "Welcome to ANC, Kate. Let me know what you find out."

CHAPTER SIX

By the time I had returned to my desk, NYCMiracles already had dozens of posts on it. A twenty-seven-year-old woman named Cathy had gone into Duane Reade in the West Village and discovered that the pain medication she needed after a recent surgery had already been paid for by an anonymous donor. She left there with $500 worth of medicine. Free. When I reached out to her through Facebook, she called me back fifteen minutes later.

She sounded like she'd been crying. "Our medical bills are more than we can manage, so I usually go without when it comes to pain medicine. But knowing that someone did this for me?" Her voice broke. "They'll never fully understand what that means."

"Any idea who did it?"

"The pharmacist said the guy paid in cash and wouldn't leave his name."

"What'd he look like?"

"Told me the guy was young, like maybe just out of high school." She blew her nose. "And that he paid for ten other people who had open pharmacy orders."

After I hung up with Cathy, more stories rolled in. The most bizarre example was a man named Hector who reported that the funeral home where he worked just received $25,000 cash by courier to pay off the funeral expenses for three families who were having services there that day.

Thankfully what happened at the Kmart in NoHo offered a solid clue. The manager's post said that right after the store opened, a woman handed him $15,000 in cash and instructed him to pay the layaway balances of as many people as he could.

"I told her no," the manager said when I tracked him down by phone later that morning. "I mean, we really aren't set up for that. But she insisted. So I got a couple of clerks, and we dug in. Took hours."

"What did she look like?"

"Hard to say. She was wearing these big sunglasses. White frames."

"Indoors?"

"Yeah. And a red scarf, tied kind of fancy around her neck. Reddish hair, I think. One of the layaway customers found out what she was doing, dropped to her knees, and started crying. That's when the woman took off."

After we hung up, I wondered if this was all a momentary blip. A brief wave of kindness in the wake of the power outage. In the days that followed 9/11, people across the globe reached out with overwhelming help and support. Maybe this was the same thing.

I'd had a lot of experience with "good" stories like this in LA. I'd broken the story about the anonymous Good Samaritan leaving $100,000 in cash on LA doorsteps. A few months later, I was able to uncover the Robin Hood–like group who was stealing from the über-wealthy and staging large-scale giving events for the poor. But what made this story different was how widespread it was—it wasn't a handful of people receiving money, like the recipients of Good Sam. It was hundreds. Maybe thousands. And it wasn't just the needy who were benefiting. Almost anyone seemed to be a possible recipient. But the scope of it meant there must be—there had to be—a group of people involved.

Were they all working together? Or was this kind of like "the wave" at a baseball game, started by a group and later imitated by copycats?

I wanted to be the one to get the answers, so I doubled down. I posted on the NYCMiracles page:

I'm Kate Bradley, a correspondent at ANC. If you have experiences with the good stuff that's spreading through NYC or tips on who might be behind it, I want to hear from you. Text me at (323) 555-9999.

"Trade you," Stephanie said, slipping a mug of coffee on the desk in front of me.

"For what?"

"Your story for mine. While I'm slogging through a report about the man who was found dead at the home of a prominent political donor in Chicago, I heard Mark is actually letting you work on a story about the good stuff happening."

"How'd you know?"

"Word gets around quickly when Mark does a rare 'nice boss' move. Especially in a reporter's first week at the network." She leaned back in her chair and crossed her legs at the ankles. "You ever think this might be the work of someone you know?"

I laughed. "I know something like five people in Manhattan. What makes you say that?"

She shrugged. "Seems odd that one of the people you profiled the night of the power outage got a brand-new van the next day. Maybe our news bosses are behind this 'good stuff' thing to get ratings or something."

I raised an eyebrow. "I'm hoping they all have too much integrity to manufacture a story like this."

Her smile faded. "Worth looking into. At least tell me you're considering the possibility that all of this is a setup for a scam."

"A scam?"

"Remember a few weeks ago some guys were all over the media for helping a woman after they saw she was paying for gas with pennies?

They started a GoFundMe for her and raised like a hundred thousand dollars from people all around the world. But they didn't give it to her. They ran off with it."

"You think someone's started all this so they can ask people to pay to join in?"

She took a sip of her coffee. "Why else would they be doing it?"

I let her question hang there. I wondered why we often leaped to assume nefarious motives when faced with things we didn't understand. Maybe it was because we were all afraid we'd look naive or uninformed if we leaned toward the positive. But if I learned anything from covering the Good Sam and Robin Hood stories, it was that we couldn't jump to conclusions before we got the facts. Before we looked at the story from all sides. "It's also possible that they have good intentions."

She pounded back her coffee. "Clearly, you haven't lived in Manhattan for very long."

An hour later I was heading down East Twenty-First Street to find a woman named Kristen who'd posted that her $12,000 bill at First Presbyterian Hospital had been paid in full by an anonymous donor. The cameraman assigned to me was a fifteen-year veteran of ANC named Chris Yamashita.

"Great to have your skills as a cameraman on this story," I said.

"Photojournalist, not cameraman," he replied, using the fancier title for the same job.

Then he started scrolling through the photos on his phone, showing me a quick slideshow of the memorabilia he'd collected from some of the stories he'd covered over the last fifteen years: a Cohiba cigar he'd received from Fidel Castro while on assignment in Cuba, a signal flag from an assignment in a nuclear-powered submarine, and a chunk of cement from the levee that broke in Hurricane Katrina.

"I like to collect something physical from every story," he said.

Otherwise, Chris was not much of a talker—a big change from Josh, my LA cameraman, who had a joke or an insight about everything we encountered on our news runs. And from the way his eyes took me in, I had the definite feeling Chris felt like he was slumming working on this "good news" story with me, a newbie at ANC.

I was wrong about that. About a mile into the ride in the ANC news van, he said, "Your dad. He's Senator Hale Bradley?"

"Yep."

"What's he doing about the shutdown? I've got friends who've been furloughed. And it's bad. They live paycheck to paycheck as it is. They're just a few hundred dollars away from having nothing. How's he helping end this mess?"

"I haven't talked to him about it. He's been too busy to return my calls."

"I hope you'll tell him—"

"I'm not here because I'm Hale Bradley's daughter," I interrupted. "I'm a reporter, not a conduit to my father or a mouthpiece for his ideas."

He nodded. "Well, there you have it."

"There you have . . . what?"

Before he could answer, my eye fell on a homeless man in front of an H&M store who was holding a large box wrapped in white paper and purple ribbon. "Stop the van, please."

Chris slammed on the brakes. "Yeah, sorry about what I said. I didn't mean—"

"Get your camera and follow me."

I jumped out of the van and ran to the man, who was sitting on the ground looking at the wrapped present, a discarded cardboard shipping box to his side. He was shoeless, dressed in tired gray work pants, frayed at the bottoms, and a faded blue T-shirt.

"Excuse me, I'm Kate Bradley. From Channel Eleven. I mean, ANC."

He looked up at me with questioning brown eyes on a face that was leathered and wrinkled. He looked to be in his seventies, although he was probably much younger.

"I'm wondering about that gift you have there. Where'd you get it?"

He smiled, exposing several missing teeth. "They delivered it to me."

"Who did?"

"Amazon."

"Amazon delivered a package to you. Here?"

He nodded. "Delivery guy comes over. Asks if I'm Reggie Booth, and I say yeah. Hands me the package and takes off."

I glanced at the shipping label, which read: "Reggie Booth, Man on Sidewalk," and the address of the H&M store. "Did you order it?"

"Got no way to do that."

"What's inside?"

He shook his head. "Fraid to find out. What if it's a trick or something?"

"Want me to help?" Our eyes locked, and I was caught in a moment of raw humanity. I wasn't looking into the eyes of a junkie or a man who had made terrible mistakes. I was looking at a man who was suffering, and this box, whatever it was, contained a glimmer of hope.

I crouched down and helped him untie the ribbon and pull the wrapping paper off the box.

When Reggie opened the box, we were both surprised to see a brand-new pair of sneakers, a half dozen pairs of socks, and some jeans.

He lifted the shoes out of the box. "They're my size," he whispered.

I hoped Chris's camera was capturing the expression on Reggie's face, which quickly morphed from bewilderment to surprise to shock and then to joy in the span of four seconds. Even if it didn't, I was sure I would never forget it.

"Guy I know. Joey. Said the same thing happened to him earlier today," he said. "I thought he was making it up. Guess he wasn't."

"How would someone know your shoe size?" I asked.

"And what size pants I wear." A glassy tear formed in the corner of his eye. "I dunno."

I spotted a packing slip in the box and snapped a photo with my phone. Underneath the Amazon logo it read: A gift note from A Stranger. The note read: We're all connected.

"What's it feel like getting something like this?" I asked.

He didn't answer. Instead, his long, bony fingers caressed each item in the box as though he were double-checking they were really there.

"Someone thinks I matter."

~

The story went viral, with viewers everywhere trying to figure out if Amazon was "in on the kindness thing" or if some Good Samaritan was actually going around Manhattan asking homeless people's names, then finding out or guessing their clothing sizes and having Amazon deliver to them. I'd called Amazon, trying to see if they'd reveal who purchased the gift for Reggie. A polite customer-service representative told me, "We never share the sender information with anyone."

Every couple of minutes, my phone chimed with yet another text from someone telling me about something good they'd experienced around the city. The next morning, the chiming became so insistent that a teen in front of me in the Starbucks line turned around, looking annoyed.

"Your phone got a bug or something?" he asked, adjusting his earbuds.

I turned the volume down. "I just get a lot of texts."

He studied my face. "What are you, some kind of celebrity?"

"Nope. Just a reporter."

That profession was apparently boring enough that he immediately turned away and started scrolling through his phone.

A few minutes later and armed with a soy latte, I glanced at my phone to see what I'd missed. I stepped toward the door and smack into Scott Jameson.

Literally.

My cup fell, and when it hit the ground, its lid popped off, spilling liquid everywhere.

I laughed. "I must look like the most accident-prone person in Manhattan—"

"You just haven't mastered the New York jostle yet," he said as a Starbucks employee jumped in to mop up the mess.

"There's a New York jostle?"

"Okay, I made that up. But the key to survival here is to never look down. Always maneuver around tourists. And never, ever look at your phone when you're leaving Starbucks."

"You made that last one up too."

He smiled. "I did. Where are you headed?"

"I was just reading a text from a man who says someone prepaid his rent for the next month. And not just his. All his neighbors' in his apartment building too."

"Everyone?"

I glanced at my phone. "He says: 'We all got letters taped to our door asking us to meet the anonymous donor by the fountain in Bryant Park at noon.' Which is where I'm heading."

"Can I tag along?"

I tilted my head. A guy with Scott Jameson's star power didn't need to join a freshman reporter on a story. If he wanted it, he could just take it. Besides, his series was all about natural wonders. In one episode, he'd spent the night lashed to the side of Yosemite's El Capitan. In another, he'd hiked the Alaskan tundra. He'd even scaled a volcano in the South Pacific and spent the night there before reaching the summit and filming his show at sunrise.

"Action. Adventure. Adrenaline. That's what you usually cover, right? Why would you want to come along on this story, which has none of that?"

We stepped aside to let a woman leaving Starbucks pass. She stopped to stare at him, then elbowed her friend to do the same. Scott had the kind of striking good looks that made people notice him. Even world-weary Manhattanites weren't immune.

"I've never seen anything like it. I keep wondering—is it a marketing gimmick? Or maybe performance art of some kind? Banksy did something with balloons here once. But then something new happens, and none of those theories make sense. What do you think is going on?"

"I don't know yet. The sheer number of things that are happening is . . . mind boggling. But things are never as they first appear."

By noon, seventeen people from a small apartment building on 134th in Harlem had gathered around the fountain in Bryant Park. Despite the hundreds of people sitting in the grass or in patio chairs in the park during the lunch hour, it wasn't hard to spot the group because they stood in a cluster, talking rapidly like people do when they're at a birthday party or other celebration.

I was nervous about allowing Scott to join me on the story. It wasn't unusual for a couple of reporters to team up, but it mostly came about on much bigger stories like natural disasters, riots, or mass shootings. Would it look like I couldn't handle this story on my own if he was tagging along?

Even though he seemed to be genuinely curious, I wasn't so naive to believe that his motives were entirely pure. This story was already getting a surprising amount of attention. Was he planning to gain some insight from our trip to Bryant Park and use it to take over the story?

The one plus to him joining was that he convinced cameraman Chris Yamashita to work with us on his day off. Without him, I'd have been stuck shooting everything with my cell phone camera because the dispatch team couldn't assign any cameramen to this story. Chris jumped right in, recording shots of the rapidly growing group and getting close-ups of their excited expressions.

Scott and I struck up a conversation with fifty-three-year-old resident Grant Hamilton, who had sent me the text. "It's like winning the lottery," Grant told us. "Plus, I didn't know most of these people in my building before all this. And now I do."

"The spirit behind the gift was even more important to me than the money," Ann-Marie Louison said. "It carried a lot of love with it." She had dressed in a brightly colored red-and-orange floral caftan and had brought a jar of homemade pickles for the anonymous donor. She told us she hoped for a photo with them so she could show her seven-year-old grandson "what a hero looks like."

But when no one had shown up by 12:25, our excitement wilted. Chris set his camera in the grass and popped a stick of gum in his mouth. "Have you considered that this is some company's campaign to get viral attention?" he asked me.

"Yeah, maybe the chamber of commerce is trying to lure more tourists to Manhattan," I replied.

"As if we need more of that," he grumbled.

"The problem with both of those theories is that if this is some kind of campaign, they'd be promoting a hashtag or account to follow. But we haven't seen that."

Ann-Marie stepped toward me. "What if this whole thing was supposed to get us out of our apartments so they could steal what we have?"

That idea struck a chord of fear, and within minutes, everyone in the group was on their phones calling nearby friends and relatives to check on their apartments. Everyone except a retired guy named Walter, who sat quietly on a café chair, slowly and deliberately peeling an orange.

"I got nothin' to steal. I'm just happy I got a month where I don't have to scrape together the rent."

"What will you do with the savings?" Scott asked him.

"Everything." He cracked a smile. "Half the fun is thinking about that."

Then three men in their twenties lumbered through the grass carrying heavy picnic baskets. "Are you people from the 134th Street apartments?" the tallest one asked.

"Yeah," Grant said.

Was this them? These guys in their baggy jeans and sweat-stained T-shirts. I scanned their faces, wondering. Did it show? Did generosity like this reveal itself on someone's face? Could you spot their compassion by the way they spoke or the way they carried themselves?

"Are you the people who paid our rent?" Ann-Marie asked.

"Nope," the taller one said, wiping sweat from his face with a red bandana. "We're from Broadway Finest Deli. Someone hired us to bring you this lunch. Sorry we're late."

The three men unpacked red-checkered picnic blankets and spread them out on the lawn.

"Who hired you?" I asked them as they laid out platters of sandwiches, salads, and cold drinks.

The one with a buzz cut and trendy clear-frame glasses shrugged. "We don't know. Someone left cash and instructions for our boss."

"That same person was supposed to meet us here. What can you tell us about who that is?" I pressed.

He felt around in his back pocket and handed me a folded paper. "No idea. But I'm supposed to give you this."

As I unfolded the paper, the group gathered around me, a few peering over my shoulder.

It read:

Dear 134th Street Apartment Residents: Sorry I can't join you as planned. You are all connected.

—A Stranger.

CHAPTER SEVEN

"There's a catch," a woman named Michelle told me on the phone. She'd called minutes after Scott and I finished recording a stand-up in Bryant Park.

"What kind of catch?" I asked.

"I went into a Le Pain Quotidien near Washington Square at lunch. The waitress said my meal had already been paid for. Which was great, right? Like my lucky day or something, because I heard this has been happening other places around Manhattan too."

"What was the catch?"

"I had to eat my lunch with a stranger. Someone else who was at a table for one."

I scribbled in my notebook. "What'd you do?"

"Look, I didn't really need the free lunch. I mean, I order the same salad every time I go there. I can afford it. And I'm really not one to eat lunch with other people. That's kind of my time to read, you know. But I was curious. So I ate lunch with a random guy."

"What was that like?"

She sighed. "At first it was strange. Then I found out he also grew up near Hawthorne, in New Jersey. Like me."

"It turned out better than you expected?"

I heard her smile through the phone. "We had a long lunch together. Then he asked me out . . . and I said yes."

I tried to wrap my head around her story. Someone was putting strings on the giving, making people jump through hoops to get the free meal. Was this all some kind of social experiment to see how far people would go for free stuff? A few years back, I'd covered a story about someone who had hidden twenty-dollar bills in parks in San Francisco and Los Angeles. People had torn up the parks, destroying flowers, dropping trash everywhere, and even smashing up manholes trying to find the money. I wondered: Was this a ploy to bring out the worst in all of us?

After I hung up with Michelle, I found Scott lounging on one of the blankets, immersed in a conversation with several of the residents and petting a chubby black Lab that had wandered into the picnic, looking for food. Scott looked surprisingly comfortable there, as if he didn't notice that a few tourists were snapping photos of him. On his series, he came off as the kind of adrenaline junkie who would kitesurf, raft, skydive, kayak, or ski anywhere to find the most stunning places on Earth. But in this setting, he seemed relaxed, gently teasing answers out of the people around him.

"You have to hear what Ann-Marie's grandson told her just happened at his school," he said. He motioned to a spot on the blanket and moved to make room for me.

"He's in second grade," Ann-Marie said, beaming. "And today all the lunches in his school were paid for. Just like our rent."

"Where?"

"East Harlem. It's a blessing because he—Dannel—just moved here from the Dominican Republic. That's where my son has been since before Dannel was born. He ate lunch alone every day since school began. But when the kids got to lunch today, they found out that everyone would get a free meal—some of their favorites—but only if no one sits alone."

"But wait till you hear what happened next. Tell her," Scott said.

"Some boys in his class invited Dannel to sit with them. This was the first time for him. He just called me to say, 'Abuela, I made a new friend. He plays Minecraft too.'"

While Ann-Marie told her story to the others, I turned to Scott. "This isn't just about giving. They're connecting strangers."

⁓

Tucked between a nail salon and a barber shop and with a faded yellow sign that had a seventies flair to it, the pizza joint didn't look like the kind of spot that a celebrity journalist like Scott would seek out.

But after we finished shooting the last of our stand-up reports, Scott had suggested we get a bite to eat. I thought we'd grab a quick sandwich and head back to ANC, but he said that if I was willing to walk an extra couple of blocks, I'd experience the "titan of all pizza." Given my disappointing experience with food in Manhattan so far, it seemed unlikely that any food here would deserve the "titan" moniker, but I'd agreed to try it out.

The line was out the door. Easily an hour wait. No combination of cheese and dough seemed worth that.

"He imports his fresh mozzarella from Italy," Scott assured me. "And a coal-fired oven makes the crust perfect every time. I met the owner's son, Vince, while mountain biking in Highbridge after I moved back from Chicago years ago. My first time here, Vince had me try the artichoke pizza, and after living in Chicago, I turned him down. Because artichokes don't belong on pizzas."

"Where I come from, we put artichokes, avocados, banana, even kimchi on our pizzas."

He rolled his eyes.

I laughed. "Did you just make a face about bananas and kimchi?"

"I did." He smiled playfully. "Stuff like that will get you banned from a Chicago pizzeria."

Minutes later, one of the guys behind the counter spotted Scott and motioned for us to come over.

"Hey, good to see you," the man said. He was a burly guy, wearing a too-tight black henley dusted with pizza flour.

"Vince, this is Kate. It's her first time experiencing New York pizza."

Vince's eyes lit up. "Where you been hiding?"

"LA."

He grinned. "Then you don't know pizza. Not yet anyway. I'll have something special for you in a couple of minutes, okay?"

True to his promise, ten minutes later he handed us a warm, boxed pizza, handcrafted by his seventy-two-year-old dad, the owner. The pizza was normally priced at thirty dollars, but Vince insisted it was on the house.

We tried to find a seat in the dining room, but it was so packed that people were standing in the aisles digging into their pizzas.

"I know a better place to go. Not far from here," Scott said as we snaked through the line and out the door. We walked a few more blocks, then stopped at a six-story redbrick apartment building. "Welcome to the best place to eat the titan of all pizzas."

"Here?" I stared, unconvinced, at the nondescript building.

"You'll see."

As we embarked on the hike upstairs, I wondered if I should be going with him. Where was the line between a collegial dinner and a date? I didn't want to give him the wrong impression of why I was there. Or have to explain later why I went to a stranger's apartment with Scott Jameson. But everything about it felt friendly, just colleagues on a mini-adventure after a long day.

"It's my cousin's apartment. But he's always traveling," he said, unlocking the door to a beautifully decorated apartment whose walls were lined with photographs and eclectic art.

He stepped over to a colorful fish tank filled with graceful fish shaped like small disks and dropped some food pellets into the water.

"You can probably guess that he runs an art gallery."

I had never seen anything like it before. The living room seemed to vibrate with energy, with pieces that ran the gamut from an Italian tapestry to a little boy's painting of a boat.

I followed him into the kitchen, where he opened the floor-to-ceiling window. "Our dining room awaits," he said, motioning outside.

A fire escape.

Stepping onto the steel platform hovering eighty feet above the sidewalk in the warm summer air immediately reminded me of the balcony scene in *West Side Story* or the fire escapes across the courtyard in *Rear Window*.

From this oasis in the city, we could hear everything: the leaves rustling in the wind, glasses clinking and laughter floating up from a nearby restaurant, and people murmuring as they walked on the street below. The rumbling city I thought I knew suddenly had a hushed, magical quality. Even the honking cars in the distance sounded like they might be the strains of some kind of otherworldly music.

"Wow" was the only word I could manage.

Scott pulled out a narrow runner rug tucked under the window and rolled it out on the steel-grate floor.

"These are the best seats in the house," he said, gesturing to the carpeted floor.

We sat on the carpet, opened up the pizza box, and dug into heaven. He was right about it being one of the titans of pizza. Every bite was a punch of flavor. While we inhaled it, Scott told me about the next season of his show, which would have him heading out across the globe again next month. On camera, he was smart, funny even, and he was surprisingly the same in real life.

"What's left to cover?" I said, digging into a second slice. "You've already dodged Taliban bullets in Afghanistan, scuba dived in the Red Sea, and wasn't that you who did a live shot from the top of the Golden Gate Bridge in San Francisco?"

"With permission," he said with a laugh. "I'm not like one of those daredevils who snuck up there last month with GoPros and got in trouble."

"That didn't make your stomach churn having to report from so high up there?"

"Probably the best view anywhere. If you remember, we got those impossible shots of all those whales breaching. That's why I love what we get to do every day. Showing people what the world looks like."

"What's next then?"

"One of the things on the list is to rappel down Mystery Falls in Chattanooga, Tennessee. It's pitch dark, and we're going to need close to two thousand feet of rope rigged at just the right angles. Plus, handheld flashes and flash guns. But I want viewers to feel the scale of it. From inside these caves, every sound—every sight—seems larger than life."

"That seems like a huge adrenaline rush. Today's story was on the opposite end of the scale."

"It is. But a lot of what we reporters do is report on the flaws, the unfairness, the bad decisions. Anyone watching TV news might think all we humans do is make mistakes. But this story is a chance to show that's not all there is."

"What's curious to me is that they're giving to everyone. They're not deciding who's worthy or not. They're just giving to complete and total strangers."

He leaned back against the balcony railing. "When I covered Hurricane Irma in the Florida Keys, people rallied together for complete strangers too. They opened their homes, brought meals, helped track down prescriptions. Donated thousands of items. Maybe this is a little like that?"

"We often see people help out in disasters and catastrophes. But many of the people they're giving to aren't in any crisis at all. I can't figure out their endgame."

"A skeptic. I get that. Especially given how many stories of manipulation we cover every day. But they told the 134th Street tenants 'You're all connected.' What do you think that means?"

"I don't know." I set down my pizza slice. "Is this all just a way to get attention or attract millions of followers? You know, like a cell phone or cable company wanting to 'connect' us through their services. Or is this a legit group, trying to bring our attention to something important? Something we just can't grasp yet."

He handed me a bottle of water. "And which do you hope is true?"

I was surprised by his question. Journalists cover what is. Not what we hope it to be. "I want to believe there's something good behind all of it. Even though that puts me in a club of one at ANC."

"I'd like to join your club," he said. Then he flashed that smile of his, the one that drew in millions of viewers each week, but here it made me feel like he saw the best in me.

"Why? We're probably only going to get our hopes dashed and find out this is just some scam. Who would possibly think there's something good behind all of it?"

"I would."

I smiled. "Because you're an eternal optimist, or just crazy?"

"Crazy, of course." He took a quick swig of water. "And because of something that happened to me a few years ago." He looked out over the darkening skyline, gathering his thoughts. His voice was quiet, reflective. "I was on a skiing trip in Colorado with my cousins and had gotten way ahead of them on this one really rough trail. We shouldn't have been out there then—it was practically a whiteout. The next thing I knew, I had flipped over a mogul and was thrown so far I was partially buried in a huge snowdrift. I got the wind knocked out of me and couldn't move. I panicked because I was pretty sure no one would be out there in those conditions. Suddenly a man comes up and pulls me out. Then my cousins called out to me, and when I turned around, the guy was gone. He'd completely disappeared. My family was in the press the next day offering a reward to whoever it was that saved my life that day, but he never came forward. I've always wondered who he was."

He surprised me. I had been holding my breath, thinking his curiosity about this story was motivated by ambition. I'd even considered that he had initially offered to help because he was curious about Senator Bradley's daughter. But his story made me realize his interest was genuine. Made me think it might be safe to tell him mine.

"When I was little, I thought the whole world was like that," I said. "People doing almost magical things for other people. My mom died in a car crash when I was five, but what I remember about it was the three guys who came to her rescue. They never identified themselves—even after reporters searched for them—but my dad always talked about how they tried to rescue her. How grateful he was that they tried. Even though I'd lost my mom, the world still had a kind of magic to it. Neighbors would come over or invite us to dinner. Friends came over with books and treats. Some of my dad's staff took me to a theme park one time, to the beach another. It wasn't until I got a little older that I realized that the world isn't like that. Most people aren't like that."

"I'm sorry about your mom," he said, softly. "Maybe we're both lucky to have crossed paths with the few people who have the altruism gene, a talent for helping others."

I thought about that for a moment. "Or maybe we all have a little bit within ourselves, waiting for the right experience to spark it into action."

As we polished off the pizza later that evening, I told Scott about my breaking-news beat in LA—covering wildfires, murders, shootouts, earthquakes, freeway chases, and other tragic events.

Surprisingly, he'd seen several of my stories, including my Robin Hood reports when they aired on the network. He tried every conceivable line of questioning and tactic to get me to divulge who the Robin Hood was behind the string of high-tech robberies in the mega-estates—even making outrageous guesses like Kim Kardashian and Chuck Norris—but I wouldn't crack.

"You are tough," he said, smiling. "I'd have better luck breaking into Fort Knox than getting an answer out of you."

"That's because you gave up too soon. Before you figured out my weaknesses," I answered, then realized how flirty that sounded.

"You have weaknesses?"

Our eyes met briefly, and the charge between us was so strong that I looked away.

My cell phone vibrated in my purse, offering a good distraction.

"You're very popular. That thing's been ringing all evening."

"I posted my phone number online saying I'm the correspondent to text or call if they have tips about any of the good stuff we're seeing."

He grinned. "So you're tough *and* bold."

I reached into my purse and glanced at the screen. Seven missed calls, and one unknown number calling me now.

I answered. "Kate Bradley."

"Hiya, Kate. You don't know me, but I run a wholesale party-supply shop on Twenty-Third in the Flatiron," the man said. "I saw your report about all the balloons that are everywhere around the city. I saw the guy."

"You saw what guy?"

"The guy who's doing it. When I came in the front door of the shop this afternoon, a guy was leaving here with six shopping bags of our bulk-pack latex balloons. Probably had more than ten thousand balloons in those bags. That's not unusual for us, really. But then I noticed they were all purple and white. So I followed him."

"You followed one of your customers? What'd he look like?"

"Shorter than me, but most people are. I'm six foot two. He was wearing a gray hoodie with the hood pulled tight around his head, so

I couldn't get a look at his face. Once he went inside his apartment, I stopped following him. It wasn't the safest of neighborhoods, and I didn't want to get myself killed."

"Where'd he go?"

"828 East Thirtieth Street. He went into the first apartment on the right. First floor."

CHAPTER EIGHT

No.

That's all the email said. One crystalline word.

I'd emailed Mark asking if I could follow up on the lead about the party-store guy, and his emphatic reply came a swift thirty seconds later. It wasn't difficult to read between the lines of his one-word answer: the government shutdown had entered its third day, and he needed me to cover it. The story about the gifts mysteriously appearing throughout the city? Over.

At least in his mind.

In mine, that meant I'd have to chase the lead before I headed into work. I set my alarm to get up early and threw on my running gear and shoes, determined to combine my morning run with a trip to 828 East Thirtieth. The address was about two miles away, a fairly straightforward path that I could run instead of slogging through town in a taxi or on the subway. And I could listen to the news rundown on my earbuds on the way there. A gold-star multitasking morning.

As I stepped outside my apartment, I almost trampled a bouquet of flowers on my doorstep.

I reached down to pick them up and realized that they were the same purple-and-white bouquets people were finding on doorsteps all around the city.

I blinked back tears. It was easy to dismiss something like this as "trivial" . . . until it happened to you. The simple flowers—given to me by someone I didn't know—made the city seem softer. Smaller.

I breathed in their sweet scent, remembering a morning when Eric had surprised me with a sprawling bouquet of the orange poppies that grew wild in his garden. I let the scent and memory envelop me: The air, soft and still. The low timbre of his voice. A lone butterfly fluttering by.

My neighbor Cora must have heard my door open because she peered into the hallway.

"Ov-va!" she said, picking up the flowers. "What are these for?"

"We all got them." I pointed down the hallway, where bouquets were stationed at every door.

She eyed the scene with suspicion. "From who?"

"The same anonymous people who are doing this all over the city."

It was the first time I'd seen her smile. "Oh good. I was worried they were from a man I know who needs a green card." She put the flowers to her nose. "Purple is my daughter's favorite. Purple dresses. Purple flowers. When she was little, she wanted everything purple."

"Enjoy," I said, then turned to go back in my apartment.

"You remind me of her," she said. "Anna. She is about your age. Thirty."

I turned to face her. "She lives here in Manhattan?"

She shook her head. "Optyne. Ukraine." She looked at me with pale eyes, pausing as if wondering if she should say more. "The war is such misery there. But all my family—my mother, brother, sisters—anyone who's left is in that village."

"Do you go back often?"

Her face fell. "Never. I come here three years ago to make money and send it back for them."

"Must be hard for you to be so far from home."

Her hand caressed the flowers. "I am fortunate. I clean homes for the man who owns this building. He lets me to pay less rent so I can send more to them. They have nothing." She gazed at the flowers. "And today? I have these."

Then she turned and disappeared back into her apartment.

⁓

The path to the address the party-store owner had given me was an easy run, but the city smells were getting to me. I'd become used to the putrid scents wafting up from the subway vents and even the wet-dog smell of the mounds of trash bags, but the stench of burning rubber and diesel-exhaust fumes mixed with a hint of burnt pretzel was making me nauseated.

I ran faster until I spotted the apartment building I'd seen on Google Maps—three stories, with an entrance flanked by sagging faux-Corinthian columns. Luckily, the front door hadn't closed properly, so I was able to slip inside. I knocked on the first door on the right.

"Who's there?" a woman asked from inside the door. I had the sense she was looking through the peephole.

"Kate Bradley." I flashed my friendliest smile. "From ANC. I have a quick question for you."

I heard her unlock the dead bolt and unchain the door. She squeezed the door open a few inches. "How can I help you?"

"I'm looking for a guy who came in here yesterday. Wearing a gray hoodie."

She opened the door a little wider, and I could see she was petite, five four at most, and in her midtwenties, with long blonde hair tied back into a ponytail. She held a fresh bridal bouquet, white roses. "I think you have the wrong address," she said with a slight drawl. "No guys live here."

"Are you sure? Someone saw him entering this apartment yesterday morning."

"Positive. I was here all day yesterday."

I nodded at the flowers. "Are you the bride?"

She laughed. "Maid of honor. My friend's getting married this weekend. She's the one who lives here. But no one came here, except a couple of bridesmaids in the morning."

"Maybe I got the apartment wrong then. Do you know if there's a guy who lives in the building who might have come in here with huge bags of balloons?"

She shook her head. "No idea. I'm from out of town. Dallas. And only here for the wedding. My friend went out to run a few errands. Why are you looking for this guy?"

"We're thinking he might be behind all the purple and white balloons everywhere."

Her face brightened. "I saw them! Not at all what I expected for my first time in Manhattan. You think the person doing it lives here, in this apartment building?"

"Actually here. A witness saw the guy come into this apartment."

She shook her head. "They're mistaken. Sorry."

After that, I knocked on all six doors of the apartment building, but no one matched the description, and no one had seen anything unusual. Everyone said I had the wrong address.

Was there a desperate clutter of cats tied to the bottom of every subway car? That's what it sounded like. A grating, incessant whine as I waited for the train to arrive later that morning, after playing real-life *Frogger* by dodging disgusting puddles of water, rust, and the unknown on the platform. And the smell. A vaguely metallic, greasy, dusty funk that surely had to be carcinogenic.

When the train finally showed up, I rushed inside, surprised to see that the few open seats had something on them. A rock maybe?

I rolled my eyes. Was someone using stones to save seats on the subway?

"It's not saved," a thirtysomething woman with thick cornrows said to me, breaking the cardinal rule of subway riding: no conversation with strangers. "They were on the seats when we got on."

I'm sure I looked like I didn't trust her.

"Go ahead, take it."

I picked up the rock and turned it over. Handwritten with a Sharpie, it read:

SOMEBODY LOVES YOU.

Tears stung the corners of my eyes. Maybe the words were true once. But not anymore. Suddenly I was missing Eric all over again. The quirky smile on his face when he was cooking up something special for me. The warmth of his hands as they skimmed my body.

I wondered if things would've been different if he'd actually come to Manhattan. Would we have been happy? Or would the sacrifices he'd made—giving up being captain of the search and rescue team he loved—have strained our relationship to the limits? Made him angry and resentful. Of me.

Why wasn't it possible to have all the things we loved all at the same time?

As I turned the stone over in my hands, I was certain about one thing. I wanted him to be happy. Even if that meant I couldn't be with him.

I glanced at the woman next to me and saw her eyes shining with moisture too. Maybe everyone was longing for something they couldn't have.

"Mine says: 'You Matter,'" she said softly. "Some people are keeping them. I guess that's okay, right?"

I nodded and clutched the stone tightly. I was never going to hear him whisper he loved me again. Or see his face light up when he laughed.

I blinked back tears. The loss of him made my chest ache. Empty. Yet somehow the stone, its message, offered a flicker of hope.

∽

"Disheartening, discouraging, deflating. That's what's on the docket. Government shutdown. Teacher's strike in Chicago. Wildfires in LA," Mark was saying to me and a few other correspondents and producers as we stood at the front of the newsroom that morning. "We got our hands full. Let's start with the shutdown. Kate."

"Working on the impact on NASA, USDA, all the acronyms," I answered quickly, because I'd already learned that speaking at a regular pace made Mark impatient.

He pointed at Stephanie. "How are you coming on the Jaymie Clancy kidnapping story?"

"I'll have a report ready by nine."

While Mark scribbled and rearranged the news-assignments list on his iPad, I used the brief lull to pitch a story idea. "The *Times* had an article this morning about a group of millennials calling themselves the Kindness Busters. They're putting cameras everywhere, trying to catch the people who're behind the good—"

"We got no time for that," Mark interrupted.

Stephanie shook her head at me, warning me not to press further.

"Wait, they're trying to bust the people doing good?" Isabelle the producer asked, furrowing her brow. "Like, get them in trouble? Or just figure out who they are?"

"That's what I want to find out."

"They catch anyone on camera?" Mark asked.

I shook my head. "Not yet, but—"

Mark's eyes were ice cold. "Then not a story."

He turned and started talking to a reporter who was covering the high-profile murder trial of a police officer accused of shooting a man during a routine traffic stop.

"Not a story," I whispered to Stephanie. "But also, not a thing he can do to stop me from calling them."

Stephanie shot me a nervous look. "Be careful."

My phone chimed and my dad's photo flashed up, so I headed to a quiet corner of the newsroom to answer it.

"Sorry I couldn't call you back until now," he said. "I've seen some of your coverage of the shutdown. You're doing great."

"You're my dad. You have to say that."

"Everything okay? Have you had a chance to run the five-mile loop through Central Park we mapped out?"

I managed a smile. Ever since I was in second grade, my dad and I had mapped out the best running trails to try out together in whatever city we were in. And although my dad was in his early sixties, he could run them nearly as fast as I could, if he didn't stop to take phone calls. "Not yet. I'm waiting for you to get here, and we'll do it together."

"Hopefully soon. You liking the new job?"

I drew a deep breath and lowered my voice. "It's tougher than I expected. And covering this shutdown isn't exactly what I wanted to be doing here."

"Still, you've only been there a few days, and you're already covering the biggest story across the globe right now."

I sighed. "I didn't come here to cover politics."

"I know it can be tough being my daughter."

"It is. But worth it. Most of the time," I said, with a small laugh. "It's Manhattan that's the problem. My crummy apartment. This job. The city. It feels like I don't belong here."

He was silent for a moment. "Could be that you're searching in the branches for what appears in the roots."

I frowned. "You always say that, Dad. But what's that supposed to mean here?"

He didn't answer. Instead, I could hear him in a rushed conversation with someone on his end.

"Sorry, Kate. It's chaos here." His voice was low, serious. "But there's something important I need to tell you. I don't want you to be surprised by it."

"Okay, I'm ready." His tone made me worry, though. Was he sick? In some kind of political trouble because of the shutdown?

Then I heard another hurried discussion on his end, but this time several voices were talking.

"Let me call you later."

CHAPTER NINE

After my run the next morning, I slipped by the newsstand to pick up a copy of the *New York Times*. I read most of my newspapers online, but there was something romantic about reading the ink-and-paper version. It reminded me of mornings with my dad when I'd read the headlines aloud over eggs and pancakes, summarizing for him what was important in each story before heading off to elementary school.

One of the first things I did when I arrived in Manhattan was to subscribe to the *Times*. But every time they delivered my copy, someone walked off with it. I suspected Artie, the neighbor who always seemed to be coming and going at odd hours. When I returned home at three thirty in the morning after working through the night on the power-outage story, he was leaving the building, hands in his pockets, head down. I'd greeted him, but he looked past me as though he hadn't seen me. Even though I had been two feet away.

I handed the newsstand guy three dollars, saw the headlines about the government shutdown, then flipped over the page. *RIPPLE OF KINDNESS SWEEPING MANHATTAN*. Below the headline was a photo of a woman whose face I recognized.

The article read:

Angie Patterson can't stop crying. She just received a phone call from Lauren Shapiro, the general manager of the Wellington Hotel, telling her that someone has made a reservation for Ms. Patterson and her family for the next three weeks. And paid for it in full. "Our apartment burned the night of the power outage," she said. "My family, we've been staying on a friend's couch. Then some anonymous person pays for us to stay in a hotel for three weeks. All I can say is it feels like a miracle."

I studied her narrow face, sharp cheekbones. She was definitely one of the women I interviewed the night of the blackout. Another woman I'd interviewed had received keys to a new van. Was someone watching ANC and helping out some of the people I'd profiled? I wondered if Stephanie was right that our news bosses were behind this story in order to jack up the ratings.

The newsstand guy held up an ice-cold bottle of water and a *People* magazine and smiled, clearly hoping I would buy something more. I shook my head, snapped a pic of the story, and texted it to Mark with the words: *The Secret Good is Growing.*

In between calls about the shutdown, I reached out to the guys calling themselves the Kindness Busters. Turned out they weren't trying to bust the people doing good. They were trying to use tech to figure out who they were. To capture them on camera. Yet despite putting motion-sensitive cameras all around Manhattan, they'd only succeeded in snapping photos of a rat carrying a slice of pizza, a few unexplained ghostly images, endless footage of cats ambling along, and a man trying to steal a bike from someone's doorstep. In a city this big, with so many people looking for them, how had the anonymous people behind this not been spotted?

As I hung up with them, my cell phone rang again. A man started talking before I could say hello, his voice barely above a whisper. "She's here. A woman paying off, like, ten thousand dollars in payday loans."

"Where is 'here'?"

"Purple Payday Loans, on Broad Street. I saw online that this is the number to call about this kind of stuff."

"What does she look like?"

"She's got big white sunglasses. Look expensive. Her hair is covered by a red scarf. You know, like Jackie O. or some kind of old-time movie star."

"What else can you see?"

"I'm in the back office now. But I remember she's wearing, like, a plaid jacket. I'm guessing she's maybe forty or so, but I can't really tell because of the glasses and stuff."

"She give you a name?"

"Nope. Paying in cash."

"Can you snap a picture?"

"Too obvious. I mean, she's the only one here. But I will if you want."

"Okay, don't do that. But see if you can stall her. I'm heading there right now."

Scott knew the fastest route to Purple Payday Loans. His master plan involved hopping in a cab for six blocks, then jumping out and running for two very long blocks, then cutting through a narrow alleyway and leaping over a trio of bottomless dirty puddles and maneuvering past mounds of black trash bags, then running between cabs on a traffic-clogged street.

"You're sure this is the way?" I asked just as a cab driving too fast through a puddle barely missed us with his splash.

We turned the corner, and there it was. Purple Payday Loans.

I had texted Scott about the lead at 520 Eighth Avenue, and he'd texted back: *Meet in lobby. I know a fast way.*

He wasn't kidding.

"How'd you know it'd be here?" I said, out of breath.

"For Eighth Avenue, you divide the address number by twenty, then add nine, and you'll know the cross street. In this case, Thirty-Fifth Street."

"What kind of math is that?" I asked as we opened the door to a narrow storefront with a purple awning.

He smiled. "The city has an algorithm. I'll explain the math later."

Purple Payday Loans was empty except for a guy behind the counter. He couldn't have been more than twenty-five, with wavy brown hair that fell below his shoulders. "Kate Bradley?"

I nodded. "Is she still here?"

He frowned. "You just missed her. I think she got wind that something was up. I tried to stall, but she took off."

"Where to?" I asked.

"Don't know. She got into a cab."

"How did she do it?" Scott asked. "Was she paying off specific loans?"

"No. She came in saying she wanted to pay off loans with cash. I told her we couldn't give up confidential information like people's names, and she said she'd pay off loans for anyone whose last name began with *M*."

"Why *M*?"

He shrugged. "Feels like it was random. But she paid off eight thousand bucks in loans before she bailed."

"And you didn't get her name?"

"I tried. She ignored me. But she was in such a hurry to get out of here that she left something behind." He pushed a cardboard Starbucks cup toward us.

"A coffee cup," Scott said flatly.

The guy lifted the cardboard sleeve. "Underneath is her name. Marie."

Scott and I exchanged glances. "That may not be her name. Everyone has a fake Starbucks name," I said.

"It's all we got."

"What about that camera up there?" I asked, pointing up to a clunky camera on the ceiling that was pointed at any customer who stood at the counter.

"That thing's ancient. Takes crap video."

"Could we see?"

He looked around. "I'm not supposed to let anyone—"

"I don't want you to get in trouble. But we'd only need to see a few seconds, if you can do it."

He ran his hand through his hair, then looked at Scott, then at me, deciding. "I guess it's okay."

A few minutes later, he cued up the grainy black-and-white video— on a machine that whirred and hummed like it was gasping its last breath—to the point where the woman was walking through the door.

He was right. Her large sunglasses and fashionable head scarf made her totally unidentifiable.

∽

My minute-long report showed the security footage and laid out the idea that a person behind the gifts sweeping through Manhattan was a woman named Marie.

Mark scowled as he watched the finished report. "I'll slate it to air," he said with an edge in his voice. "But this is the last time you run out and do a story I don't assign you. Are we clear?"

I nodded, but inside I was still clinging to the stubborn belief—or was it simply a hope?—that my job was to find stories, not wait for approval to follow my instincts.

Luckily, the response on social media was strong enough—ANC's ninety-three million followers on Twitter retweeted the story nearly five hundred times and posted two hundred mostly positive comments—that it ended up airing multiple times throughout the night and into the morning.

When I arrived at my desk the next morning, Stephanie was heading out, with a cameraman in tow. She shot me a mock frown. "I spend days working on the huge crime wave in three major cities and don't get half the love you're getting on this story," she said. "And look, you even got fan mail. Mail room dropped it off."

I lifted the envelope from my desk. My name handwritten in black ink. No return address and not stamped, which meant someone had dropped it off instead of mailing it. I hadn't been on the air enough to have viewer fans yet, and I knew so few people in the city that I had no idea what to expect inside.

I ripped open the envelope and found a single sheet of white paper with a scrawled message:

KATE, STOP LOOKING FOR MARIE. I'M WATCHING YOU.

I shuddered. Back in LA, I'd done a series of reports about escalating gang violence and received death threats. One came in an email: *I know where you work, where you live. I will pay you a visit soon. It will be the worst day of your life.* For two long weeks after that, the station had an off-duty police officer with me 24-7. I was spooked the entire time and lost my appetite and ten pounds. I'd kept a brave face through it all yet couldn't muster the courage to go anywhere except my apartment and the newsroom.

With trembling hands, I held the letter by its right corner to avoid smudging any fingerprints, in case there were any. I headed through the newsroom, where I found Mark at the assignment desk reviewing some footage of a tropical storm brewing in the Gulf of Mexico.

"Nutcase," he said after scanning the letter. "Now that you're at ANC, get used to it. We get them all the time."

"Should I give it to security?"

He looked it over again and handed it back to me. "Don't think so. Can't imagine anyone actually threatening you for looking for the person behind all these good things happening."

"But he—or she—says, 'I'm watching you.' Feels creepy."

I could see I was testing his patience. "Of course they're watching you. That's what viewers do," he said, then rushed off to talk to someone else.

His reasoning didn't do anything to quell my anxiety. I was on edge, my chest clamped tight, as I walked home from the subway that night. I had the feeling that I was being watched. A guy with a man bun glanced at me, making casual eye contact, and I felt a shiver run through my body. Then a woman carrying a black tote bag followed behind me in step for an entire block before turning onto another street. *Spooked.*

Inside my apartment, I locked the door and slipped the chain into position. Pulled down the cheap vinyl blinds. I flung myself onto the couch but was immediately assaulted by the loud grinding sounds of metal upon metal, punctuated by crashing thuds as though someone were dropping a concrete ball on the floor. Who was doing construction on one of the apartments at this time of night? Upstairs, the neighbors were playing country music, but even the driving beat and earsplitting volume couldn't drown out the grinding.

At least the woman in the window across the way was there again, her very presence giving me a feeling of certainty when everything else felt decidedly off the hook. Tonight, she was working on a dress in lavender brocade, and in the soft light, its folds and flares and lace gathered around her like she was the subject in a baroque painting.

I tried to take my mind off it all, ease the tightness in my chest, by straightening the apartment, then sorting through the mail. Most of it was junk mail addressed to Janet and her boyfriend, because despite my filing a change of address, the post office was erratic about forwarding my mail.

Then I saw it, tucked between a flyer advertising one of those food-delivery services and another for a blonde real estate agent. It was a postcard of Times Square. Torn in the corner. On the back it read:

KATE, STOP LOOKING FOR MARIE. I'M WATCHING.

They knew where I lived.

CHAPTER TEN

My dad was worried. He was trying to sound calm, but I could feel his anxiety through the phone. He'd never been particularly good at hiding his feelings, and the telltale signs were there. The catch in his voice. The careful choice of words. "Have you talked to the police?"

"I can, but what could they do? It's not a threat to say you're watching a reporter on TV."

"It is if you drop a postcard at her office and her home mailbox."

He was right, but he'd called me as I walked the final few blocks to the ANC studios, and I was surrounded by too many people on the packed sidewalk to be honest with him about my fears. "I'll let my bosses know. Now, what's your news, Dad? What were you going to tell me the other day?"

He drew a deep breath. "I've been seeing someone. Her name is Julia. And I want you to meet her."

"Already?" I suddenly sounded like I was ten years old.

"I've been seeing her for a while now."

My voice rose another notch. "And I'm just hearing about her?"

He sighed. "I didn't want to bother you about her if I didn't think it was going to work out."

I stopped, slipped into the entrance to an electronics store. "Work out? As in . . . how?"

"Assuming we can get this shutdown resolved, I'm coming to New York with her next week."

I realized I had become one of those annoying people shouting into their cell phones on the streets of Manhattan, so I lowered my voice. "Was she the woman you took to the British prime minister's dinner at the White House?"

"Yes. She was with me."

"Dad, she looks like she's . . . I don't know. Forty maybe? And you're sixtysomething . . ."

"I know how old I am. And yes, she's forty-five. I'd really like you to go to the Metropolitan Opera with us when we're there."

"The Met? You hate opera. A ball game, sure. Maybe even a Christmas concert given by the symphony. But—"

"She's been on their board for years. And this is what she loves. Art. Music. Opera."

Everything my dad didn't like. He was a history buff who binge-watched historical documentaries, who lived for visits to museums—and read every informational plaque—and whose bookshelves were lined with biographies of practically every American historical figure from John Adams to the present. When the NPR station he listened to played anything resembling opera, he'd always switched it off.

"I'll put it on my calendar," I said, but I knew I sounded like a sullen teen.

"I think you're going to like her."

"Of course I will. She's forty-five. We were practically in high school at the same time."

He laughed. "Bring Eric. Julia got us all third-row-center seats."

I heard the joy in his voice and couldn't bear to tell him that Eric and I were not together anymore.

❧

The Christmas carols had started at five in the morning. "Christmas Will Break Your Heart." "Where Are You, Christmas?" "Blue Christmas." Instead of the usual upbeat jingle bells, chimes, and happy horns, these were the most depressing songs of the holiday, a string of melancholy wails. If it had been December, I might have forgiven the neighbors for these loud laments, but Christmas was months away, and no one should ever play somber songs at those decibels before the sun had risen.

Nothing had worked. I'd covered my ears with noise-canceling headphones, but even though they muffled the sound, they didn't mask it entirely. A few nights before, when they'd played Mongolian throat singing at high volumes, I'd used a broom to knock on my ceiling, and when that failed to get their attention, I'd actually left the apartment to get away from the din. I'd even read up online about radical solutions—blaring bagpipe music or police sirens in retaliation—but ultimately rejected all of them.

When Prince's "Another Lonely Christmas" came on, I'd had enough. Bleary eyed, I threw on some slippers and ran up the stairs. With my heart pounding and my anger at full bore, I mustered up my toughest face and stood at the door, my fist poised to knock.

But along with the music, I heard something soft and muffled. Crying. Mournful. Grief stricken. I put my hand down. Then headed back down the stairs.

On my run a little later, I couldn't stop thinking about whoever lived in that apartment and what they were going through that they were playing sad Christmas songs and crying at five in the morning. But what could I do when I knew nothing about them? The name "Waters" was scrawled on the mailbox slot, but the sticker was so old it was probably the last name of a previous tenant. All I knew from the heavy tread of their footsteps above was that at least two people lived there. Still, I couldn't stop thinking about them.

I stopped to gaze at a bakery's gorgeous window display. In the warm yellow light, the shelves in the window were lined with fresh blueberry tarts, chocolate baby Bundt cakes, cream-stuffed cannoli, delicate macarons, and sugar-dusted doughnuts. I always avoided stores like this because the calories per square inch could do serious damage to a reporter's on-air career, but a cloud of vanilla and nutmeg smells lifted on the air, inviting me to explore inside.

As I scanned the shelves, my thoughts drifted again to the upstairs neighbors. Wondering. Could I do anything more than feel sorry for them?

So much of my own life felt beyond my control: My frustrating new boss, my father's sudden girlfriend, my depressing apartment and irritating neighbors. My breakup with Eric. I wondered if doing something for them—even if it was small—might make me feel like I had the power to affect *one thing* in my life.

I ordered a dozen assorted delicacies. Then, with the sun rising behind me, I balanced the bright-blue box on my right hand and raced through the streets of Manhattan back home. Giddy with excitement, I scurried up the stairs and placed the box on the neighbors' doorstep.

I scribbled a note:

Hope your day gets better. Your neighbor.

❧

ANC's head of security, José Valles, was frowning. Maybe that was his perpetual look, because between his beefy build, broad face, and buzz cut, he seemed like someone who rarely smiled. Who had suspicions about everyone and everything.

He scanned the "stop looking for Marie" letter and the postcard, his breath coming in deep sighs; then he searched something on his laptop before fixing an intense pair of brown eyes on me. "The person did this more than once, so it's not a casual threat. Don't go anywhere alone. Or late at night. Lock your doors. Be sensible. But I don't think these are enough to warrant a beefed-up security detail on you."

"Any ideas on why they might not want me to find Marie?"

He shrugged. "Maybe finding her will lead to the letter writer and they've got a criminal history. Or maybe they're worried that if you find Marie, she'll be locked up for what she's doing."

I raised an eyebrow. "Locked up for helping people?"

"You're a reporter," he said, a dark expression crossing his face. "People are arrested all the time for reasons that don't make sense."

He was right. And it made me think for a moment that maybe finding Marie might be putting her in danger. Maybe some people would harass her for not choosing them or make death threats because she'd helped the "wrong people." The world was filled with hordes itching to be offended, to post inflammatory messages or to "take her down" on Twitter. Just because Marie was doing good things didn't make her exempt from the wrath of social media trolls. Maybe that's why she was hiding.

With so many people looking for her, might she stop all the giving to reduce her chances of being discovered? Yet the uptick in the number of gifts people were reporting seemed to suggest that she wasn't afraid of getting caught. As if she knew she was several steps ahead of all of us.

Later that morning, I checked in with the Kindness Busters and learned that all their tech—GoPro cameras, motion sensors, even a drone—still hadn't turned up anything. The leader of the group—who would only identify himself as Peter Venkman, the name of the character Bill Murray played in the *Ghostbusters* movie—told me that Manhattan had "too many people and too much stuff going on, making it easier to do kindness under cover of the crowds."

But tech aside, what puzzled me was that no one had come forward claiming to be behind the secret good, nor had any of their friends or neighbors. When reporters had searched for an anonymous Good Samaritan in Boston who had left blankets and gloves for the homeless in city parks, one of her friends had told reporters who was behind it. Here, no one was talking—no neighbors, no friends—which seemed almost impossible, considering how many people had to be involved.

I considered the idea that dozens, maybe hundreds of people were behind it. That someone started it, and now legions of copycats were running around riffing on the original idea. But despite the journalists swarming the streets of Manhattan and the tech work by the Kindness Busters, not a single person had been spotted. Which made me return to my theory that this was a small, covert group with a compelling reason for secrecy.

If cameras and drones couldn't spot them, then how would I ever find them? Even if I had an entire team devoted to it, I couldn't have "spies" in every restaurant, flower shop, party-supply store, hospital, and pharmacy in Manhattan. The scope of what they were doing was too big.

As I sat at my newsroom desk, I suddenly realized I could harness a power few people had: the ninety-three million who followed ANC on Twitter.

I journeyed upstairs through the vast warren of ANC offices until I found one of the social media directors, Amanda Rockwell. I told her what I wanted to do, and she looked at me with a tired expression through oversize glasses.

"Yeah, I kind of love the way Manhattan is these days. The balloons everywhere. People are less pushy. Even on the L train. Someone paid for my coffee at Starbucks today. But why do we need to know who's doing it?"

"Well, for one thing, we work for a news network. Finding out is what we do. But you know why else I want to find out? Because I want to know why someone would spend so much time and money giving to complete strangers. Aren't you curious?"

"I guess I assumed they'd eventually tell us. And we'd find out it was some company who wanted to make us feel good about their product. Branding or something. Or maybe a promotion for a movie or a play on Broadway . . ."

"What if it isn't?"

She frowned. "Why else would they do it?"

"That's what we need to find out."

Amanda made sure my tweet was posted that afternoon. It read: "SECRET GOOD: Who is behind the cash, flowers, balloons, free meals, free rent, paid-up hospital bills, etc. in Manhattan? ANC wants to know. Email any and all tips to ANC reporter KateBradley@ANC.com."

"Your story just got interesting," Mark was saying the next morning in the newsroom. "You know those gift cards on windshields all around town? Some guys used bolt cutters to break into a parking lot in the East Village to get at them this morning. And when other people saw what they were doing, it started a stampede. Hundreds of people flocked to that parking lot. A teenage boy got trampled. Couple of guys got in a fistfight, and one of them ended up in the hospital."

"All because of twenty-dollar gift cards?"

He nodded. "Yep. The whole thing snarled traffic in the area for forty-five minutes."

"You want me on it?"

"Nope. I already sent MJ," he said, referring to another journalist at ANC. "Keeping you on the shutdown story. But you know what I think the point of all this supposed kindness is?"

"A marketing gimmick?"

He shook his head. "To expose that we're all selfish. Greedy. We're seeing it here. People will do anything for twenty bucks."

"That's cynical." Listening to him, I wondered if I was hearing myself in fifteen years. The only difference between us was that I kept stubbornly looking for proof otherwise. I wondered if he, too, had searched for goodness in others and never found it. Then the cynicism slowly settled in, and like concrete curing over time, it hardened and became solid.

He shrugged. "Reality. People only do good things for two reasons. You want to know what they are?"

"Enlighten me," I said, but I could see my sarcasm was lost on him.

"Because we think there might be some kind of benefit to us. Or because we think it will make other people respect us more. That's it."

I relaxed my face, hoping to hide any trace of my mounting frustration. "Those are the only reasons someone might be doing kind acts for strangers? Some are estimating they've already spent a half-million dollars. You're saying they're throwing around that kind of money just to prove that we're all inherently selfish and greedy?"

He blew out a breath and looked at me as though I were a foolish child. "It's a game, Kate. You notice how many followers that NYCMiracles page has? A hundred thousand, right? But people are only interested to the extent that they might get something out of it. And the people who're doing it? They're exposing humanity at its selfish worst. That's why they're hiding in the shadows. Why they don't want you to figure out who they are."

The report from the scene in the parking lot played over and over again on ANC and other networks. It was a horrifying mash-up of cell phone video showing people shouting, shoving, pushing, and scuffling with each other, occasionally punctuated by shots of victorious people holding up twenty-dollar gift cards as though they had just won the Super Bowl. One woman even snatched a gift card from the hands of a kid wearing a dinosaur T-shirt. It took two police officers pushing through the mob to break up the fights and disperse the crowd, but not before an ambulance was called.

The story played so often that even I had the sense that there was a contagion of violence and an epidemic of bad people everywhere—all of which completely wiped out any memory of the secret good that had swept across the city. Was Mark right about this whole venture exposing the worst in all of us? And if it was, then surely all the acts of kindness would end. The people behind it had proved their point.

CHAPTER ELEVEN

The gift cards continued. In fact, judging from the posts on NYCMiracles and the texts I was receiving, the giving was *increasing*. Someone had left cash to fill the gas tanks for weary motorists at a station in Lower Manhattan. Dozens of people living on the streets reported getting packages of clothing and shoes delivered to them by Amazon. And droves of lucky Manhattanites arrived at bodegas and coffee shops to find their meals had already been paid for.

Sure, there were a few conspiracy theories still floating around suggesting that we check the flowers and balloons for listening devices. Maybe Google was listening in on our conversations through these gifts? But a guy named Noah who had found a gift card on his windshield summed it up best in his text to me: *I was raised to believe that strangers are dangerous. We can't trust them. But seeing what these strangers are doing makes me wonder if maybe we've got that wrong.*

As I grabbed a cup of coffee from the kitchen, my phone chimed, alerting me to a text from Scott.

Want to swing by my office? A friend of mine is here. He's got intel on the gift cards.

I smiled. I'd teamed up with other reporters before, but there had often been a competitive tension or disagreement on how to approach the subject. Working with Scott had none of that. It wasn't that we agreed on everything, but he seemed to trust my instincts. I was beginning to trust his too.

On my way.

Scott's office was somewhere on the seventh floor, the plush, light-soaked level that housed many of the network's brand-name hosts and their prime time shows. The floor was a hive of activity, so I had to navigate past a newsroom and around producers scrambling to start a production meeting for one of our political-news shows before I found his office at the end of a long hallway.

The first thing I noticed was that his walls were covered in photographs. Framed collages of press passes decorated one wall, while behind his desk was a huge photo of dolomite formations, shrouded in fog, and rising high from Vietnam's Ha Long Bay. A wardrobe of shirts, ties, shorts, and T-shirts hung on a rack in the corner.

"Kate," he said, rising from his chair. He was dressed casually. Dark jeans, equally dark polo. White Adidas. "This is my friend Richard. We went to high school together. He's a quant jock at one of the management-consulting firms here."

"Quant jock?" I asked, shaking his hand.

"Financial modeling. Analysis." Richard was tall, with a super-lean build that made me think he was either a marathon runner or gifted with the metabolism of a hummingbird.

"Another name for a numbers genius," Scott said. He motioned for me to have a seat on the couch. "He's noticed something important about the gift cards."

Richard opened his laptop. "My wife found one on the windshield the day this all started. I got curious, so I began plotting the streets where the cards were found, based on what people were posting on social media. The data sets can be a little wonky, because lots of people who get the cards don't post about it. But there is a pattern. Most are around the Morningside Heights area."

"I just moved here from LA. Where's that?" I asked.

He pointed to a map on his laptop. "A neighborhood that borders the Upper West Side and Harlem."

"Home of Columbia, Barnard, and a bunch of other universities," Scott added.

My thoughts were racing. "What if the gift cards are the work of some college students running a social experiment? A few years ago, Harvard did a study where they gave college students twenty dollars to spend on either themselves or someone else. They were trying to see if people were happier if they kept the money or gave it away."

"And?" Richard asked.

"The people who gave the money away reported greater happiness."

Scott's eyes lit up. "Maybe a similar experiment is at play here? It would explain a lot."

"Another thing I tracked," Richard said. "Most people report getting the gift cards in the early-morning hours. Before six. Which means they're being delivered in the dead of night—four or five in the morning. Maybe earlier."

"College students are up at those hours," Scott offered.

I pointed to the map on Richard's laptop. "The area looks relatively small. Maybe thirty blocks total. We could probably canvass the whole thing by running it tomorrow morning."

Scott nodded. "Easily."

"You guys really are hard core." Richard shook his head. "You're actually going to run the entire neighborhood to try and catch these people in the act?"

"Absolutely," I answered.

"Of course," Scott added.

He stared at us, wide eyed. "For a story?"

"Yes, but I need to be careful," I said. "Someone's been sending me messages, telling me to stop looking for Marie."

The color drained from Scott's face. "Are you kidding me?"

I shook my head. "I got notes both here and at my apartment. I showed them to security."

"Does José have any idea who's sending them?"

I shook my head. "None."

His tone was serious. "We have to be smart about this."

"If you ask me," Richard piped up, "and I know you haven't—it'd be a heck of a lot safer if you took a car or taxi. Or hired a detective to do this work."

I was silent for a moment, thinking. I had to be sensible, but I refused to live in fear, confining my life to my apartment and the newsroom. "I want to do this," I said quietly.

"Then I'll run with you," Scott volunteered. "And I'll make sure we're not followed by any crazies. What time tomorrow morning?"

"Four?"

"You know, you two are cut from the same cloth." Richard closed his laptop. "But you're both nuts."

$\sim\!\!9$

"This is a problem," I was saying the next morning when Scott showed up for our run. I pointed to his Yankees cap. "The cap isn't enough of a disguise. Everyone's going to recognize you. And when they do, our friends leaving the gift cards are going to scatter."

"You didn't recognize me when you first saw me in this cap."

"I had just been run over by a guy on a bike. We can't hope everyone is going to be dazed and confused like I was."

"What do you suggest?"

I looked at him: mussed hair, blue eyes, a hint of stubble on his jaw. Not much was going to keep people from looking at him. "Hoodie. Tied tight around your face. That's all I got."

"Fair enough." He removed the cap and tightened the hoodie so only his eyes, nose, and full lips showed. "But then you've got to wear the ball cap." He placed it on my head and smiled. "Looks better on you anyway."

Morningside Heights before dawn was hushed, faintly aglow. As we ran at a clipped pace, Scott was easy to talk to as he pointed out a famous diner, Tom's Restaurant, whose exterior was used as a stand-in for the fictional café in *Seinfeld*, and called out all the colleges and universities in the "Academic Acropolis."

I learned that he had studied political science at Yale, but otherwise, Scott didn't talk much about his past, steering the conversation either to something we were running by or to questions about the people we were hoping to find.

Ninety minutes later, after scanning every car and peering at every awake person—even following some for a few blocks—we'd covered a lot of ground but hadn't discovered anything.

"Maybe this is a bust," he said, slowing to a stop at a street corner. He unzipped his hoodie, revealing a slim-fitting black *Zoolander* T-shirt underneath.

"You're only saying that because you're beat," I teased.

He shot me a boyish grin. "You think so, do you? Truth is, I've got a better idea. You know what sounds really good right now? Waffles. With warm syrup."

"You know what sounds even better?" He looked up at me, and there was that spark again. "Another two miles. If I don't get some kind of foothold on this story, I'm going to be stuck on the government-shutdown political beat forever."

"There are worse things, you know. And research shows waffles will help you face the reporting challenges ahead."

His doe-eyed, hungry expression was convincing. Almost.

"I'd like to see your research sources."

"Okay. Want some proof? They're the reason I made it through an ice-climbing expedition in the Canadian Rockies for one of last season's episodes."

"Waffles are."

"Serious. The extreme cold—not to mention three hours of climbing up sheets of ice right after dawn—were knocking us out. It's a scary climb with no margin for error. But our cinematographer kept coaxing the team, saying, 'Get this done, and we'll all be eating plates of waffles.' It worked."

"Okay, somewhat convincing." Why was I always smiling around him?

Out of the corner of my eye, I noticed movement down the block. The slightest blur in between the cars parked within inches of each other in a tight line.

I touched Scott's arm and gestured. In the dim predawn light, someone was weaving between the cars. Their back was to us, and from my vantage point, I couldn't tell if it was a man or woman. They could have been casing the cars to see if people had left them unlocked, but it looked like they were stopping briefly at each one, making some kind of hand movement, then moving on, heading away from us.

We ran softly, making as little noise as possible. "Hope this doesn't end up being someone passing out junk mail flyers," I whispered.

Then we saw it. A gift card wrapped in a purple ribbon perched on the windshield of a Honda Civic.

We picked up the pace and caught up to the guy pretty quickly. "Excuse me," I said. "Are you doing this, putting gift cards on these cars?"

The guy turned around. He was handsome. Perfectly symmetrical features, square jaw, deep-set blue eyes. He looked like he wanted to bolt. "Yeah. That's not a crime or anything, is it?"

"No. We've just been wondering who's behind it. And now we know. I'm Kate Bradley," I said, extending my hand.

Scott removed his hood. "Scott Jameson. From ANC."

The guy looked at Scott, then at me. "Aren't you on that *Wonders* show?"

"Yes. But what we'd like to know is . . . who are you?" Scott asked.

"Name's Logan," he said, with a hint of a southern accent. "But this isn't what you think. This is my first time doing this. I'm not the guy who's been doing this all over."

"You're not?"

He was young. Barely out of high school. Wearing blue jeans with a belt and a navy-blue polo, tucked in. "I'm just visiting. From Kentucky. Here staying with my aunt and uncle for my cousin's graduation."

"Why are you doing this?"

"I saw all the news about the gift cards and thought I'd join in."

I gave him a skeptical look. "Just like that? You thought you'd put gift cards on windshields?"

"I started a new job a few weeks ago, so I can't afford to do very many." He scanned the cars on the street. "I'm doing, like, what, six total."

"You're from Kentucky, but you're putting gift cards on windshields for six people you don't know in Manhattan?" Scott asked.

"When you say it that way, it sounds kind of strange. But, yeah. Some guy from here helped me out when the airline lost my luggage on the way in through Dallas. So why's it weird if I kinda do the same thing and help out a few strangers before I go back?"

Scott and I looked at each other. He had a point.

He shrugged a backpack onto his shoulders. "Look, it's cool meeting you both. But I have a plane to catch, so I'm gonna run."

"Mind if we snap a photo of you in case we can use it for the news report?" I asked, bringing out my phone.

He looked at us, then his phone, deciding. "I guess."

As I snapped the photo, he looked away, ruining the picture.

We had no real leads. None.

Which made it easy for Mark to say no to staying on this story. And with the government shutdown finally over after a tense two-thirty-in-the-morning agreement between the parties, he assigned me the aftermath. That meant I spent the morning looking into how long it would take the airline industry to get back to normal after the shutdown had created flight delays and chaos at major airports around the country. After a morning interviewing FAA officials and a flight captain for American Airlines, I headed back into the newsroom and into the kitchen for a late-afternoon cup of coffee.

Scott was there, talking to a man I recognized as one of the legendary producers at the network, Michael Kim, a gruff-voiced machine of a man. Michael's conservative gray suit and tie were an instant tell that he was one of the top brass, not someone you'd see in the newsroom kitchen very often. Scott towered over him and was dressed for adventure: strong, tanned legs beneath blue cargo shorts and a trim white henley. He was barefoot and held a pair of water shoes.

"Kate, there's someone I'd like you to meet," he said, motioning for me to come over.

"Is there an Amazon rain forest somewhere around here?" I asked, nodding at the Oakley sunglasses slung around his neck.

He smiled. "I'm shooting a promo in the studio. Green screen is the closest I'm getting to the rain forest right now. Michael, meet Kate. I've been lucky to work with her on some of the stories about all the good things happening around Manhattan."

"I've seen your reports," he said, shaking my hand.

"You know, one of the rumors going around is that the whole thing is an operation cooked up by some of the news bosses here to boost ratings."

He must have thought I was kidding. "Well, it is boosting ratings."

"And it's strange that two of the people I included in my reports during the blackout ended up getting help."

He shrugged. "I get the feeling you already know that it's not the executive news team at work here. What your observation does prove is that whoever *is* responsible is watching you."

Watching you. My pulse quickened as I tried to put it together. Why were the people doing this good stuff watching *me*? Why didn't they want me to find Marie?

Michael clapped a hand to Scott's shoulder. "I'll catch up with you after I've nailed down the details."

As Michael left the kitchen, Scott turned to me. "I've been thinking about the gift cards guy, Logan. Why does a guy wear a backpack at five in the morning if he was only putting gift cards on five or six windshields?"

"Maybe because he was heading to the airport afterward?"

"My guess is that there were more gift cards in that backpack. And we stopped him before he could give them out."

"I've been wondering about him too. I checked a photo of the gift card he was giving out against one of the original ones you found on your windshield." I scrolled through some photos on my phone and showed one to him. "They're identical. Same gift card. Same exact shade of purple ribbon."

"So maybe he's not the copycat he says he is."

"A guy who's visiting from Kentucky for his cousin's graduation just happens to use the exact same ribbon and gift cards that hundreds of people have already received? What are the odds of that?"

He shrugged. "Could be the ribbon and gift cards are pretty common, though. Maybe we should check out a couple of Duane Reades or CVSs tonight?"

"Good idea," I said. "Except . . . not tonight." I sighed. "Tonight, I've been summoned to the Met with my dad."

"Opening night. *Barber of Seville*. Lucky you."

"Seats at third row, center. I'm planning to leave at intermission."

"You're not excited?"

"Screeching sopranos. Hammy acting. Hardly."

"It's a wacky story about love and disguises. You're going to be wowed."

"'Wacky.' 'Wowed.' You did hear me say that I'm going to the opera, right?"

He laughed. "I *envy* that you're going to the opera."

"Seriously?"

"I've been going since forever. First my mom or my aunts dragged me; then I actually grew to love it."

"Maybe you'll go in my place?"

"Third-row center? Sure. But I'm pretty sure your dad wouldn't like that."

"Actually, I have an extra ticket. All yours, if you want it," I said, then flushed red. It sounded like I was asking him out. Like I'd planned it. But I'd begun to feel so at ease around him that the invitation tumbled out before I'd considered how he might interpret it. "I didn't mean that to sound . . . well, it's not like I'm asking you—"

"I'm in. But I know your motives."

My eyes traveled over his face. "You know my motives."

"You're only inviting me so you can duck out at intermission and your dad won't notice because I'm there."

"My dad won't even notice I'm there. He's asked me to the opera to meet his new girlfriend. Apparently, she's on the Met board and loves opera."

He raised an eyebrow. "And from the way you say that, I'm guessing you don't like her?"

"I haven't met her. All I know is that she's seventeen years younger than my dad."

"Looks like it's shaping up to be a miserable evening," he said with a wicked smile. "*Barber of Seville*. Dad's new, younger girlfriend. Can't wait."

"You're serious."

"On one condition."

"Let me guess. You want to bail at intermission too."

"The opposite. You owe me a dollar for every time you laugh tonight."

I smiled. "You're on. You won't get enough to buy a cup of coffee."

CHAPTER TWELVE

Julia was an expert at working a room. Or in this case, the lobby of the Met before the performance. Dressed in a stunning royal-blue sheath dress with a China-inspired print, she seemed almost to glide across the lobby on my father's arm, shaking hands, exchanging hugs and kisses and brief pleasantries. From across the lobby, I couldn't hear what anyone was saying to her, but I could see her face light up when she introduced my father and the surprised looks from her friends when they realized who he was. As she spoke with one distinguished-looking couple, her hand slowly slid down my father's arm until their fingers intertwined. They exchanged a brief glance, and I caught the look on his face. Happy.

She seemed younger than the forty-five years my father claimed she was. Delicate bone structure with a toned body that looked like she spent a lot of time in a yoga studio. I studied her, wondering if I could figure out anything from watching her. Was she in this for the money? For the prestige of being a US senator's girlfriend?

Girlfriend. Even the word bothered me. Ever since my mom died, it had always been the two of us—we hashed out the news together on the phone, I'd attended endless political fundraisers and dinners as the senator's daughter, and when he was in town, we'd keep up our traditional five-mile runs together. Would Julia change all that?

"Want to tag team interrogating her?" a voice from behind said.

I whirled around to find Scott. Sleek in a black pin-striped suit, he looked like he had stepped out of a magazine ad. The cobalt-blue tie made his eyes appear a deeper blue. Wow, did he clean up well.

"You're looking at her like she's the subject of your next interview. Or interrogation."

"I'm trying to figure out if I'm going to like her or not."

"Probably easier if you actually met her, no?"

He waited for me to agree, and then we made our way through the crowd. When my dad spotted me, he and Julia excused themselves from their conversation with a young couple.

"You must be Kate," Julia said, taking my hand in both of hers. Her voice was higher than I expected. Breathy, like she was some kind of ethereal being. "I'm Julia. I've been looking forward to meeting you."

I glanced at my dad, and his eyes seemed to be saying: *Please like her.*

"Me too," I said.

"And you must be Eric," she said, turning to Scott.

"Scott, actually."

Julia's cheeks flushed. "Oh, I'm sorry for getting that wrong."

"This is my colleague at ANC, Scott Jameson," I said.

I could see my dad was trying to figure out where Scott fit into the picture, and I kicked myself for not telling him that Eric and I had broken up. He recovered quickly. "I've seen your show. *Wonders of the World*, is it? The last one I saw, you were in Patagonia climbing some impossible mountain."

"Mount Fitz Roy. I did a segment on the two million acres some billionaires bought up and turned into national parks."

"That seems to have stirred up some controversy with the locals."

"They were trying to make the case that unspoiled wilderness is more valuable than any of the minerals or timber that can be stripped from it."

"Compelling story," my dad said. He nodded, as if he were thoroughly engaged in the discussion, but I could see he was still trying to understand why Scott was here and not Eric. "I'd like to hear how it turns out."

"And I want to know all about the secret good sweeping through our city. The story you've been working on, Kate," Julia said. "Tell me you have some idea who's behind it."

I smiled. She was already making it hard for me not to like her.

∽

The Barber of Seville was bubbly, wacky, and funny. The young Count Almaviva's many disguises and ruses to make beautiful Rosina love him for himself—not his money—had all of us, even my dad, laughing.

Midway through the performance—and yet another of the count's disguises, this time as a sailor—I looked over at Scott, and his eyes were lit up. Anyone watching him on TV would think he was largely an adventure junkie, but seeing him in this setting made me realize he was more than that.

"You were right," I whispered. "I am already wowed."

His eyes met mine. "It gets even better."

But it was during one of the quieter moments, the tender anthem to love sung at the very end, when the two meant-for-each-other lovers found out they could be together, that Scott looked at me again, and his mouth curled into a faint smile, making me feel warm all over. No words were whispered. Our bodies weren't even touching. Yet it felt as though we were having a silent communication buzzing between us. I could actually feel his joy, and I had the sense he knew mine. When the performance was over, the entire audience stood, giving the cast a warm ovation. We both lingered a fraction too close, his fingers gently brushing against mine.

Then Julia swept in, introducing us to a woman in a mustard-yellow tweed coat and oversize glasses who was seated in front of us. I had the feeling she was a major donor to the opera because a man in a stylish suit, likely a Met executive, stood beside her, hanging on every word.

"This is Nan Fremont," Julia said, introducing her to my father and me, but before she could make the introduction to Scott, Nan interrupted.

"I already know this one," she said, hugging him briefly. "Wonderful seeing you, Scott. When is your mother back from Singapore?"

"Next week," he answered.

"Give her my best." Then she gestured to a young woman next to her who was wearing a striking geometric-print dress. "This is my niece, Elizabeth. We're throwing her a thirtieth birthday party at Masa next month. I'll send you an invitation. You should come."

"Thank you. I'll check my schedule," he said.

By the time we left Nan, my dad and Julia looked like they were planted in a conversation with a small group, so Scott and I said our good nights and made our way through the lobby and out the door, but not before a man with a shock of jet-black hair threaded through the crowd, calling Scott's name.

"I'm glad I caught up with you," he said, then launched into a three-minute monologue about a gala at the Natural History Museum—an event that Scott had apparently also attended—before asking him to emcee a fundraiser at Hayden Planetarium and then eventually letting us go.

"So, this is what it's like to host a hit TV series on ANC?" I asked as we stepped outside into Lincoln Center Plaza. "People invite you to their nieces' birthday parties at five-star restaurants. And they stalk you in the Met lobby, asking you to emcee fundraisers."

"I don't think it has anything to do with my show."

"No?"

"I'm guessing you haven't googled me."

"Nope."

"And you don't know anything else about me?"

"Okay, now you're scaring me. Are you Ted Bundy's brother or something?"

He laughed. "I like that your first guess is that I'm some kind of serial killer."

We stopped in front of the famed Revson Fountain. I'd seen it in countless movies, but tonight, lit by the glow of hundreds of white lights, it somehow seemed even more magical.

"Here's my second guess. Elon Musk's love child?"

"Closer." He smiled. "My mother is Virginia Biltmore."

Virginia Biltmore was a billionaire heiress to a textile fortune. A New York socialite known for her many marriages to high-profile men.

I looked at him in surprise. "I had no idea. I never googled you because I thought I knew a lot about you from watching nearly every episode of *Wonders*. I'd never have guessed you were the son of an heiress."

"I'll take that as a compliment."

"Is that why you always change the subject every time I ask about your past?"

He flashed me a smile. "I didn't realize I was doing that. But I guess the answer is yes. Being her son comes with a whole set of assumptions about who I am. People expect me to be the flashy Manhattanite going to all the marquee parties or hanging on a yacht in Sag Harbor. Or running one of the family's many businesses. But I'd rather be tracking a column of macaroni penguins on the ridge of an old volcano crater in Antarctica."

"Chasing penguins does sound more fun. Especially ones you call 'macaroni' penguins."

"That is their actual name, you know." His eyes brightened. "How about you? It can't be easy being Senator Bradley's daughter."

"It's a long story."

"Then give me three sentences."

"Okay, here goes. Everyone assumes I want to get into politics. Even my dad doesn't understand why I don't follow in his footsteps—the trail has already been marked for me. In many ways, it'd be a lot easier than being a reporter. But I'd rather be running after a story than running for office."

"That's more than three sentences," he said, with a grin. "But I can see we both have our stubborn streaks when it comes to what our parents would like us to be doing."

I laughed. "Who are you calling stubborn?"

His lips parted in a soft smile. "Both of us. Definitely."

I took a seat by the fountain, and he settled in next to me. As we watched the water jump and dance in a carefully choreographed water ballet, the sound of the rushing, splashing water drowning out the city noise, Manhattan felt kind of spellbinding. I could see why people might fall in love with this city.

"I'm glad you enjoyed *The Barber of Seville*," he said, his tone all serious. "But now I've got an important question to ask."

"A question?"

The corner of his mouth lifted into an impish grin. "Any thoughts on when you're going to pay up on your debt?"

"My debt?"

"Twenty-two dollars. A dollar for each time you laughed tonight."

The warm look in his eyes sent my pulse racing. "Are you sure it was twenty-two times? You were counting?"

"It might have been twenty-four. I did take my eyes off you occasionally."

CHAPTER THIRTEEN

The email was insistent: *Come to our store on West 28th Street. I've seen the person who is buying all the purple and white flowers. Lulu.*

I wrote back: *What did he/she look like? Can you send a photo?*

Just come. Holiday Flower and Plant. 5:30 am tomorrow. Before we open.

I sighed. I couldn't imagine any good reason she wouldn't tell me the information by email. And from my experience on countless other stories, a sketchy email like this probably wouldn't lead to anything. But I was curious enough that I agreed to meet her. Besides, the Flower District was a few blocks from my apartment.

At five thirty the next morning, I arrived at West Twenty-Eighth Street and scanned the one-block area of Chelsea for the store. Instead of bus fumes and sewer smells, the air was thick with the scents of wisteria, hyacinth, and roses. Outside the store, workers were stacking the gum-splotched sidewalks with cartons filled with fresh carnations and perfect long-stem roses in every color.

I found Lulu standing beneath a faded green awning with the words HOLIDAY FLOWER AND PLANT, ESTABLISHED 1938. She was barely five feet tall with lush dark hair and a smooth, lineless face. "Every morning it's crazy here with trucks and customers coming in and out," she said with a soft, melodic accent that sounded like she came from the

Philippines. "Hundreds of people everywhere, it's always elbow to elbow, so I wouldn't normally have noticed anybody in particular, you know. But yesterday, one guy stood out. He was in an army uniform."

"Fatigues?"

She nodded. "He was loading up dozens of cartons of purple coneflowers and baby's breath. And rolls of our purple ribbon. People don't usually buy so many purple flowers like that."

"Do you have a photo? A name?"

"He paid in cash, so we didn't get a name or address. No photo either."

"What'd he look like?"

"In his twenties. I think. African American. Tall. Muscular."

I hid my frustration. "That could be lots of people."

"That's why I asked you to come. There *is* a way to find him." She lowered her voice and looked around to make sure no one could hear her. "I wrote down the license plate number of his van. My husband's a cop. I asked him to run the license plate."

"And he did?"

She nodded. "I'll tell you what he found out, but I need you to promise you won't tell anyone how you got the information. My husband would lose his job."

"Why is he willing to risk his job telling me this information?"

She shook her head. "All the flowers and things they're doing are nice, but they are very strange."

"Strange. How do you mean?"

"My husband's seen it all working for the NYPD: break-ins, shootings, beatings, gang violence. So we can understand why someone might steal or do bad things. Maybe they're hungry or have no money to live on. Or have a drug or alcohol problem. But why would someone pay for meals or the rents for people they don't know? What's in it for them?"

She was right. We'd grown so accustomed to hearing about crimes and thinking about the motives behind them that, when faced with someone doing the opposite of crimes, we were immediately suspicious of their motives.

She scrolled through her phone. "Here's the email from my husband. The van is registered to Kevin Raley. 145 West Twelfth Street. When you figure out why he's doing this, would you let me know? Hope it's not something illegal."

"I will, thank you."

"Oh, and one more thing. He wasn't alone. A girl was helping him."

∞

Kevin Raley's address was a well-maintained six-story apartment building on a tree-lined street in Greenwich Village. I passed through an entryway door decorated with elaborate wrought ironwork and found his last name scrawled in black ink near the top of the old-fashioned doorbell panel.

I cleared my throat and pressed the button. A male voice squawked through the speaker. "Can I help you?"

"This is Kate Bradley. From ANC. I'm looking for Kevin Raley."

"What for?"

"I'd like to talk with him about a story we're doing."

A few seconds later, the door buzzed. I grabbed the handle and stepped inside a mosaic-tiled entryway. A door down the hall swung open, and a man wearing a baseball jersey stepped into the hallway.

"I'm Kevin Raley. How can I help?"

Although part of the description matched—he was tall and African American—he was a paunchy man, at least fifty, with hair graying at his temples. I had a hard time imagining him wearing army fatigues.

I walked toward him. "I'm doing a story about all the things happening around the city: flowers, gift cards . . ."

His eyes brightened. "I've been hearing about that."

"Someone said they saw you and your van in Chelsea yesterday buying a truckload of purple flowers."

"You think I'm somehow involved in all that?" he said, obviously surprised.

"Someone at the flower mart said they saw you."

"They saw *me*?"

"They said you were wearing army fatigues."

He laughed. "Do I look like I wear fatigues?"

"So you're obviously not in the army."

"No. My son Joe is, though." He narrowed his eyes. "Wait, how did you find me? My vans don't have signage on them. Is there some kind of trouble?"

My stomach clenched, but I smiled anyway. "The opposite of trouble," I said, trying to dodge his question. "Could your van have been at the flower mart in Chelsea yesterday morning?"

He nodded, crossing his arms. "One of them could. Nearby anyway. I own a bunch of vans that are out every morning delivering to hotels and office buildings. Are you talking about the one on Twenty-Eighth? We deliver to the Hilton and DoubleTree nearby. But they wouldn't have been at the flower mart."

"Your son. The one in the army. Could he have been on Twenty-Eighth yesterday morning? Maybe driving your van?"

He shook his head. "No."

"Maybe I could talk with him?"

"He's not here. He's with family in the Bronx."

"Could I call him?"

He sighed, not the way people did when they were tired, but a shuddery sigh like he was on his last thread of energy. "He's only in town because his sister—my daughter—just passed away," he said, sadness in his eyes. "He's in for the funeral."

I looked at him in shock and felt my head go light. I wasn't afraid to ask questions. Ever. But all my questions suddenly seemed unimportant. "I'm so sorry . . ."

His voice became heavy, dense. "You couldn't have known. My son's been through the worst of it. Took him two days to get here from Afghanistan. First to Istanbul, then bad weather had him rerouted through Dallas, and finally here. No way he's the guy you're looking for."

I reached out to shake his hand. "Thank you for talking with me. I'm so sorry about what your family is going through. Looks like we got our wires crossed."

"We need one lead to pan out. One. That's all," Scott was saying, as if it would be easy. It was nearly eight o'clock after a long day spent reporting on the after-effects of the government shutdown, and he'd swung by my desk on his way out. Wearing a sleek charcoal-gray suit and white shirt, collar open, he looked like he was heading out for an important event.

He sat at the empty desk next to mine as I filled him in on the dead end with Kevin Raley.

"We did make some progress," I said. "One of the interns looked into the purple ribbon. He could only find one place that sells the style of ribbon that's been on all the gift cards and flowers. Holiday Flower and Plant in Chelsea."

He eased back in his seat, shaking his head. "We're supposed to believe that the guy—Logan, was it?—went all the way to Chelsea and got that same exact ribbon so he could put it on a few gift cards?"

"He lied to us. He's part of the secret group. I'm sure of it."

"And now that he's left town, we've got to find a way to track him down."

Out of the corner of my eye, I spotted Mark rushing through the newsroom, a heavy leather briefcase in one hand, his cell phone pressed to his ear. He headed toward us.

"Why are you two still here?" he asked.

"Getting ready to leave," I said.

"Waiting for someone," Scott answered.

"Then I'll cut to the chase. Is there . . . something going on between you two?" he said, pointing to Scott and then at me. "Someone told me they saw you at the fountain in front of the Met last night, and it looked—"

"We were—"

He pointed to Scott. "You, I'm not responsible for. But the network won't like any gossip on your end either." Then he pointed at me. "But you, I am. My job is to keep things sane around here. I can't have you two adding to the . . . drama."

My cheeks flushed. "Nothing is going—"

"So, you're not—"

"C'mon, Mark, do you have any idea how hard it would be to go out with Senator Bradley's daughter?" Scott said, in an attempt to inject some levity into the discussion. "You have to undergo a full background check, endure an interview with Homeland Security, and complete the entire national security questionnaire."

"It's only a hundred thirty pages," I said, laughing.

Our humor wasn't working on him. "Andrew wants to see all of us in his office tomorrow morning. Nine."

"Why? We're only working on a story," I said.

"Keep it that way," Mark said, then marched away, starting another call.

Scott leaned in and lowered his voice. "I should've warned you about the rumor mill. Gossip spreads faster than the actual news around here."

"Any idea what Andrew wants to talk to us about?"

His head dipped lower, closer to mine. "Mark was probably just trying to scare us from ever going to the opera together again."

"It's working," I whispered.

"There you are," a woman's voice said.

I turned to see a woman with luminous blonde hair in a formfitting white dress. She walked toward us with the graceful posture of a ballerina and the delicate facial structure to match.

"I went to your office, but they said you were in here," she said.

Scott rose, his face flushed. "Paige, this is Kate."

She smiled. "Nice to meet you." She glanced at the watch on her slender wrist. "We should get going. You know how Lauren and Blake get when we're late."

CHAPTER FOURTEEN

"Listen to me, damn it!" Raymond was shouting in the hallway. On his phone. At eleven o'clock at night. His booming bass voice was so loud and agitated that even with my door and windows shut, I could hear its hammering cadence as I headed to bed. Words like *lies* and *failure* punctured the air.

Even worse was the smoke. He had been out there so long that it smelled like he'd powered his way through an entire box of very cheap cigars.

I considered shouting at him to be quiet but then decided not to. Raymond was easily double my size, and the threatening words he was using made it clear he was white-hot angry. I thought about calling the police, but I knew in big cities like LA and Manhattan, it'd be hours until they arrived.

When his phone argument continued for another ten minutes, I decided to poke my head into the hallway. My plan was not to say anything. Only to look at him and hope he realized how loud he was being.

It didn't work.

He yelled another obscenity-laden tirade into the phone, then turned to me, his face dark with anger. "Can I help you?"

"Is everything okay?" I asked.

He stepped toward me. "Mind your own business, will you?"

"It's past eleven."

He stopped talking and looked to be on the crispy edge of anger, as if he were going to come over and punch me.

"I gotta call you back," he said, then swiftly hung up and jammed the phone into his back pocket.

He strode toward me in silence.

My first instinct was to run inside my apartment and lock the door. But nearly every day on my breaking-news beat in LA, I'd encountered someone in such a spitting rage over something that had happened that I often wondered how they functioned in life. If I was lucky, it was only words they spewed. But a guy once slashed my tires over what he thought was an unflattering story, and a mom of three keyed my car because she was angry about my live coverage of a street protest. Along the way, I'd developed a system for dealing with anger: *Show no fear. Lower your voice. Listen. Find your story.*

I stood there, my heart hammering so hard I felt it pulsing in my throat. And then the moment suddenly had a heightened feel to it, as if I were in a nightmare, unable to move, my feet bolted to the floor.

My words came out breathy. "What's going on?"

As he stepped closer, I noticed a hint of moisture in the corners of his red-rimmed eyes. Tears.

"Someone stole from me. They've told lies." His face was red, swollen. "And now instead of building, I'm shutting everything down. Layoffs. Teardowns."

"I'm so sorry."

There was no mistaking the heartbreak in his eyes. "Just when you think you got it right, y'know? You treat your crew the best you know how. You try to be the best boss. Hell, I know I yell too much. But then they talk behind your back. Lie. Steal from you."

"Maybe you can get back some of what they stole."

His voice was raw with emotion. "Impossible."

I'd misjudged him. I had decided that his abrasive talk and his tough-guy looks represented all he was—a shark. But beneath his shark persona, might there be a goldfish inside?

Anyone seeing him shouting all these days on the front steps would have found him frustrating. Fear inducing. Could it be that he—like so many people—was reeling in pain, disappointment, and loss and hiding that behind a tough exterior?

"Trust no one," he said. "If you do, you're just gonna get screwed."

"I've got to hope that's not true."

"It's easy to have hope when you're young. When you haven't had too many things taken from you."

"You got a raw deal from someone. But most people? Most people are not like that."

He glanced at me with mournful eyes. "I wish I could believe that's true."

I'm not sure where the words came from, but they slipped out as though I'd planned them. "Tell me what I can do to help."

His voice was icy. "What can you do, anyway? You gonna go help me shut down the construction site? Tell my crew they don't have jobs anymore?"

"If that would help you? Okay."

He cracked a smile. "You know what? I actually think you *would* do it."

My voice was steadier than I felt. "Sometimes things just . . . suck. Things happen that make us feel like this is going to be the way it is forever. And we get stuck in this bubble, feeling like we're the only one going through this crap. But we're not alone. Tell me what I can do to help."

His shoulders sagged as if the tension in his body were a balloon that had just burst. He opened his mouth to speak, but no words came out.

"Don't know," he managed to say. "The best thing you could do is . . . exactly what you're doing. If some jerk had been hollering in the hallway like I've been, I would've thrown something at them instead."

I smiled. "That was Plan B."

"It's late," he said, quietly. "But thank you, Kate."

We both turned and started back to our apartments. When I got to my door, I stopped.

"Raymond?"

He swung around to look at me. "Yeah."

"I hope things get better. I'm pulling for you."

"The numbers are astounding," Andrew was saying in his office the next morning. Dressed in a slate-blue shirt with a white collar and cuffs along with tortoiseshell glasses, he looked decidedly scholarly. "It's impossible to tie specific stories to ratings on the channel, but the views on social media and YouTube are through the roof. Millions. And the numbers grow with each story you've filed."

Andrew's office was stunning: breathtaking views of the New York City skyline, a spacious seating area with buttery-soft leather couches, and a credenza lined with fresh pastries and a high-end coffee maker.

While Scott and I sat on a couch across from Andrew, Mark stood, his arms crossed, looking annoyed. "Sounds like a numbers error."

"Yeah, the team thought so too," Andrew said. "Which is why it took so long for us to get the data. But the stories about the good stuff happening are outpacing every single story on the channel now."

I couldn't believe what I was hearing. "Even all the government-shutdown stories?"

I sensed that Mark already knew the answer to that question and didn't like it. In fact, from the way he was biting his lower lip, it seemed like he didn't like anything about this meeting at all.

Andrew glanced through some numbers on his tablet. "People are hungry for hope. That's why I want to try something unusual. I want to put you both on this story."

"Both of us?" Scott asked.

"I saw the piece you did together at Bryant Park with the people who had their rent paid. You two have great chemistry on air. Putting you on this together will distinguish our coverage. And we need that. Because we got competition. Lots of it."

"CTN and Fox are both working on large-scale coverage of this story," Mark said. "CBS too."

"And we know that how . . . ?" I asked.

"We're that good," Mark said.

"Scott, I've cleared it with Michael," Andrew continued. "I know you're up to your ears in prep on the *Wonders* series. But it's up to you to decide if this is something you want to do."

"Count me in. I want this."

Andrew rubbed his hands together. "Great. But first, I need some clarity on the lead you were following—this person named Marie. I saw the report you shot at the payday-loans company. What else do you know about her?"

I shook my head. "Nothing. It's a dead end."

He turned his tablet toward me. "Dead end or not, someone doesn't want you to find her. They sent this video at four this morning." He swiped the screen and pressed play. The video was shaky; then, when it came into focus, I realized it was footage of my apartment building in the early evening. Shot from across the street. A few seconds into the video, I walked into frame and up the steps. As I fumbled to get my keys out of my purse, a man's voice intoned: "Stop looking for Marie."

A chill ran up my spine.

"Holy hell," Mark whispered.

"I've got security looking into this," Andrew said, stopping the video. "But they haven't been able to trace where it came from."

"Maybe Marie might actually be who we're looking for," I said. "I mean, why else would someone go to all this trouble to scare me into *not* looking for her?"

Andrew smiled. "I like that your first instinct is to see this as a possible clue. But I don't like the guy's tone. Or his persistence. José in security told me about the postcard that came here and to your apartment." He closed his eyes and rubbed his forehead. "I don't like how this is rolling out. I've hired an off-duty police officer to drive you to and from the newsroom."

Mark looked at him in shock. "Don't you think that's overkill?"

"We can't take any chances," Andrew said. "I want the entire team to be cautious. Let's avoid nighttime coverage or investigations where you're out on the streets by yourself, Kate."

I frowned. "Some of my best reporting has been done—"

"I know I'm clipping your wings. But let's be smart about this."

∞

Anxiety braided in my chest. I felt like I was on a tightrope again, balancing so precariously that a fall simply felt . . . inevitable. I fantasized about going back, escaping to the comforts of LA. I thought about walking the beach in my bare feet, the foam of the waves lapping at my sand-crusted toes. Then I closed my eyes and imagined eating Korean barbecue tacos from the food truck parked on La Brea most Friday nights in summer and felt the tension—the knot in my stomach—slowly release. But alluring as the fantasy was, I knew instinctively going back wouldn't solve everything. I could only go forward and face whatever danger and uncertainty lay ahead.

One solution was simply to do what they were asking: stop looking for Marie. I was mulling over that option when Scott showed me a story some Wall Street types had posted on NYCMiracles.

"You've got to see this," he said, pointing to the post on his iPad. In the photo, four finance types dressed in custom-made shirts and dark Prada suits stood next to a man in a wheelchair. "These guys found gift cards on their windshields and donated them to Gary Harpe, a veteran who, in summer months, is always tooling around Wall Street in his wheelchair."

I shrugged. "People do that all the time. Give to the homeless."

"This is different. They've seen this vet every day. Handed him some change and then moved on, never giving him another thought. Yet finding a thin piece of plastic, a gift card, disrupted their routine. They started talking to him. One of them found out he'd been in the marines a few years ago. And then they hatched a plan and got him a position at their big-name firm. That's why we have to find Marie. To understand what inspired this movement. This change."

I looked at him in surprise. I'd never worked with anyone who cared about a story as much as I did or so easily saw beyond the obvious to lock in on what was really important.

As we headed out to record our stand-ups, relief seeped into my veins. Being back in the field in front of the camera, telling the story, was helping me regain my bearings. Making me less afraid.

Scott's part of the report had him perched high atop a turret in Belvedere Castle, a fantasy stone-facade structure in Central Park, where Chris captured a breathtaking wide-angle shot of a sea of purple and white balloons bobbing all around, with the Manhattan skyline as a backdrop.

"Everywhere you turn, something good is happening," he said, opening the report. "Maybe it's cheery balloons on your morning commute. Or perhaps you woke up to find your rent or your utilities have been taken care of. Your prescriptions or your cupcake order paid for by a stranger. You might have been one of the thousands to find a purple gift card on your windshield. Or you've had your meal paid for at the coffee shop or at your favorite bodega. Perhaps you've connected with a stranger over a free meal at a restaurant, or your child has made new friends because of a no-one-eats-alone free meal at school. Whatever it is, people throughout Manhattan are all experiencing the same feeling: joy."

"Balloons. Flowers. A few dollars," I continued, standing by a construction site on Leonard Street where someone had left bouquets of purple flowers on a backhoe. "They're simple. Ordinary. Most times we might even overlook them. But they take on a whole new meaning when we see them spread throughout our city day after day. And when they are given to us by an anonymous person or group. Yet we cannot even agree who might be behind it. Witnesses have described many people: a soldier in uniform, a teenage girl, a guy in a hoodie, a woman in a red scarf. Despite hundreds of surveillance cameras throughout the city, no one has been able to capture them on camera except for this one grainy photo of a woman who was spotted paying off strangers' debts at a payday-loan company. We believe her name is Marie, but that's all we know."

Then we showed our only solid clue: the photograph of Marie. We hoped someone who recognized her would come forward. But, dressed in a red scarf and sunglasses, almost anyone could have been beneath that disguise.

❧

"I met the Marie you're looking for." The woman's voice was hoarse on the phone later that night.

"Why do you think it's her?" I asked, balancing my phone on my shoulder as I packed my bag to go home for the night.

"Well, those glasses, for one. They kind of stand out. For two, she was wearing the same Hermès scarf as in the photo, but around her neck instead."

"Hermès scarf? How do you know?"

"I used to work at Neiman Marcus. Recognized it right away. It's vintage, from the nineties."

"Still, many people might own that scarf."

She cleared her throat. "True. But something happened on the flight that made it hard to forget her."

"Flight?"

"I'm a flight attendant for American Airlines. A few weeks ago, we were boarding a plane from Dallas heading to New York City. This woman, Marie, got on—she was flying first class and was one of the first to board. She flagged me down and told me she'd found a letter on her chair—2A—and asked if I knew who put it there. I said no. But she was persistent and asked the other flight attendant too. She said the letter was on her seat when she arrived. But we told her that was impossible because the cleaning crew had just finished working on the cabin, and there's no way they would have left any papers on a first-class seat. Then she started crying."

"Why?"

"We couldn't figure it out. I offered to take the letter and find its owner. I figured it had hate speech or something else offensive. Maybe a swastika or something. But she wouldn't let go of it. She pressed it to her chest like it was something valuable."

"What did it say?"

She drew in a deep breath. "My coworker and I didn't know what to do because she was so upset. That's when I looked up her name on the passenger manifest. Marie something. I don't remember her last name. I asked her what we could do to help, and she didn't answer."

"She never told you what it was?"

"Eventually she did. A big storm was heading our way, and every plane was grounded, so we had to ask all the passengers to get off the plane. Right before she got off, she showed me the letter."

"What did it say?"

"'And we know all things work together for good.' Romans 8:28."

My thoughts raced as I researched Romans 8:28. Although I found thousands of interpretations of it online, the one thing most everyone agreed about the passage was this: It didn't say all things were good. It said they all worked together for good—even the bad and even the disappointing.

I had no idea why this passage had had such an effect on Marie that day, but I had the feeling that it was an essential part of understanding who she was and why she was doing all this.

I wondered if she was trying to make it *become* true.

I felt safe, and a little pampered, as I was shuttled from the newsroom that night by Gavin, a taut off-duty police officer in his early forties who looked like he could windmill-kick his way through all of Manhattan. Still, I worried that I'd put myself in more danger by sharing another photo of Marie on national TV.

As we left the safety of the car and Gavin escorted me to my apartment door, I was troubled by a sense of dread. My eye fell on every person on the street, looking for signs that they were paying too-close attention to me. I was relieved by the ones preoccupied with their phones or immersed in conversations. But I couldn't shake the feeling that someone was watching me from the shadows. From a distance.

Inside, the apartment building was in chaos. Ram Board was taped to the hallway floors, and every surface seemed to be covered in a fine layer of yellow dust. A metallic chemical smell like formaldehyde or paint thinner permeated the air. Upstairs, the neighbors were playing rhumba music, and it sounded like they were rolling bowling balls across the floor.

I tried saying good night to Gavin, but the sound of the grinder—or was that a saw?—in the apartment down the hall drowned out my voice. Then, just as Gavin was about to leave, Cora stumbled out of her apartment in tears. My first thought was that she was reeling from all the noise and the smells, but her face was unusually pale, and she looked like she'd been crying.

I followed her back out the front door, with Gavin trailing right behind me. "Kate, you really shouldn't—" he started.

"Is everything okay?" I called to her. I wondered if whoever had been watching me had somehow spooked her.

She turned around, her lips trembling. "My daughter, Anna, is very sick. She's the one in Ukraine I told you about."

"Sorry. What are the doctors saying?"

"I need to go to her. But I don't have a way to do that."

She turned and started to walk away.

"Wait, where are you going?"

She kept walking. "To work."

"Let us drive you."

She turned around, and the change in her face was immediate—a look of utter disbelief. "Why would you do that?"

"Would you?" I whispered to Gavin.

I could tell he was reluctant—I'm sure it wasn't part of ANC security protocol. But when he saw Cora's expression, even this guy, who looked like the street-fighting inspiration for *Mortal Kombat*, joined in.

Inside the car, Cora's spirits seemed to lift a little. With puffy eyes, she told me that all the doctors had fled her family's village in Ukraine and that the nearest one was many miles away. She talked about the friend who had offered to loan her $200 toward the thousands she needed for the plane fare but then had to withdraw the offer when she landed in the ER with a broken ankle. And then she divulged that all her savings weren't enough to buy a plane ticket and that she "didn't believe much" in credit cards, so she didn't have one.

As we dropped her off, I noticed a change in her. A lightness in her eyes—in her whole body—I hadn't seen before. Had this little thing

Gavin and I had done for her—this simple car ride—had this effect on her?

It made me think that maybe small things could make a big difference. An ordinary balloon had changed the city. A simple bouquet of flowers had brightened countless lives. Could it be that the biggest problems could be solved by the smallest gestures, person to person? If that was true, then could I find a simple and ordinary way to help Cora?

As I exited the car, another thought struck me so hard I almost stumbled on the way up the steps. I knew what to do.

I raced into my apartment and dug out a vinyl pouch adorned with goofy vegetable characters that I'd had since middle school. Inside I kept a stash of emergency cash, a little more than a thousand dollars, a habit my dad had instilled in me when we moved to earthquake-prone Southern California.

I placed all of it into a paper envelope and hurried across the hall, careful not to be seen. As I slipped it under her door, a remarkable feeling came over me. Relief. Joy. Pure happiness that I'd rarely felt since I'd moved here.

I returned to my apartment feeling surprisingly richer than I had been before. But as I went to close the window shade, my stomach clenched.

Someone was standing on the sidewalk directly across the street. Looking up at my apartment.

My breath caught high in my throat. From my slightly higher vantage point, their face was obscured by a dark-blue hoodie and the drooping branches of a sycamore tree. Whoever it was—man or woman—stood with their sneaker-clad feet together, their fingers gliding across the faint screen of their phone. Then they shoved the phone in their pocket and folded their arms across their chest, turning their body from side to side as though looking for someone.

As if they sensed me at the window, they looked up at me. In the fading evening light, I had the feeling that our eyes met, even though I could not see them. I shivered.

They hurried into the darkness.

I braced my arm against the window frame, trying to catch my breath. But not even this chilling visitor could take away all the joy I felt about the envelope under Cora's door.

CHAPTER FIFTEEN

"You're on Page Six of the *New York Post*," Stephanie said when I reached my desk the next morning. "Well, your dad and his girlfriend are. I think this is you in the background."

Getting written up on Page Six wasn't a goal of mine or my father's. Page Six was celebrity journalism, usually reserved for reality-TV stars, squabbling politicians, pop-culture icons, and brand-name philanthropists. The stories focused on scandal, style, and gossip, so I was curious about what they were saying about my senator dad.

She swiveled the laptop toward me and pointed to a photo of Julia and my father holding hands as they entered Lincoln Center. A woman with dark hair walked behind them. I could see why Stephanie thought it was me, but it wasn't.

The caption read: "Senator Hale Bradley, 62, attends opening night at The Met with Julia Pearson, ex-wife of New York governor Mark Abbott."

"Did you know she was the governor's ex?" Stephanie said.

I cleared my throat, surprised that Julia had been married to another high-ranking politician. And not just any ordinary one. A governor who was under scrutiny for possible money laundering. "My dad never told me her last name."

Looking at her photo, I wondered if my dad was just another rung on the political and social ladder for her. Maybe I was jumping to conclusions, but this new information made me question her agenda. Yes, plenty of women married men seventeen years their senior, but none of those other men were my father. I was troubled by the possibility that she was simply using him but equally confused by the feeling that came over me. *Protective.*

It'd always been the other way around. When I was little, he was the one protecting me, urging me to "make good choices" about friends and the people I spent time with. "Don't let people use you," he'd always said. Was Julia using him?

Not that I had much time to mull that over. Because Mark suddenly appeared at my side.

"Thousands of New Yorkers have reported getting anonymous texts this morning," he said without much enthusiasm. "They say things like 'We are all connected' or 'Do something nice for someone today' or 'I believe in you.' Either of you get one?"

"Now they're sending texts?" Stephanie said. "These guys are everywhere."

"Jocelyn on the tech team got one and is looking into it," he said. "Looks like it came from one of the anonymous text services. Untraceable."

"Wow, I see it," Stephanie said, staring at her phone. "Usually Twitter is the aggregator of venom, but not today. It's blowing up about these texts. People can't believe it."

Mark sighed. "Look, this story might be getting record views and tweets, but it's forgettable. And I'll tell you why."

"Let me guess," I said, letting my impatience show. "People are inherently selfish and greedy."

"That, and we are living in an age of fear. Most Americans are living in the safest place at the safest time in human history, but the stories that grab our attention—the ones with staying power—are the ones that make us anxious and afraid: we're on the edge of doom, the country is divided, our leaders can't be trusted. That's what people care about."

"You're wrong about that," I said. Anger flashed in his eyes. I had the feeling few reporters had dared to openly disagree with him. "Yes, there is trouble, chaos, and tension. But there are far more people doing small gestures and big things to make the world better."

He shrugged. "Think what you want. But what they're doing is not going to change anything."

"It already is."

⁓

I want to tell you about something that happened on a road outside Dallas. I think it's connected to the story you're reporting. Sincerely, Gary Reyes.

The email was one of the hundreds that had poured into the station since my report aired the day before. I'd skimmed past it the first time because a possible connection to the back roads outside of Dallas easily fit into "way out there" territory.

But the email jogged something in my memory.

"Didn't that guy Logan say that he had a connecting flight through Dallas?" I asked Scott as we sat in his office later that morning sifting through the tips viewers had sent in.

Scott looked at me. He was overdressed for the occasion, still wearing a gorgeous indigo-blue dress shirt, unbuttoned at the neck, from an earlier ANC hosts photoshoot. "How do you remember details like that?"

"That's why he was giving away the gift cards. Remember? Because some stranger had helped him with his luggage on a connecting flight through Dallas. Here's a viewer that wants to tell us about something that happened outside of Dallas."

He leaned back in his chair, stretching his tall frame. "Okay. I'm trying to catch up here. But it seems like a big leap to think that an event fifteen hundred miles away is somehow connected to what's happening here."

I rubbed my forehead. "Yeah. I feel like I'm grasping at straws here," I said, moving the note to the "no" pile.

But something was pulling me back to it. Reporter's instinct, maybe. Or maybe it was simple desperation. "But then again . . ."

He smiled at me. "Then again?"

"That guy Kevin Raley, he said his son Joe's flight had been rerouted through Dallas."

"Coincidence, maybe. Could be we're only seeing patterns in random information."

"You're saying we're crazy?"

His eyes were dancing. "Obviously we are. But it doesn't mean we're wrong."

I read the note again.

"Why do I feel like you're going to call this guy?" he asked.

Emboldened by his admiring smile, I called the number and put the phone on speaker. "Because I am."

"Gary Reyes," a man answered, but the rumble of road noise overpowered his voice.

"Gary, this is Kate Bradley from ANC. I got your email."

"Wow. For real, this is Kate Bradley? Let me pull over."

While we waited, Scott shot me a quizzical look. Now that we had the guy on the phone, I had the feeling we'd just taken a dive down the rabbit hole.

"In your report, you mentioned that a US Army soldier might be behind all the good things sweeping through New York City," Gary said, the noise around him quieting.

"Right. A woman at the flower mart reported seeing a soldier buying a truckload of purple flowers. But it turned out to be a dead end."

"I saw him."

"You saw a soldier on the back roads of Texas."

"We had a terrible storm here a few weeks ago," he said, his Texas drawl in full bloom. "Winds were ferocious. A bunch of tornado sightings. We got three inches of rain in just a couple of hours. I wouldn't normally have been out on the road in a storm like that. But I'd left my house keys at the towing-company office and had to go back and get them. Lots of the highways were flooded, you know, so I took 4305. It's narrow and pitch black along that route, but it was faster than taking the interstate. Have to say I was pretty angry at myself for having to drive that empty road late in the night like that. But I'm glad I did."

I reined in my impatience and tried to get control over the interview. "What does this have to do with the soldier?"

"I'm getting to that. I saw a car, you know, alongside the road. It was raining like crazy, there are downed trees and brush along the road, and I see this car almost in the drainage ditch. A guy gets out, and he's wearing an army uniform."

Scott and I exchanged glances. This was a waste of time. I tried not to sound annoyed. "So you helped him?"

"I gave him a tire, yeah, but it took two of us to change it. Water swirling around us. Both of us were covered in mud, and I told him that whenever I'm in the middle of the toughest jobs, I always imagine myself on a warm beach in Hawaii sipping a piña colada. We laughed about that. When we finished, we were soaked to the bone with rain and mud, and he asked me for my business card—"

"What does this—"

"A week later I get an envelope addressed to me at the towing company. I don't ever get mail there, so that was strange. Inside was a pair of airline tickets to Hawaii. Wrapped in a purple ribbon. Same stuff I'm seeing all over the photos in Manhattan. No name or anything on the envelope. But I knew. I knew they were from him."

Scott and I looked at each other in surprise.

"Did you get his name?" I asked.

"I never did ask him. But I remember seeing his last name on his uniform."

"What was it?"

"Raley."

∾

"No luck," I told Scott on the phone as Gavin drove me back to my apartment later that evening. "I called Joe Raley's dad, and he told me Joe is now stationed at White Sands Missile Range in New Mexico."

"Will he put you in touch with him?"

"Definitely not. He doesn't trust the media and asked me why I kept pursuing this, as he called it, 'crazy idea.' Then he told me not to come back. Said the whole idea that his son might be involved in some secret 'operation' was disturbing the family."

"They're probably overwhelmed, after the funeral and all."

As I left the car and headed to the front door with Gavin a few feet behind me, Artie scurried down the steps, his hands in the pockets of his hoodie.

"Hey," I said, but he kept going, ignoring me.

"There's only one way to find out. Let's track down Joe Raley at White Sands," I said, unlocking the front door.

"It won't be easy getting through the army red tape."

As I stepped into the hallway, Gavin suddenly pushed in front of me. "Call 911!" he shouted.

That's when I noticed the door to my apartment was slightly ajar. I remembered pulling hard on the handle in the morning, straining to lock it.

"I have to hang up," I said. "Someone's broken into my apartment."

"I'll be right there."

CHAPTER SIXTEEN

I'd been robbed.

I felt like I was going to cry, but there was no time for that. My hand was trembling so hard that it took a huge effort to connect with the phone in my purse and dial 911.

Shards of broken glass and dishes littered the mini-kitchen, as if a monster had barreled into the room in a rage, hurling every glass, jar, and bottle to the floor. Even my mother's favorite cobalt-blue Depression-era glass bowl, the one reminder of her that I'd brought to Manhattan, had been thrown to the floor, broken into awkward, ugly pieces. My laptop was gone.

The next thing I noticed was tufts of cotton scattered throughout the apartment—the stuffing from the couch cushions they'd torn apart. Any sense of safety or trust I thought I'd had was torn up and scattered on the erratic path the shadowy figure had taken through my apartment.

Detective Steve McGregor, a hefty guy in his forties, showed up fifteen minutes later but seemed bored by the whole situation, lethargically surveying and photographing the scene and asking me questions in a dreary monotone. Even when he was examining the smashed glass in the kitchen window, his only words were, "That's gonna be expensive."

But when I showed him the postcard and told him about the video shot from across the street, he started flinging rapid-fire questions at me: Did ANC have any suspects? Did I have a security system? Cameras? What was on the laptop? Who knew it was here?

I crouched down and picked up two halves of a broken plate. Was this payback for continuing to report about Marie? If that was the case, wouldn't they have made that clear by leaving a message for me? Or did they assume I would just know?

While the detective photographed the wreckage, I tried to steady my nerves. I opened the blinds and gazed at the woman in the window across the street. Tonight, she was working with a shimmery fabric that rose like silver, puffy clouds from her sewing machine and glittered in the light. I envied her, so engrossed in her voluminous, frilly fabrics that the chaotic world around her disappeared.

Raymond and Cora had seen the detective arrive and stopped in to see what was going on. In a blurry haze, I told them what little I knew. Saying it aloud was strange, like I was delivering a news report, not something that had actually happened to me. Raymond promised to call the landlord and offered to install a padlock so I could lock the front door that night.

Had they seen anything? I'd asked. Cora thought she had seen a car driving slowly down the street earlier. But she didn't remember the description. Raymond saw Artie rushing into the apartment building earlier in the afternoon, angry about something.

Artie.

Why had he been leaving the apartment building in such a hurry? And just who was he?

I asked Cora and Raymond about him, but neither of them knew anything.

"Would you look into him as a possible suspect?" I asked the detective. "He lives in 2B."

Toward the end of the meeting with the detective, the tears fell. I had tried to hold them back, but when I looked around the room and realized that everything here—everything—had been ransacked or ruined, exhaustion kicked in, and the tears slipped out seemingly of their own free will.

It wasn't just the brokenness of it all that got to me; it was the time I'd have to spend repairing or replacing all that was lost. I tried to rally some optimism by convincing myself that it wasn't so bad. How hard could it be to replace an entire kitchen of dishes and glassware? A laptop. Probably not too difficult, but add to that getting the couch re-covered and coordinating the window repair, and the minutes started adding up to hours and days. All just to put back the apartment to the wretched way it was when I left it this morning.

"Kate?" I heard Scott ask as he knocked gently on the open front door. "Everything okay?"

He did a quick sweep of the room with his eyes, then put his arms around me. "I'm so sorry."

I might have stayed there forever. It felt so good to rest my head against his chest, feeling calm for just a moment. My hand clasped his jacket as if absorbing every bit of warmth and comfort it offered. We both lingered in the hug too long, but he covered it well by talking casually, as if it were absolutely normal for us to be standing there with our arms around each other.

"I would have gotten here sooner, but the Uber driver got lost," he said. "The guy had glow-in-the-dark stickers on his ceiling."

"You're kidding."

"He was also wearing a cowboy hat and singing along to 'Happy Trails' and 'Tumbling Tumbleweeds.'"

I relaxed into a smile. "How come I never get Uber drivers like that?"

"You doing okay?" His forehead was creased with worry.

"Are you Mr. Bradley?" the detective asked, making me realize how long we had been holding each other.

Scott let go of me and extended his hand. "Actually, no. Scott Jameson."

"I thought you looked familiar. Well, I'm finished up here," the detective announced, hiking up his pants a little. "I'll be in touch when I'm further along in the investigation. I'm going to be talking to your neighbors." He handed me a business card. "In the meantime, I'd suggest you stay somewhere else until this place can be secured."

After he left, Scott and I surveyed the living room again. "You okay?" he asked.

"Honestly? No," I said, then realized, with my puffy eyes and smeared mascara, I must have looked like someone straight out of a telenovela.

"What's his theory? Does he think it's related to the postcards you've been getting? Or just some random guy?"

"He didn't know." I looked around, shaking my head. "Ironic, isn't it? Here I am chasing a story about all the good happening around the city, even arguing with Mark that people are not inherently selfish and evil. But seeing this, experiencing what people are capable of . . . maybe I've been naive."

"Don't change, Kate," he said. "You're not naive. You're . . . hopeful. We could all use a little more of that."

My eyes met his, and I thought I was going to cry again. It was the nicest thing anyone had ever said about me. And hearing it now, when I had succumbed to fear and sadness, made it even more meaningful.

I tried to laugh it off. "You only think that because of the story we're working on together. But it's easy to be hopeful in the face of so much good like that." I lifted a lamp from the floor, revealing my most treasured copy of *Harriet the Spy*, its cover newly torn. I sighed. "Not so easy when you're faced with a reality like this. This has been my favorite since third grade."

He took the book from me and dusted off some tiny shards of glass. "Yeah, this definitely sucks. But you haven't been naive. Bad stuff like this happens, but it doesn't take anything away from all the good things that are going on too."

"Now who's the one sounding like an optimist."

He smiled. "We're a rare breed in this city."

Something about the way he said *we* made me feel warm.

I drew a deep breath and glanced at my watch. Ten thirty. "This 'rare breed' needs to get a hotel reservation and get some sleep. We've got to hit the ground running tomorrow morning."

He turned to face me. "Why don't you stay at my place? I've got an extra bedroom, and if we get an Uber driver who isn't a singing cowboy lost on the range, we can get there in ten minutes."

Everything about his invitation seemed right. But also totally wrong. What would people think if they found out I'd stayed the night at Scott Jameson's apartment?

"Thank you, but a hotel probably makes more sense. You know what Mark would say if he heard we—"

"Mark's got a big enough ego. Let's not make it bigger by allowing him to make decisions for us. Besides, I've got one advantage over the nearest hotel."

"What's that?"

"Waffles. I have a state-of-the-art waffle iron and a killer recipe that would make Gordon Ramsay cry. And maple syrup straight from Mont Rigaud in Quebec."

He made me smile. "What is your obsession with waffles?"

"It's the cure for all bad things. Especially robberies and vandalism."

I laughed. "A robberies and vandalism cure? As much as I want one, I don't want to inconvenience you and Paige."

"She's not . . . we don't live together."

"I just don't want to make this . . . awkward."

"Look, it's late. Why don't you grab a few things and get some shut-eye at my place? No weirdness, promise. It'll be like you're sleeping in an ashram."

"An ashram?"

"You know, peaceful. Quiet. But with waffles."

⟡

Scott's guest bedroom was comfortable and well appointed, with a mattress that came straight from heaven, so I fell asleep easily. But an hour later, I woke up, my heart pounding, a thick, pulsing knot roiling in the pit of my stomach.

My thoughts bounced between two fears. This was a random robbery and further proof that where I was living in Manhattan was not safe. Or: whoever had been sending the menacing letters and videos demanding that I stop looking for Marie was escalating the threat.

That thought sent a chill through my body. How far would they go to stop me from looking for Marie?

My throat and lips were parched, so I left my bed and padded toward the kitchen to get a glass of water. I kept the lights off so I wouldn't disturb Scott, but I didn't need them because the lights of the city floated through sheer curtains in the living room, casting a liquid blue-white glow throughout the room.

The apartment had been tastefully decorated, the walls covered with framed wildlife photographs. An inspiring shot of a hawk floating over powdery snow with the stately Grand Tetons in the distance hung over the fireplace. Across the room, a stunning photo captured a tiger by the side of a calm stream and under a canopy of dense foliage. The dreamy expression on the tiger's face in the dappled light made my pulse slow.

"You can't sleep either?" I heard Scott say.

I turned around as he stepped out of his bedroom. He was wearing a pair of navy-blue knit lounge pants and was shirtless for a brief moment before he pulled a slim white T-shirt over his head.

"Yeah. I hope I didn't wake you. I was just admiring this one." I nodded to the tiger photo.

"Still my favorite. We were filming in India at the Bandhavgarh National Park, and we were actually looking for a four-horned antelope when I just stumbled upon him. The scene just kind of begs you to linger."

"He almost looks like he's meditating."

"Or dreaming. Like we both should be."

As we stood together gazing at the photograph, I felt an undeniable pull between us. I pushed the feeling away, chalking it up to the magical lighting and a heavy dose of exhaustion.

"I'm starving. You hungry?" he asked.

"Are you suggesting waffles at midnight?"

"As much as I hate to admit it, it's actually too early for waffles. But I bet you didn't eat dinner, either, and I know a great place to get a late-night something. You up for a quick walk in the city?"

"Where do you have in mind?"

"You'll see."

∽◌

A few minutes later, we were headed down the hushed streets of Manhattan in search of a street vendor Scott assured me would "change my mind about eating street food after midnight."

"What I need is something to change my mind about the city," I said. "I feel like this robbery is a sign that I shouldn't be here."

"You know what? I felt the same when I moved back here."

"But you grew up here."

"I'd been working in Chicago for a couple of years, and the day I moved back, I got on the A train, and a deranged guy got on behind me and shoved me. Then he started getting into people's faces—nannies, businessmen, everyone—and shouting. I told him to stop. He pulled a knife and was waving it around like he was going to stab all of us. Right then, I thought, 'I'm done with this place.' We're all crammed onto this island, and our complicated lives end up colliding with each other. The trick is finding your place and knowing that it gets better. You're in the trial phase. The city is testing you."

"If this is a test, I'm definitely failing."

"Maybe this will change your mind."

We turned the corner and a gyros food cart was right in front of us, its brightly lit orange-and-red umbrella standing out on the dark street. And like everything in NYC, even in the wee hours of the morning, there was a line: A guy in camo pants and a yellow sweatshirt. A pony-tailed woman in black yoga pants. A man lugging an oversize stuffed penguin.

"After midnight. I'm pretty sure my stomach knows this is not a good idea."

As we stood in line, my eye drifted down the street to an old man shuffling down the sidewalk. Wearing a black beret and brown sport coat that was too large for his thin frame, he seemed out of place in the grit and graffiti. I wondered where he was going at this time of night, but in the city that never sleeps, people walked around at all hours.

Then a woman walking two pugs came from the opposite direction and stopped in front of him, blocking his way. I couldn't hear what they were saying, but I was instantly on edge. My nerves still raw from the break-in, I didn't have the energy to cope with more conflict. But as much as I wanted to turn away, I knew I couldn't. Shouldn't.

Whatever the woman was saying to him seemed to confuse him, because he kept shaking his head. He tried to get around her, but she stepped in front of him, blocking him again, holding up a paper shopping bag.

Then she pulled something out of the bag—a bakery box—and presented it to him, lifting its flaps so he could see what was inside.

His eyes lit up, and then he reached out, slowly, gingerly, and squeezed her hand. My heart swelled at this simple moment. I had no idea if she knew the man or what exactly had taken place, but I could feel the kindness transfer between them.

Under ordinary circumstances, I might not have noticed something like this. Yet somehow in my grief about my apartment, in my heartache for all the ways my life had gone off the rails, I was suddenly struck with wonder. In all the chaos, anger, and upheaval, was kindness all around, just waiting for us to notice it?

I ran after her. Any exhaustion I felt earlier was gone as I chased her down the street.

"Wait up!" I shouted.

She kept walking.

I caught up with her. "Excuse me, but what did you just give that man?"

She eyed me suspiciously and withdrew the earphones from her ears. "What's it to you?"

"I'm Kate Bradley. From ANC. Covering the secret good sweeping through the city."

She broke into a big smile, exposing a gap between her two front teeth. "I like those stories."

"Did you give him something?"

"I gave him a cake I made. Strawberry shortcake."

"You know him then?"

"Not really. I see him out here every night around this time when I'm walking these guys," she said, nodding toward the pugs. "He always seems so lonely. And kind of sad. So when I saw all the nice things people in the city are doing for each other, I thought, what the heck, I can do something too."

"For a complete stranger. In the middle of the night."

"I guess it sounds kind of strange. But it didn't feel that way. It felt good, you know?"

"Are you one of the people who started this whole thing?"

She laughed. "Wish I could say that I was that creative. But, no."

I thanked her for talking with me, and when I returned to the gyro truck, I filled Scott in on the exchange.

"I think you sprinted that entire block in under fifteen seconds," he said with admiration in his voice.

"It's a skill set. You track tigers in India. I track people in the city. But seeing what that woman did made me wonder if maybe good things are happening all the time, but we focus most of our attention on what's broken."

"You're right. ANC did a story a few weeks ago about a couple of homeless guys who got into a fight with a lone NYPD officer at the Twenty-Eighth Street subway station. That story was everywhere. Even my aunts were talking about it. But that same day, a blind man tumbled on the tracks at Columbus Circle, and five bystanders rushed to get him to safety seconds before the train pulled into the station. You can guess which one got more attention."

"Why are we obsessed with hearing about a fight, but when people do good things, we act like it's something trivial?"

The gyros guy slid out order through the window. "Kept 'em warm for you."

"This will make you love Manhattan," Scott said, handing one to me. I didn't think I could stomach a gyro loaded with chicken, onions, french fries, and rich tzatziki sauce on thick naan-like pita in the middle of the night, but after the first bite, I was sold.

"I'd say the city is growing on you," Scott said as I went in for a second bite.

"You've been trying to convince me through my stomach. But this place has got to have more than good food to help me forget that my apartment is in a state of mayhem."

"Sounds like you're throwing down a New York City challenge."

"Is there actually such a thing?"

"Not really, no. But we New Yorkers are notoriously smug about our city."

"For what reason, I still don't know."

He faked a look of annoyance. "Challenge accepted. What time is it?" he said, looking at his phone. "Only twelve fifteen. How fast can you run?"

I smiled. "Is that a trick question?"

He squeezed my hand. "Then let's go. They close at one."

CHAPTER SEVENTEEN

Wherever he was taking me was in Central Park. As we ran in the warm pools of light beneath its old-fashioned streetlamps, I tried to guess. "Belvedere Castle? Conservatory Water?"

"Nope. But we're almost there."

The roar of traffic had died down to a whir in the distance, and except for the two of us, this section of the park seemed empty. Even though the wind had picked up a little, I was surprisingly warm. Being with him had that effect on me. Our relationship was easy—the kind of relaxed friendship that had been so natural to make in college but was becoming more complex as I entered my thirties. Yet I felt something growing between us—something more than a friendship—and I wondered if I was imagining it. Maybe I was so desperate for connection in this city that I was mistaking his friendliness for something more.

Then suddenly we left the part of Central Park I knew, the one I'd seen in movies and TV, and we slowed to walk down a stone path that wound through gardens crowded with flowers whose sweet and pungent scents whispered in the air.

"What's your favorite Shakespeare play?" he said.

"You're asking me that because . . ."

"Because we're in the Shakespeare Garden."

Then it all made sense: the rustic fences, the wooden benches, the hedges and shrubs that looked as though they had been lifted from another time.

We stopped in front of a long, curved stone bench with an eagle's wing carved into the end. "I know it doesn't look like much. Tourists pass it thousands of times a day and don't realize its magic. Why don't you sit here . . . ?"

I sat, thinking he would join me, but instead, he walked to the other end of the forty-foot bench. To my complete surprise, he pulled out his phone and began scrolling.

"They call this the whispering bench. It's the one place in the city you can whisper and the other person can actually hear you," he said, but his voice seemed to be coming from the stone bench itself. "Full disclosure, I'm using a Shakespeare app. So no, I'm not quoting from memory."

"You're actually going to read Shakespeare to me?"

"What else would you do on a whispering bench in a Shakespeare garden after midnight?

> I know a bank where the wild thyme blows,
> Where oxlips and the nodding violet grows,
> Quite over-canopied with luscious woodbine,
> With sweet musk-roses and with eglantine:
> There sleeps Titania sometime of the night,
> Lull'd in these flowers with dances and delight."

I'd always imagined that if a man read Shakespeare to me, it would feel corny or contrived. But as in any Shakespeare play, a lot of what happened had to do with the characters' intentions. This wasn't a grand romantic gesture to woo or impress me. Scott was working to help me forget about the city that had crumpled me and instead make me fall for the place he'd grown to love.

"What'd you think?" he asked.

"I think I want one more."

It took him a minute before he began reading again:

> "It is not night when I do see your face,
> Therefore I think I am not in the night.
> Nor doth this wood lack worlds of company,
> For you in my respect are all the world.
> Then how can it be said I am alone
> When all the world is here to look on me?"

Beneath a canopy of trees and surrounded by a thicket of flowers, listening to him read words written hundreds of years ago, I felt the tension easing in my chest. My breath slowing.

There was an intimacy in the way he read the verses, but even though I knew they were only said to cheer me up, I couldn't help but wonder what it might feel like otherwise. That feeling, the yearning for something more, took me by surprise.

He walked over to me, his hands in his pockets. I thought he might declare that he'd won the challenge. But instead, he surprised me. "I know it's going to take more than gyros and a whispering bench in Central Park to make up for what that maniac did to your apartment, but I hope this is a start."

His words swirled around me, as if infused with magic. "It's working. Except for the french fries in the gyros."

He gripped his chest in mock pain. "You didn't like the fries? That's the best part."

"Maybe I should try them before midnight next time."

Then big fat raindrops danced along the sidewalk in a quirky rhythm. And stopped.

Seconds later, it began to pour. Not like the sprays of rain I'd experienced in Southern California, which were mostly wind and a little drizzle. This was dense rain that fell in sheets and shrouded the streetlamps, transforming their drowsy light into something mystical and otherworldly.

"So this is rain," I said.

I leaned my head back and let it hit my face, an action that seemed childish but then wonderful as I reveled in the soft, cool feeling on my skin. The smell of it. Every drop erasing the tension, rinsing it away.

When I lifted my head back up, his eyes drifted across my face. I felt like he had something he wanted to say, but instead he was quiet for a long moment.

"Let's get out of these wet clothes," he said finally. While the statement was practical, his tone sounded almost seductive. "You ready?"

The rain suddenly grew more insistent, pounding us as though a cloud had opened up above us. He took my hand and we began to run.

There are moments when things turn. When time seems to slow, and we suddenly realize we are experiencing something we're probably going to remember forever. Maybe it's goose bumps or a lump in our throat that first signals it.

For me, it was the way my hand felt in his. Buzzing. Alive.

The rain didn't stop, but we did. About two minutes into our attempt to escape Central Park and find a taxi, Scott paused and scanned the landscape.

"Are we lost?" I asked.

He shook his head. "No, but I know a shortcut. Do you mind getting a little muddy if it means we'll shave a few minutes off our run?"

"Is this going to be another jumping-puddles-and-running-down-alleys adventure?"

He smiled. "Probably."

Then he took my hand again and led me through a stand of elm trees, then onto a dirt path that meandered between shrubs and rock outcroppings, beneath tall trees and down a gentle hill, with the earthy smell of the rain-soaked leaves rising up around us.

We rounded a huge sycamore and nearly ran straight into . . . a Christmas tree. Or at least it looked like one, a fir tree decked out with laminated photo ornaments tied to the tree with ribbons and bows.

"I thought this was just a rumor," Scott said, approaching it slowly. "An urban legend."

He lifted an ornament, a laminated portrait of a tabby cat with the word "Rockstar" written beneath it. There were dozens more like it with photos of pets and short tributes.

"I know people who've walked this park for years, and they all say this doesn't exist. But here it is," he said. "The Secret Holiday Memorial Tree to Pets."

I didn't quite grasp the significance of this secret tree devoted to the memory of strangers' pets. Instead, I was pulled in by his excitement for it. I might've expected someone with his background to be cynical, certainly reserved, about a discovery like this, but he was so comfortable in his own skin that he approached it, like seemingly everything, with a sense of wonder. Somewhere along the way, I'd lost that ability to immerse myself in a simple moment. But with the rain falling thick and hard, I felt a shift inside me.

"Take a look at this one," he said, picking up a laminated photo of a collie that had fallen to the ground. He was standing so close to me that I could smell the woodsy scent on his skin, and it threw me off balance.

"Squirrel hell and dog heaven are the same place," I read.

He grinned. "Now that we've found it, we have to make a vow of secrecy about its location," he whispered.

"A vow of secrecy may be a difficult promise for two journalists to keep."

He turned to look at me, and the charge was there again, stronger than before. He reached up to move a wet lock of my hair from my face and lingered there for a moment. Then he leaned in, as though to kiss me, his eyes locked with mine in an unwavering gaze. Emotion squeezed my chest. I felt his jacket brush up against me. Then his lips hovered over mine briefly before they settled into a gentle kiss.

Suddenly he pulled away, taking away his warmth.

"I hope I didn't—" he said.

"No, it's . . . okay—"

His lips curved into a smile. "Let's see if I can remember the way out."

Waffles. Fluffy, warm perfection. Crowned with a dark-amber maple syrup straight from the gods.

"Now I get why you're obsessed with these," I said in Scott's kitchen the next morning, polishing off the first one out of the waffle iron.

Standing in the sun-drenched kitchen wearing Levi's and a gray T-shirt, he looked more relaxed than I'd seen him before. And somehow more handsome.

I had never been attracted to famous men—I'd grown up around well-known men orbiting my father, and I never found any of them any more alluring because of it. But here I was, falling for a man who was a familiar face to millions.

After our almost-a-kiss the night before, I could see he was as nervous as I was, his hands busily whisking and combining ingredients, his eyes focused intently on what he was doing, then lifting and taking me in as though he were seeing me for the first time. "Needs a little more amaretto liqueur," he said absently, but the way he was looking at me made me feel light headed.

When he stood next to me demonstrating his secret waffle iron technique, I could feel the exact distance between our bodies, down to the millimeter, and a shiver of excitement raced through me. I felt powerless to ignore the new feelings, even though I knew all the reasons I shouldn't have them.

"This will help you regain your strength." He placed a second waffle on my plate. I smiled at him, finding him irresistible. "Doctor's orders."

"I'm having serious doubts about your prescription, Dr. Jameson."

"You don't approve of my remedy? Ouch." His eyes lit up as he baptized the waffle with syrup. "You'll be singing a different tune later."

"You mean when I'm comatose on the couch?"

He smiled at me. "If you lapse into a coma, I promise I'll bring you back to life," he said, but I was pretty sure we were no longer talking about waffles.

My phone vibrated on the counter. The caller ID on the screen read: "Office of the Mayor."

I laughed. "Telemarketers are really getting sneaky. Pretending to be the mayor."

"Maybe it *is* the mayor?"

I didn't think that was possible because I didn't know the mayor of New York City, Fred Trester, and he didn't have my cell phone number. Scott's expression was urging me to answer it anyway. I put the call on speaker. "Kate Bradley."

"Kate, Fred Trester. I hope I'm not calling too early."

"Not at all," I said, heat rushing to my face.

Scott and I exchanged surprised looks. As far as I knew, the mayor of New York didn't call journalists on their cell phones. Especially ones he'd never met.

"I ran into your father at an event last night, and he shared your number with me. I don't know if you saw the *USA Today* front page yesterday, but they're now calling Manhattan the 'Good City.' I was telling your dad that my office is planning to give a civic award to the people who started this movement. We're announcing the award—and the ten-thousand-dollar reward—at a press conference later today. Your dad told me you're covering the story for ANC and suggested I call you about it."

"My dad convinced you to call me personally?"

He laughed. "As I'm sure you already know, he's very persuasive."

"He is. But aren't you worried that many people are going to say they're behind it so they can claim the reward? How will you ever know who's the real deal?"

"Our cameras recorded four people leaving balloons around city hall the night of the power outage. Before the emergency lights kicked on."

"How did they—"

"City hall cameras operate on battery backups. You can't make out much, even with cameras that can see in the dark. But two images are pretty clear."

My breath hitched in my throat. "What did they see?"

"We're not sharing this with the press or the general public. But your father says I can trust you. And that you might be able to help us find them."

"Yes, to both. Can someone in your office send me the photos? Not for broadcast, of course. So we'll know who we're looking for."

"Will do. Two of the people are impossible to make out in the images we have. The third one is clearly a soldier. He's wearing army fatigues."

"I've been trying to find someone with a similar description. What about the fourth person?"

He sighed. "We can't see her face. She's wearing a scarf around her neck. We think she's a little older."

Marie.

When Scott and I walked to ANC that morning, it felt like we had stepped into an alternate universe.

It started with a text we received from the newsroom—cell phone video showing State Representative Randall Feldman riding a bus through Lower Manhattan. In the video, he was sitting next to a woman who appeared to be doing a job interview over the phone.

"Can I put in a good word for you?" the state representative asked.

When she handed him the phone, he proceeded to give a personal recommendation about her work ethic while the woman looked on with shock and delight.

Then, farther down the avenue, we spotted a sign in the door of a high-end wedding shop reading: FREE WEDDING DRESSES FOR VETERANS. In front of one of the buildings a block from the ANC studios, someone had left out a large cooler with a note saying:

Delivery People: Water and Gatorade inside. Enjoy your day.

At every turn of the eye, good things were happening.

Even the newsroom. "Has everyone in New York gone soft?" Mark was saying to some of the news team. As he pointed to something on his iPad, he looked like someone who'd seen a ghost. "A few minutes ago, a man slipped off the platform and got his leg stuck in the gap between the train and the platform at Fulton Street. You know how busy that station is. But get this, at least fifty passengers stepped off the train— they all got off—and pushed on the train car so the guy could free his leg." He shook his head. "Doesn't sound like the Manhattan I know."

"This won't either," Isabelle said, joining us. "Forty NYPD officers and their K-9 dogs just paid a visit to a seven-year-old girl in Queens with a brain tumor. Since when do police do something like that?"

"I got something to top all of that," Stephanie added. "Some viewer just sent us cell phone video of a man in first class on a Delta flight leaving LaGuardia. Bet you're thinking it's some kind of fight, right? I know I did. But instead, some passengers recorded him giving up his first-class seat to a mom and her baby who were heading to Children's Hospital in Philly."

"What the hell is going on here?" Mark's voice was almost a whisper. "Is this what those balloons-and-flowers people started?"

"The *New York Times* just did a piece calling them 'miracle workers,'" Scott said, looking at his phone.

"And we just got a big break in the story," I added. "The mayor called me this morning. He's announcing a civic award and a reward to—"

"The mayor. Fred Trester. Called you. Himself," Mark said in disbelief.

My face was flushed with excitement, but at least my voice was calm. "He said they have recordings from city hall cameras the night of the power outage where they can see the people putting up the balloons. He shared them with me confidentially."

"The mayor shared—"

I showed him the grainy black-and-white photos taken with night vision cameras. The first one was zoomed in on a guy with tightly cropped hair. Dark eyes on a broad face. Army fatigues. "I think this one is the soldier I've been searching for—Joe Raley."

Then I flipped to another photo of a woman wearing a head scarf. The image was blurry because she was in motion, but it was clear enough to tell that she had a tall, slender build like the woman on the Purple Payday Loans footage. "This is Marie. The key to all this is finding her."

"Something tells me a reward isn't going to be enough to make her come forward," Mark said.

He was probably right. But Scott and I were determined to get viewers to help us find her. We put together a report cramming in as many of the good things happening as we could in three minutes and replayed the footage of Marie from Purple Payday Loans.

"We're looking for this woman," I said in the report.

"Her name is Marie," Scott added. "If you have any information on who she might be, call ANC."

My phone rang ten minutes later.

The woman's voice was soft, insistent. "I met your Marie. I recognize those glasses. That scarf."

"How do you know her?" I said, flipping open my notebook.

"It started with a wrong number. She was calling someone else—a nephew of hers named Jordan. But it turns out that's my name too. She left a message saying something like, 'Jordan, I'm just calling to say I love you and I'm thinking about you. I hope you're having a good day.'"

She stopped talking, and I heard a soft tremble in her throat. Was she crying?

"Then she said, 'I know you're going through some tough times, but I want you to know you mean a lot to me. I made that recipe for your favorite cookies, and I want to bring them to you. Love you.' I know that call wasn't meant for me, but I played that voice mail over and over."

"Can I ask why?"

She cleared her throat, but her voice still shook. "My life was a mess. My husband had left me. I'd lost my job. I was having a hard time keeping it together. But her call came at just the right time. It made me feel special."

"But the call wasn't for you. It was for someone else."

"I know. But you have to understand, her call was kind of a . . . buoy for me in the worst of times. I finally got the nerve to call her back and tell her that she'd left a message on the wrong number. I don't know how I had the guts to do it, but I ended up confessing that her words meant so much to me. And you know what?" She started to cry. "She came over to my apartment with those cookies. And she told me . . . she said to always remember that what I was going through wasn't going to be forever. That I would be okay."

"But she didn't know you."

Her voice shook. "It didn't matter that she was a complete stranger. I just loved her from the moment I met her. I know it's hard to believe that I could feel that way about someone I barely knew. She had so much joy and love in her."

"Did she tell you her last name?"

"I never asked."

"And you're sure she was the woman in the photo we aired?"

"Positive. She even had those same glasses."

"Lots of people could have those glasses. How can you be sure it's her?"

She drew in a deep breath. "I just know. You never forget someone like that."

"Do you have the number she called you from?"

"After I saw your story, I tried calling her. But the number's been disconnected."

CHAPTER EIGHTEEN

You got time for coffee today?

The text was from my dad. Who didn't text. And didn't drink coffee.

Sure. But aren't you in DC?

NYC. Meet you at 3:15 at Eleven Madison Park.

Eleven Madison Park wasn't a coffee place. It was a gastronomic destination—and it wasn't even open until 5:30 p.m.

The Coffee Bean down the street is easier to get to, I texted, trying to smoke out why he wanted to go to Eleven Madison Park.

This is better.

As I took a cab to the restaurant's upscale location on Madison Avenue, I tried to figure out why my dad was in New York when so much was going on in Congress, and why he wanted to meet here. He had never been one for grandiose restaurants with celebrity chefs. He loved an occasional fine steak but never seemed all that interested in restaurants bedazzled with tasting flights and sixteen-course meals, all of which had won this restaurant international acclaim. This seemed like Julia's doing.

The restaurant seemed empty. Then I spotted my dad in a booth in the corner, talking on the phone. I sank into a lush walnut-and-mohair chair and gazed at the breathtaking room with its floor-to-ceiling windows and knockout views of the park.

"My daughter just arrived," he said, beaming. "I'll call you later."

I scanned the restaurant. "What's all this about?"

"Julia and the owner, Danny Seitz, have been friends since they were at Columbia together. I had lunch here earlier, and Danny suggested I stay and make my calls here, instead of running back to my hotel."

"Why are you here?"

He sighed. "Why am I anywhere? Fundraising, of course. Elections aren't far around the corner." He brightened. "And I'm here to see you, of course."

"This is the nicest place we've ever been together," I said. "Something on your mind?"

He met my gaze. "You don't miss a thing."

His hand shook slightly, and suddenly I was worried. Was he ill or just nervous?

"I've asked Julia to marry me."

I stared at him. Blinked. In my entire life, I had never imagined him saying those words.

He broke into a smile. "She said yes."

"Of course she did. But isn't this kind of sudden?"

"Not really."

I leaned forward. "Dad, you've known her for what, six months?"

"A little more than six months."

"Doesn't it bother you that she's the governor's ex? I mean, their divorce wasn't even final until a year ago."

His face darkened. "What are you getting at?"

"I don't know. Is it possible she's just social climbing?" I said and immediately regretted it. It sounded like I thought the only reason Julia might love my father was because of his position. "I didn't mean—"

"Any man," my dad started, then stopped. "Any man who's in his sixties and is seeing a much younger woman has to ask himself those questions. But Julia isn't like that."

"Then what does she want?"

He looked at me in surprise. "I'd hoped that once you'd met her, you'd be happy about this."

I sat there, trying to catch my breath. I knew my own breakup with Eric was coloring every emotion, making me bitter.

With a sour taste in my mouth, I moved the flawless porcelain coffee cup and saucer in front of me, squaring it with the plate. "She's too young. Newly divorced from a governor who's under criminal investigation for money laundering. You've been together for a few hundred days. And she's changing you—making you go to the opera and having you hang out in glorified manors like this one. It doesn't seem to me like you're making good choices."

"You're making a lot of assumptions, Kate."

Suddenly I missed the mom I never really knew. I wished she could speak to him and tell him what a mistake he was making. She had died before I could make many memories of her, but what I knew from the photos I'd seen and the stories reverently whispered by aunts and uncles was that my parents had the kind of love that lasted. They had taken their time to be sure. Word was, they had dated for three years before my dad got the nerve to propose. Love had a clear path—you didn't plunge into it recklessly. It happened slowly, on a reasoned, measured timeline.

Why wasn't all of this so obvious to him? Couldn't he see what was happening?

"I hope you'll grow to love her as much as I do," he said. "We're getting married next month."

I couldn't talk. My brain was telling my mouth to speak, but no words came out. Then I did something I'd never done before. I walked out on my dad.

I had a bad habit of walking out—sometimes storming out—when I didn't like the way things were going. I'd done it a few times at Channel Eleven—once when a big investigation I'd been covering got taken away and assigned to a junior reporter for reasons that made no sense. My boss, David Dyal, said I was "too rigid," expecting decisions to always follow a logical progression, when the reality was that the process was often more "fluid" than that.

"Fluid decision-making" sounded like an excuse for making bad ones.

My dad was doing the same thing. He was being impulsive, mercurial, as though he had succumbed to some kind of fever. Who married someone after knowing them for only six months?

By the time I reached the sidewalk, I was embarrassed about running out on him. I heard my heartbeat in my head. Thumping, urging me to go back. To apologize.

I didn't.

I knew my instincts were right about Julia. I just needed a little time to cool down my nervous system and investigate.

In the cab on the way back to the studio, I accessed the LexisNexis database and looked up Julia Pearson. The first images that came up were of her with the governor on the campaign trail, at a film festival or two and several fundraisers, and during his swearing-in ceremony with the New York State seal in the background. In every photo, she was always camera perfect, dressed head to toe in understated but luxe designer outfits.

I learned that after college she worked in Africa and Latin America to help aspiring women entrepreneurs build their own businesses through the microcredit-enterprise model. After she earned her MBA from Stanford, she started a foundation to support women entrepreneurs. She met then-governor Drew Abbott on a blind date set up by a mutual friend in New York.

It all looked so good.

Until the stories became all about the investigation into her husband's money laundering. I dug through a dozen or so articles, looking to see if she was implicated, but it seemed to be isolated to the governor's dealings with a fugitive Malaysian financier. Julia didn't seem involved. Still, I did a deep dive on court records and requested a few transcripts.

After the mayor announced the civic award and cash reward that afternoon, hundreds of people came forward claiming they were responsible for the balloons at city hall. None of them matched the people in the grainy photos.

Social media lit up. It seemed like anyone who didn't claim they were at city hall that night thought they'd seen Marie.

One woman in Colorado swore she went to church with Marie but then admitted she hadn't been to church for two years. Another man offered unconvincing photographic proof that Marie had been on the teacups ride in Disneyland last week. The strangest tip came from a man who said that the woman in our photograph looked exactly like his grandmother, only she had died twenty years ago.

Our spirits wilted. As Scott and I, with help from Isabelle, sifted through the calls and emails, we discovered many of them were bizarre Marie sightings—Vegas card dealer, truck driver in Iowa, swimsuit model at Mardi Gras. The tips were more likely to lead us to Elvis than Marie.

Except one. "Linda. Compass Car Rental," Scott said. "Says Marie rented a car from her."

"Where?" I asked.

"Dallas."

Was it a coincidence?

Scott called the number and put the phone on speaker.

"Compass Car Rental," a woman answered in a practiced customer-service voice. "Linda speaking."

"Linda, this is Scott Jameson and Kate Bradley from ANC. We got your email. You think you rented a car to Marie?"

"I *know* I did. The night of the big storm. August seventh. All the planes out of Dallas were grounded, and we had a mad rush to get rental cars. People were shouting and shoving. Everyone was crying or mad. And this young man. He had been one of the first to get to the counter. He was very charming . . . good looking. My rep thought his driver's license looked fake, so he called me over. I think the guy was trying to flirt with me, which was kind of ridiculous, since I've got kids his age. So that made me suspicious, you know. He was talking me up, explaining how he needed to get to Manhattan in time for a graduation. And that's when Marie came up to the counter."

"What'd she look like?" I asked.

"She had on the same scarf. Like in your report."

"Did she rent the car?" Scott asked.

"First she spoke to the guy—I couldn't hear what they said—then he hugged her. Like a really big hug. She said she lived in Manhattan, then rented the car and offered to drive him. She had elite status, so she was one of the lucky ones to get a car that night."

"And you're sure her name was Marie? What was her last name?" Scott asked.

"Positive. But I'm . . . not allowed to give you her last name. Customer privacy."

"And the man? What did he look like?"

"Dark hair. Blue eyes. One of those charming types. Don't remember much else except he had a fake driver's license from Kentucky."

Scott and I locked eyes. Could this be Logan?

"Linda," I said, carefully, "as you know, the mayor of New York is giving a civic award and reward to the people behind this movement. We think the Marie you met is part of it. Can you tell us her last name?"

"Sorry, but I can't."

"Would you ask the manager?" I pressed.

"I am the manager. And my boss will say no too."

"Maybe they'll make an exception? Everyone wants to know who she is."

"I know," she said with a laugh. "Even here in Dallas. It's all over the TV."

"Please ask your boss if they'll let us have her last name," Scott said. "We don't need an address. Just a last name."

"We'll call you tomorrow to check in," I added.

As we were about to hang up, Linda added, "One more thing. I guess I should've told you up front. Marie wasn't alone. She came up to the counter with two other people. One was a young woman. Blonde. The other was a man in uniform. Army, I think."

CHAPTER NINETEEN

Standing on Thirty-Fourth Street in front of a guy handing out flowers to military wives and widows, Scott and I delivered our report for ANC. "Thousands of New Yorkers have found themselves the recipients of acts of kindness by a secretive group no one has been able to identify. Their rent or hospital bills have been paid. Or they received a free meal or flowers on their doorsteps. These stunning acts have taken the city by storm, but it may be an actual storm thousands of miles away that brought the people behind it together."

"The storm was massive," Scott continued. "Its ferocious winds dumped three inches of rain, downed power lines and trees, and spawned countless tornados in the Dallas–Fort Worth area of Texas in early August. Yet the Secret Four—the people who are behind the kindness movement in Manhattan—were four strangers engaging in one simple act: getting a rental car to escape the storm. What happened after they left Dallas is still unknown, but ANC is piecing together the story of who these people are and why they engaged in the largest ongoing giving event in recent history."

Mark didn't scowl when he saw the report, which was the closest thing I'd seen to him being happy with my work. The story snapped up tens of thousands of views online within a few minutes. Then millions. For a story that wasn't about a political scandal, a string of murders, or a natural disaster barreling toward a major city or coastline, the response was surprising.

Still, we had no foothold on finding any of them. We hadn't yet located anyone named Joe Raley at White Sands. And we had no way to find a guy named Logan somewhere in the state of Kentucky. At least none of the other networks had anything concrete either. ABC even had anchor David Muir reporting live from the streets of Manhattan on what they were calling the "Secret Good," but they had come up empty handed too.

As I was packing up for the night, a text buzzed through. From my landlord: *I've fixed the window. Changed the lock. New key in your mailbox. Sorry about what happened.*

My apartment.

Consumed by the search for Marie, I'd forgotten all about the destruction there. Now the anxious feelings rushed back at me. I sank into my chair, closing my eyes for a moment.

"Everything okay?" Scott asked.

I opened my eyes. "Yeah. Just gathering the courage to deal with the cold, harsh reality of my apartment cleanup."

"Want some help? I'm pretty good with a broom."

I laughed. "I'd like to see these broom skills you're claiming."

"I won the Broom Championships two years running. You doubt my skills?"

Our eyes met, and I fell into his gaze. "You've already done more than enough."

The next thing I knew, we'd been standing in front of the ANC studios talking for fifteen, maybe twenty minutes longer. Somehow, we ended up talking about the time he spotted a sleeping hump-back whale while shooting underwater near Tahiti last season. "She'd doze—vertically—for about ten minutes at fifty feet, then drift to the surface for a few breaths. Those minutes with her were surreal. You almost don't believe it's really happening to you."

Despite his beautiful tale, I found my mind wandering. In the orange-red glow of the fading sunset, he seemed even more handsome, if that was even possible, and although we were standing a professional distance apart, it felt as though a magnet were pushing us together.

I forced my mind to pay attention to what he was saying. But my emotions didn't follow along. Instead, as I listened to him tell his story, I felt a spark of the unexpected. Something I couldn't describe. Some might call it joy. But this was more. It felt as though my whole world was filled with possibility and unfolding in front of me.

"I see Gavin is still waiting to take you home, so I should let you go," he said. Then he leaned in for what I thought would be a quick, casual hug.

It started that way, but then neither of us pulled away. And the moment suddenly became liquid and warm, vibrating with promise. My heart was pounding so hard I wondered if he could feel it through my blouse. As we lingered in that hug for longer than we should have, I was certain he could read my feelings, even though neither of us moved or said a word.

"Be safe," he murmured in my ear. I heard the silky warmth in his voice, and it only made me want to stay longer, just exactly where I was.

The apartment was worse than I remembered. In addition to everything being in complete disarray, fine sprinkles and shards of shattered glass were everywhere. And maybe I was imagining it, but the apartment had a sour chemical smell. Maybe from the window repair?

Gavin had inspected every inch of the apartment and confirmed it was secure, but as he stood in the living room taking it all in, he shook his head. "I think you should get a cleaning crew and stay in a hotel for a few more nights."

"Yeah," I said, because it was the only word I could manage.

"Want me to drive you? The Hilton's up the street."

"No," I said. "I need to get some things together first. I'll take a cab."

He squared his jacket. "You shouldn't head there alone."

"I'll be fine."

He didn't move. "You'll get me fired if I don't take you."

"Okay, how about you get something to eat and come back in an hour?"

He seemed to like that idea and took off. Then I went to work assessing the damage, putting a few things back in their place, and packing a suitcase. Thirty minutes later, I heard a knock at the door, and figuring Gavin was returning early, I flung it open.

Artie was standing in the hall, his hands shoved in the pockets of an oversize hoodie.

"We thought you were home," he said.

"I am," I said uneasily.

"I'm Artie. From upstairs." For the first time, I got a good look at him. Thin and pale with dark circles under his eyes. He didn't make eye contact.

I tightened my grip on the door handle. "What can I do for you?"

His speech was halting, unsure. "Cora told me to have you come to the apartment upstairs."

"What for?"

He looked down. "She said to come get you."

"Don't you think it might be good if I knew why?"

His voice was monotone. "Will you come with me and find out?"

I thought about closing the door. Calling the police. But what would I tell them? A strange guy in my apartment building was asking me to meet a neighbor in another apartment? Instead, I grabbed my keys and the pepper spray the production coordinator had given me the night of the power outage. "Lead the way."

I followed him at a safe distance up the stairs, but even though I'm sure I looked calm and maybe even brave on the outside, inside I was worried I was making the stupidest move of my life. I placed my fingertip on the trigger of the pepper spray, ready for anything.

Artie didn't say a word.

The second-floor hallway was empty and completely quiet, save for the muffled sound of a TV set coming from one of the apartments. It was also dark. One of the lights wasn't working, which made the already dirty-gray walls look more depressing.

We headed down the hallway. Then suddenly he whirled around. "Did you lock your door?"

"Yes," I said, but my answer sounded weak. Why would he ask me a question like that?

"Good." He turned back around and headed into the apartment at the end of the hall.

I knew better than to follow him inside. "Ask Cora to come out here if she wants to see me." I planted myself firmly in the hallway.

He looked at me strangely. "Okay."

Then he opened the door, stepped inside, and closed the door behind him. If he came back with a knife or some other weapon, I'd be ready. Or at least I thought so.

Instead, Cora rushed out into the hallway. "Why are you standing here? Come inside." She beckoned to me with her hands. "You must see." She took my hand and hurried me into the apartment.

Raymond, Artie, and a couple I didn't recognize were gathered around a table in the living room. Steam rose from a pot of soup. My stomach rumbled at the scent of fresh bread.

"Surprise!" they all shouted.

"I don't understand . . ." Did they think it was my birthday?

"I talked to the owner," Cora said. "You can stay here until you get your apartment fixed."

"And my company's cleaning crew will come tomorrow to do a full cleanup of your apartment," Raymond added. "Free, of course."

I looked at him, then Cora, searching for an explanation. "This is all . . . great. But why?"

She took my hands in hers. "I know you left the money under my door so I could go see my daughter. Because of you, I'm getting on a plane tomorrow morning."

"It was a nice thing you did, Kate," Raymond said. "On my end, I know that you put up with a lot of crap from me. Just glad you didn't blow my head off the other night."

"You were so loud," Cora said, frowning. "I couldn't sleep."

"I appreciate what you said to me," he said quietly.

I was so overcome with emotion I couldn't speak. I tried to let their words settle in, but all I kept thinking was how strange and wonderful it felt to be appreciated for something so small. So easy. And then another feeling floated in, layering itself on the wonder: I felt like I belonged to these people. To this moment.

"You must see what the Andersons got for you," Cora said, taking my hand and leading me into the bedroom. "Beautiful, yes?"

The room was stunning, like something out of a high-end furniture catalog. The kind of bedroom I wished I'd have time to shop for and the eye to put together: a gorgeous turquoise patterned duvet with perfectly coordinated throw pillows in rich textures.

"They both work at West Elm," she whispered. "So they got it on discount."

"I don't—"

"We're the Andersons," a woman's voice said from behind me. "Holly and Dan." She extended her hand.

"Thank you. This is beautiful. But I don't understand why you are—"

"We're your upstairs neighbors," Dan said quietly. Neither of them looked like the people I imagined when they were playing their music at earsplitting decibels. Instead, they seemed like any other couple you might see on the street—he a little on the hipster side, with a scruffy goatee, and she the companion to that, with a blonde ponytail and wearing a vintage seventies dress.

"You probably want to kill us right now," Holly said. "We don't blame you. We just wanted to find a small way to thank you."

I felt my cheeks flush. "For what?"

Dan laughed. "Well, for putting up with our loud music, for one."

"And for your note and the treats," Holly said.

I shook my head. "Those are hardly reasons to give me . . . this."

Holly lowered her voice to almost a whisper. "They are, actually. This is hard for me to say, but . . . we've been trying to have a baby, and . . . I miscarried again." Her voice cracked. "We've been in shock. Dealing with it, for the third time. We'd lost hope. Your note came at the right time."

She reached out to hug me, and suddenly I felt connected to her even though we had just met.

"Hug later. There's more," Cora said, ushering us out of the bedroom.

Then she walked me through every sumptuous dish on the table. Manti dumplings, kebabs on a bed of rice pilaf, stuffed peppers.

"Artie made this for you," she said.

"He's a line cook at Cafeteria," Raymond said, sampling a stuffed grape leaf. "One of those twenty-four-hour joints. Which is why he has such odd hours."

"These are my recipes," Artie said, slowly. "I hope you like them."

I drew a deep breath. "It all looks amazing."

"I'm sorry if I frightened you earlier," Artie said.

I didn't know what to say. Moments before, I had thought he might harm me. I'd pegged him as dangerous. But instead, he seemed to be someone who struggled to be comfortable engaging with other people. In place of fear, I was overcome with the realization that even the person who looked away, who seemed to ignore us, might also be struggling to find connection.

"No worries," I said. "I've been a bit jumpy since the break-in."

"I am happy I can do this."

My eyes misted. I knew I hadn't earned any of this; nor did I deserve it. But somehow their beautiful gestures were stealing my breath away. And the people who were once frustrating, annoying strangers were beginning to look like friends.

CHAPTER TWENTY

"It's time to move on," Andrew was saying in his office the next morning.

I'd had a restless night's sleep in the upstairs apartment, and even the double espresso I'd just finished wasn't taking the edge off my exhaustion. Or helping my patience.

"You can't be serious," I said, my voice raw. "This story is getting bigger every day. Even the president mentioned it in his press conference yesterday."

His face tightened with frustration. "Can I be straight with you? I want you to drop it."

I stared at him in disbelief. "Drop the story that's been getting record ratings?"

"What are the chances we're going to find these people among the thirteen million who live here? Police and FBI aren't looking for them. All we have is a gaggle of reporters trying to chase them down. And not even you have a solid lead."

My cranky tone didn't seem to be working, so I tried a softer approach. "Look, bad things like fires and murders, they happen fast, right in sync with our news cycle. But good stories like this, they take time to discover. And uncover. I just need more time."

He shifted in his seat. "Let me give you some advice, Kate. You know what story you should be covering right now? What story would be moving your career forward? Millions of taxpayer dollars have gone into settling employment-discrimination claims against a handful of state representatives and—"

"The news can't be only about what goes wrong," I interrupted. I saw a quick flash of surprise flicker in his eyes and had the feeling reporters didn't interrupt him often. Or if they did, they didn't have long careers at ANC. But I was already in too far to back down. "It can't just be about chaos, unrest, and people doing bad things. This story we're trying to tell is just as important as ones about spikes in crime waves, escalating violence, and how divided we all are. This story is proof that small acts can bring about big change."

He looked at me, a defeated sigh escaping his lips. He wouldn't win this argument by claiming the story wasn't worthy of more time. He knew I was right. And that meant that he had to reveal his actual motives for wanting me off this story.

He leaned forward, resting his forearms on his thighs. "When we talked about you coming to ANC, you told me you wanted to cover stories of substance. Right now that's the Supreme Court, rising hate crimes, immigration policy."

"Politics," I said quietly.

"It's a big step for you, but that's what we want you to do."

I looked down at my hands. I didn't come all the way here to lose everything I cared about: my boyfriend, my friends, and the stories I wanted to cover. I swallowed my anger and leveled the only weapon I had left: the truth. "Andrew, I want to stay on this story because I'm in awe of what these people are doing. When was the last time either of us can say that about a story we covered?"

He looked out the window, his jaw tight. "I do remember what it's like to be passionate about a story you simply must tell. But let me give it to you straight: clinging to this story is a bad career move."

I opened my mouth to say something, then shut it.

"You probably already know this, but a lot of eyes are on you here. A kind of scrutiny you didn't have in LA."

"Why?"

He waited a long time before answering, letting the seconds tick by. That's when I knew he was finally going to tell me what his real agenda was. "Because the top brass at the network don't like seeing a prominent senator's daughter fail."

His words sliced through my confidence. They thought I was failing.

I took a shaky breath. "I'll work harder then," I said, more solidly than I felt. "I know—"

"You can't fail on this one, Kate. Either find who's behind it—today—or you've got to move on."

⌒☉

"Her last name is Rivera. Marie Rivera," Linda from Compass was saying on the phone later that morning.

"Can you give us a physical address? Email?" I asked, jotting quickly in my notebook.

She sighed. "Well, that's where it gets interesting. The email address we have on file isn't working. It's been returned as undeliverable."

I rested my head in my hands and rubbed my eyes. "What about her driver's license? That must have an address."

"It does. It's an address in Crown Heights. But when we googled it, we saw that the apartment building had been demolished about six months ago."

I tried to hide my frustration. Unsuccessfully. "So we don't even know for sure that she lives here in New York City anymore?"

"No, we don't. But when she was at the counter, she told us she had to get 'home' so she didn't miss an important appointment. That's at least something."

At least something. But not proof.

After I hung up with her, I looked up the name Marie Rivera in the Whitepages online. There were plenty. Twenty-three, to be exact. Then Scott and I began eliminating possibilities. From the photos, we'd guessed that Marie was over fifty, so we excluded anyone who was under forty and over seventy. That narrowed the list down to a dozen.

But as I was scrolling through the listings, I noticed the "Family Members" section and remembered talking to the woman named Jordan who had met Marie after she had accidentally left a voice mail for her nephew with the same first name.

We found only one Marie Rivera with a relative named Jordan. She lived in the Bronx. Could this be her?

Even though we knew that the "relative" databases online weren't always reliable, it was the strongest lead we had to date, and with time slipping away, I knew I had no choice but to pursue it. Minutes later, we were heading to the Bronx in an ANC news van, with Chris at the helm.

My pulse was hammering as we pulled up in front of the crumbling two-story house with faded yellow vinyl siding. A tiny concrete "front yard" was fortressed by a white iron fence. A battered green Ford baked in the hot sun out front. It hardly looked like the launching pad for the country's largest giving event.

"She gives away millions but lives in a place like this?" Scott asked.

"Doesn't seem right," Chris said, peering at his GPS app. "But this is the right address."

My stomach roiled. I had a sudden sinking feeling we were wasting our time. That we were on the edge of failure. I'd worked on plenty of stories that hadn't panned out before. But I'd never floundered on a story this big. Maybe the top brass was right: I was failing.

I thought about bailing. Had the feeling the others were thinking the same. Instead, I sucked in a deep breath and forced myself to keep it together.

"Let's see what's going on here," I said, swinging open the van door.

As the three of us strode up the front walk, a tabby cat watched us through a set of bent metal mini-blinds in the window. We couldn't find a doorbell, so I knocked.

Long moments later, a woman in her early sixties opened the door. She wore a blue tunic with white slacks and a black orthopedic boot on her left foot. I studied her reddish-brown hair and sharp blue eyes, but without the distinctive glasses or scarf, she didn't look like a definitive match.

"Hi, I'm Kate from ANC. And this is Scott. Are you Marie Rivera?"

She nodded, then glanced at Chris's camera, puzzled.

"We're here because we believe you're the Marie Rivera that's behind all the good stuff happening in Manhattan," Scott said, his natural charisma on high beam.

She placed a hand on her chest. "I've been hearing about her on the news." She talked slowly, her breath labored. "But while I have the same name, I'm not her."

Scott and I exchanged glances. If she was Marie, we knew she wouldn't confess. But she sounded pretty convincing that this was a case of mistaken identity.

"Do you have a nephew named Jordan?" I pressed.

She eyed me warily. "Yes. But how do you know that?"

Scott answered. "The Marie we're looking for has a nephew named Jordan. Also, someone matching your description was spotted renting a car in Dallas during a big storm."

"My description? That's impossible. I've never been to Dallas."

"Where were you during the blackout?"

"Right here," she said, nodding to her boot. "Not getting far with this."

"You weren't at city hall?" Scott pressed.

She shook her head. "I haven't been to city hall in ages. And certainly not like this. Why would I go?"

I could feel this hurtling to yet another dead end, but I still had one last volley.

"Maybe we do have the wrong Marie," I said carefully. "How long have you lived in this home?" I remembered Linda from Compass saying that Marie had moved recently because the Crown Heights apartment building in the address on her driver's license had been demolished.

"Almost five years." She looked at me and then Scott. "I'm a retired teacher living on a pension. Do you really think I could be behind this, or are you just hoping it's true because I have a similar name?"

My spirits sank. Andrew was right. It was time to move on. We were never going to find Marie.

⁓

"Welcome back to the real world," Mark was saying the next morning. I'd spent another restless night in the upstairs apartment, and my nerves were frayed. The whole commute into work, I'd been dreading this moment with Mark. Figured he'd use this opportunity to put me in my place. I wasn't wrong.

"Now that you've come to your senses, you might try covering important stories," he continued, his tone laced with arrogance. "Things viewers actually need to know. Growing terrorism. Old diseases outwitting our antibiotics. Did you see the researcher we had on this morning who said the next global pandemic is a matter of when, not if?"

My assignment was not that, of course. Instead, he had me cover a billionaire political donor who had just been charged in a Florida prostitution sting. Scandal. To say I was miserable was an understatement.

I'd failed to find Marie. Now I was back to being the senator's daughter covering politics. And a giant failure on my first big story at ANC.

I trudged back to my cubicle and noticed that someone had left a vintage copy of *Harriet the Spy* on my desk. The book was expertly wrapped in red ribbon, and the cover showed Harriet roaming her Manhattan neighborhood clutching a spy notebook under her arm.

No note or card.

"That was my favorite when I was a kid," Stephanie said, dumping a tote bag on her desk. "Is it your birthday?"

"No."

"Part of the kindness thing? Or from someone else?" Her knowing smile made me think she had a hunch about who was behind it.

"No idea." I faked a puzzled look, but my stomach was doing a nervous flip. It had to be from Scott. He was the only one who knew that my own copy had been torn in the break-in. He'd thought about me, hunted down this rare treasure, and bought it for me. All of that was making my head spin.

I threw myself into reporting on the political-donor scandal, but after a long day of the endless repeat of the story, I realized that hearing about this billionaire who was hiring prostitutes wouldn't really make a difference in viewers' lives. The millions of people who watched my report about him weren't going to be better off because they knew every detail of what he'd done. Instead, the story was just another example of the bad things people did.

Yet what Marie was doing was changing us. All around the city, we could actually see it happening. People paid for coffee for those in line behind them. A group of strangers formed a human chain to rescue a boy who fell in the lake in Central Park. A high school cross-country team took a dozen shelter dogs on their morning run. The list of "good" stories was rising from dozens to hundreds by the day.

As Gavin drove me back to the apartment building that night, I felt regret creeping in. I'd given up on Marie too easily. There had to be a way to convince Andrew to put me back on the story. A way to find her.

As I stepped out of the car, I noticed something scrawled on the sidewalk in white chalk:

STOP LOOKING FOR MARIE.

CHAPTER
TWENTY-ONE

The police found the guy who broke into my apartment. Twenty-five-year-old Roy Jackson was inside a Chinatown apartment when the tenant arrived home to find him ransacking her place. When the police searched Jackson's apartment, they found my laptop, wiped clean, along with a slew of other electronics he'd stolen.

My palms were sweating as Detective McGregor told me the news on the steps of my apartment building the next morning before I headed into work.

Jackson was in jail. My upstairs neighbor Artie had had nothing to do with it.

I was relieved. Grateful that they'd found him. Yet still angry. The robbery had thrown me down a bizarre wormhole, saddling me with a crushing to-do list to put my life back together, most of which I'd still been avoiding, and making me believe everyone around me couldn't be trusted. I'd even suspected Artie, simply because his late-night hours and his lack of social skills seemed unusual.

But as glum as I still was, what I suddenly realized was that the robbery had also given me another perspective. So many people had rushed in to help me—Scott, the detective, my neighbors, the landlord. Even complete strangers like the Andersons.

The good guys outnumbered the bad guys by at least ten to one.

"Is this new?" the detective asked, bringing me back to the moment. He pointed to the chalk writing on the sidewalk.

I nodded. "Do you think Jackson's been doing this? Is he the one sending the notes?"

He snapped a photo. "He's a crash-and-grab kind of thief. Not much thought behind the stuff he does. I don't think he wrote this."

"Maybe you could do a handwriting analysis?"

He frowned. Clearly, he didn't like me making suggestions for how to do his job. "I'll work on it. You got any idea why this person wants you to stop looking for Marie?"

"Lots of possibilities. Maybe she's in trouble or in hiding. Perhaps she does business with criminals. For all we know, she could be in the Witness Protection Program."

His eyes narrowed. "Be careful. Those are big reasons for not wanting to be found. And someone who does stuff like this, he's more cunning than petty thieves like Jackson. He's putting calculated thought into what he's doing. And that's far more dangerous."

Mark was obsessed with my report about the Florida prostitution sting that had ensnared a major political donor and several other high-profile individuals. He found the story so compelling that he went on and on about it that morning, walking me through the excruciating details of what he wanted in a follow-up report. In his mind, any story about scandal, people behaving badly, celebrities, sex, or violence was highly newsworthy, even if it didn't represent most of what was happening in the world.

While he was talking, my phone chimed, and another text from my father flashed up. This was his third text this morning, and I'd lost count of how many he'd sent since I walked out on him. I promised myself I'd call him, but first I needed to find out more about Julia.

After Mark headed off to another meeting, I scoured the transcripts of the ex-governor's court documents I'd ordered. I'd been mulling a couple of theories: Maybe Julia was in financial trouble and needed my father to bail her out. Maybe she wanted a higher profile for her foundation, and being a senator's wife would do that. Perhaps she wanted to burnish her reputation after being married to the governor embroiled in scandal.

I hoped the transcripts would point me in the right direction. But despite scanning hundreds of pages of her husband's court proceedings, I found nothing connecting her to any of it.

I went back to the LexisNexis database. In the place of any proof of financial trouble, I found articles about the work she was doing to encourage women entrepreneurs in Vermont and in far-flung rural areas of India. Instead of evidence of her being a social climber, I found photos of her sitting on a schoolroom floor in El Salvador, her hair tied back in a ponytail, listening to young girls playing the violin.

I closed my laptop. Even without any indication of an agenda, her marriage to my father still troubled me. Maybe my instincts, honed by years uncovering manipulation and deceit, were right.

Or maybe I was uneasy for another reason: I didn't want things to change.

∽

My dad answered my call on the first ring.

"I was beginning to worry about you," he said. He didn't sound angry, but my dad was better at hiding his negative emotions than I was.

"Sorry it's taken me a while to get back to you," I said sheepishly. "And sorry for walking out on you."

"I don't understand. Why are you so upset that I'm marrying Julia?"

I'd placed the call while standing outside the ANC building, a mistake because the stale odor of cigarettes lingered there. The low groans of the buses lumbering by grated on my nerves too.

"I'm not upset," I said. *Upset* seemed like a term for frail women who couldn't control their emotions. "I'm concerned. It's all happening really fast, and it doesn't make sense. It's not like you to be impulsive."

"This isn't impulsive. I know this is what I want to do."

I leaned my head against the concrete wall. After all the years of it just being the two of us, I knew my dad. He was deliberate and systematic in his thinking. Before he reached a decision on any issue, he'd have sifted through all the facts and research, evaluated what experts were saying, and outlined the strategies to fix the problem. Then, when he talked about his decision, his voice was measured, deliberate. But that wasn't the case here. When he talked about Julia, his decision to marry, the cadence of his voice was one I didn't recognize: breezy, unrestrained.

"Is she pressuring you to get married?"

"Kate, this is something we *both* want."

"Then what's the hurry?" I asked, my voice unsure. "Remember when you were looking for an electric car a few years ago? You researched all the models for nine months before you decided on one. You spent more time on that decision than you have about a person you're about to marry."

"The two are not the same, and you know it," he said sharply, then softened his tone. "When you meet the right person, you know it. Sometimes you take a leap like this because you can't imagine your life without them."

I swallowed the knot that had formed in my throat. "It seems like you're rushing into this, Dad. Like you haven't thought this through. Maybe you should give yourself more time. Call off the wedding for now."

"Call off the wedding?" He blew out a breath. "Kate, you're being unreasonable. It's a little embarrassing, to tell the truth. I'm not sure how to explain to Julia why you're acting this way."

Unreasonable. Embarrassing. My sadness, my fear, transformed into straight-up anger. I bit out the words, letting him feel my frustration. "You're ruining our family."

He was silent for a long moment. Then he had the audacity to ignore what I said. "I've got to run. Julia and I are late for a fundraiser."

CHAPTER
TWENTY-TWO

The text rolled in at 6:55 in the morning, just as I was finishing my run. A number I didn't recognize:

Kate, you are invited to participate in a concert at Floyd Bennett Field at 50 Aviation Road tonight only at 8:00 pm. Free. There is more that connects us than divides us. Marie. This invitation is non-transferable.

I looked up Floyd Bennett Field in Brooklyn and learned that in its heyday it was the site of flights by Amelia Earhart and the start and finish point for Howard Hughes's record-breaking flight around the globe. But the airfield had been abandoned since the early seventies, and the photos I found were of buildings in serious disrepair, with rusted beams, peeling paint, and sprawling vines taking over spaces that once housed stately airplanes. I couldn't imagine why anyone would want to host a concert in such a depressing venue.

Plus, I wasn't sure this was an actual invitation from Marie.

In the newsroom later that morning, I checked around to see if anyone else had received a text, but no one had. I figured it was a fake. But after a quick check on social media, I realized I wasn't the only one to receive an invite. Thousands of people were posting about the unusual invitation, and the hive mind had as many conspiracy theories as there were questions.

Most were worried that the concert was a sham like the Fyre Festival in the Bahamas, which turned out to be nothing like the advertised hype. But since no promises were being made about the concert except that invitees could "participate" in it, that theory faded quickly. Others thought this was a scheme to make money off Marie's name. Midmorning, Scott texted me that he had received the same invitation, and we made a plan to share a cab to Floyd Bennett Field later in the afternoon.

I don't know what I expected when I got into the taxi with him. But I didn't imagine that I'd actually feel nervous sitting with him in the back of a shabby cab. Everything about him was distracting—broad shoulders beneath a flawless creamy dress shirt, blue eyes—and the pull was so strong that I had to look out the window every few minutes.

I needed to distract myself, so I asked him about *Harriet the Spy*. "I have a very important question to ask you."

He raised an eyebrow. "It sounds serious."

"It is." My heart was racing. "And you have to promise to answer honestly."

"Well, you're either about to propose to me or—"

I laughed. "Propose to you?"

"Or you're about to ask me a deeply personal question. I know that look, Kate. It makes people you interview want to tell you everything you want to know. Or it can look like you're about to ask someone to marry you, vote for you, or lend you money."

"The same look can mean all those things?"

"Yes. And it's very effective," he said with a mischievous smile. "Now what kind of question are you going to ask me?"

His eyes were dancing. So distracting that I stared at the back of the head of the taxi driver for a moment before looking back at him.

"I want to know if you were the one who left the vintage copy of *Harriet the Spy* on my desk."

He stared at me blankly. "What happened?"

"I asked around the newsroom, and no one knew anything about it. You're the only one who knew my copy had been destroyed."

"True." His eyes met mine in an unwavering gaze. "And even if I did it, I wouldn't tell you."

"Why?"

"I like the idea that wondering where the gift came from brings you a little happiness."

"Wait, you're not going to tell me. Because . . . you want me to be happy?"

"Exactly."

I wanted to hug him. Kiss him. Both. My emotions were spinning out of control.

I sobered. It was too soon after my breakup with Eric to feel this way. If nothing else, my feelings were completely unprofessional.

I tried to get things back on track. Remember why I was there. "FNN is saying this whole thing is a sham," I said as we neared Floyd Bennett Field. "That it's just someone capitalizing on Marie's name recognition."

"They're just saying that because no one in their entire network was invited. Same for ABC."

"None of the other networks were invited? That's odd. Makes me wonder if this is the real deal or if we are a bunch of gullible suckers, so eager to find her that we'll head an hour outside of Manhattan on the off chance we might see her."

"Depending on the hour of the day, I've been leaning toward: we're all a bunch of gullible suckers."

"My only hope is in the last sentence in the text, where it says: 'There is more that connects us than divides us.' Not the kind of wording scammers use. Plus, it's spelled right. And with good grammar."

"Good grammar." He laughed, and then his gaze traveled over my face, making me feel warm. "I've missed working with you, Kate."

His words were soft like a caress. I wanted them to be true, but I was afraid I was reading more into them than he intended. "We've only been apart for twenty-four hours."

From the look in his eyes, I could see that wasn't the response he was hoping for.

Away from the bustle and buildings of the city, Floyd Bennett Field was bathed in darkness. Hundreds had shown up without invitations and had been corralled off to the side, waiting to see if they might get in after all. After a security guard checked our phones to confirm we had legit invites, we followed a lit path of lanterns that stretched as far as the eye could see.

At the huge corrugated metal door to a former airplane hangar, a dozen or so ushers were handing out square white envelopes.

"Do not open until instructed to do so," they told each of us. "No exceptions."

Their serious warnings only made me impatient to open mine. I felt the envelope to see if I could guess what was inside. Surprisingly flat. Maybe paper. Money?

The hangar was filled with at least five thousand people, a guest list that was far bigger than Scott and I had imagined. But what immediately caught our eye was the sumptuous feast laid out along the walls beneath yards and yards of café lights: steaming trays of meats and seafoods, silver chafing dishes containing everything from fried-chicken comfort food to elaborate dishes with exotic names, and tables piled high with decadent sweets. Everything about it felt like a celebration. But of what?

The warehouse had been restored, or at least repaired and upgraded enough to function, and now had all the stage, lighting, and equipment you'd see in a traditional concert space. Steel-riveted beams stretched in a geometric pattern above our heads, but there was no roof. Standing underneath a glittery vault of stars, completely invisible to us in the city, I felt as if we had been transported to someplace far away and magical.

As we snaked our way through the dense crowd, we couldn't find anyone resembling Marie, and none of the dozen or so people wearing earpieces or headsets knew where to find her. Finally, we found a security guard who seemed to know what was going on. "We've all been hoping to spot her, but none of us have," he said. "Best you can do is talk to Jeff. He's the producer in charge." He pointed to a guy wearing a red polo and a headset standing by a set of speakers.

Jeff had the weathered look of a producer who'd seen it all. Deep wrinkles around his eyes. Shaggy hair in desperate need of a stylist's attention. A death grip of a handshake.

"Can you tell us how this concert with Marie came about?" I asked after Scott and I had introduced ourselves.

"I've been doing concerts for, what, twenty years, and I've never seen anything like this before. This lady calls me up, tells me she's the Marie that's been all over the news, explains exactly what she wants. The next day some courier guys show up with a bunch of file boxes full of cash. I took it straight to the bank to make sure the money was real."

"What did she want to do?"

"You'll see in a minute. Standard concert stuff we do all the time. And a ton of secrecy. We aren't allowed to talk about any elements of the concert in advance, but otherwise, none of us—not even me—know anything about her."

"Is she here?" I asked.

"Told me she'd come, but I don't know what she looks like. I mean, she could be anyone here."

I scanned the packed hangar. If she wasn't wearing the sunglasses or scarf, I'd never find her.

"Did she give you any clue as to who she is? Why she is doing this?"

"Nothing." He shook his head. "Short and sweet. Whole thing was very straightforward."

"Everything?" Scott asked. "Organizing a concert like this would involve a lot of moving parts. Was there anything that stood out? That seemed strange?"

"Not really." He shrugged and adjusted his headset. "I guess it was a little odd that she insisted that this one construction company had to do the work to get this place ready. I mean, we usually hire local for a job this small, and they were based somewhere down south. But we figured she owned the company or something. Lots of our clients have quirky requests like that."

"What company was it?" I pressed.

He leaned over to another guy in a red polo, who was adjusting one of the microphones. "Frank, who did the work here? You remember the company name?"

Frank turned to look at us through oversize black frames. "The guys were from Kentucky. Name starts with an *H* . . . Hagerty Construction."

I tried to google the company, but the cell reception was poor, and the page wouldn't load. I scribbled the name in my notebook.

"Gotta run," Jeff said, then left us standing there as he headed to talk with a lighting team.

As we made our way through the crowd again, I scanned every face. Was goodness obvious? Did generosity like hers make her stand out? Or was it hidden in the woman leaning on the walker? Or the woman with a face leathered by too much time in the sun? I already knew what questions I would ask. Things I wanted to understand. All I needed was five minutes.

And we weren't the only ones looking for her. As we swept through the crowd, the one word we kept hearing in many conversations—even those in languages we didn't know—was *Marie*.

"Someone told me Marie is a Russian spy," a woman said, her friend nodding in confirmation.

"I heard Marie made her money in Silicon Valley," a man whispered to two wide-eyed women. "Some highly classified tech start-up."

We reached the back of the hangar, with no sign of her. And just as I was about to give up, I caught a glimpse of a red scarf in the crush of concertgoers in front of us.

Marie.

I pushed through the crowd, dodging a tall man in cowboy boots, to where I'd seen the scarf.

Instead I was standing in front of a bear of a man with a winged sleeve tattoo. Standing with him was a woman with frizzy black hair and bright-silver shoes, but no scarf. Both of them gave me vacant stares, clearly confused as to why I was looking at them as though I had just made a huge discovery. I felt like an idiot.

Had I imagined it? Was I so consumed with finding her that I'd mistaken a glimpse of something in the dim light for Marie's red scarf?

Suddenly the lights went out, plunging the packed-to-the-gills hangar in darkness. Then the crowd broke out in applause as a young man with curly hair bounded across the stage into the spotlight.

"Welcome, everyone! I'm Trevor, and you all are the lucky ones invited to this event by Marie. And in case you've been under a rock lately, Marie is the person who's been all over the news because of all the remarkable things happening in our city. Now, you're probably wondering why you're here and what we're supposed to be doing. Let's find out, shall we? You know you've been dying to find out what's in those white envelopes. So go ahead and tear them open!"

The hangar erupted with the sound of envelopes being torn open. I unfolded the paper inside. It was a letter:

Every one of us is fighting to find peace.
In a world filled with despair.
We're missing someone.
Losing someone.
Worrying.
Pushing back fear.
Your moment of kindness
To someone you don't know
To someone who can never repay you
Has the power
To bring hope in the darkness
And to lift
In ways you can never imagine.
Be the light in someone's darkness.
—A Stranger

It was only when Trevor started singing a melody set to the words that we realized it was a song—part pop, part anthem, a gospel beat with a bit of a reggae rhythm.

"For this first song, you are the singers. That's right, all of you. And after we've rehearsed and brought out the band and amped up the lights, you can record this special night and share it on social media. Now, I know some of you may not feel like singing. And that's okay. Do what makes you comfortable. But I promise, every single one of you is going to be blown away by what it feels like to be surrounded by five thousand voices singing the same song."

Then he proceeded to rehearse us through the song—cajoling us to enunciate, to sing louder and not so raggedly, to try again, to not lose focus in the middle, and to not get ahead of each other—until by take five we sounded seriously good.

And he was right. There was nothing really comparable to singing with five thousand others. I felt carefree, carried away by a sense of belonging. Like singing "Take Me Out to the Ball Game" in the seventh-inning stretch, but more magical. Meaningful.

Once we'd rehearsed the song a sixth time, twenty-five musicians rushed onstage, and Trevor introduced them simply as "Marie's Band." Then the lights suddenly switched into arena-style mode, transforming the hangar into a high-energy concert. The crowd buzzed in anticipation.

"Before we sing again, I'm gonna ask every one of you to either link arms or put your arm on the shoulder of the person next to you," Trevor said.

Instead of either of those options, Scott took my hand and slid his fingers between mine. For an instant, I wondered how it might look for us to be holding hands publicly, but then my thinking mind shut off because something about his fingers interlaced with mine felt intimate. Exciting.

We sang. Surrounded by five thousand others and the band, the simple words on paper turning into something that gave me goose bumps. It felt like a modern-day prayer. Loud, unguarded, joyous. As I looked all around me, everyone linked together arm in arm and swaying in unison, I couldn't find a single cynic or even anyone who was holding back. Even the thirtysomething guy in the Deafheaven T-shirt next to me.

When the song was over, the crowd erupted in applause. But Trevor wasn't letting us rest on our laurels. "Let's do it again. This time, look around. Everyone around you is different. Everyone is a complete stranger. But it doesn't feel that way, does it? We're not as divided as it seems. Now get your phones out and record this one, because it's going to be special."

It seemed like everyone there recorded the next performance, and this one, buoyed by emotions that had grown stronger with each repetition, was bursting with confidence.

When the song was over, the crowd broke into applause again, and the band began playing an upbeat song. All around us, people were hugging, many with wet eyes, talking to each other as if they weren't strangers at all.

"I had no idea you had such a beautiful voice," Scott said, without letting go of my hand.

I smiled. "You are hard of hearing."

His eyes traveled over my face, his gaze catching mine and holding it a second. Then he leaned in, his lips brushing mine. I felt the tension in his body, his heart thudding in his chest. I breathed in his scent, locking it into my memory. His hands moved through my hair, drawing us closer. I felt like I was falling. His kiss was deliberate. So intense it made me dizzy.

He was the one who broke away first. "We shouldn't do this."

CHAPTER
TWENTY-THREE

"Why?" I asked, even though I knew all the reasons.

"You're making this tough." His breathing was labored, as though he'd been running. He laced his fingers through mine. "Looking like you do. Smiling at me. You're making it hard to do the right thing."

My pulse was racing, emboldening me. "What is the right thing?"

The band started a dreamy ballad, which only made him more attractive in the soft light.

"Going back to the way things were. Working on a story together. Keeping things uncomplicated."

"They were getting complicated before."

He flashed a half smile. "No one's going to see this for what it is. Or what it might be. The gossip mill will talk about it like it's some sordid affair."

"How will they even know?"

"They'll know. And it'll be hardest on you. Instead of seeing you as the hugely talented reporter you are, they'll only see you as 'Scott Jameson's girlfriend.'"

"What about you?"

He moved a lock of hair from my face. "They'll all hate me. Think I'm the luckiest guy in the world."

I laughed. "Right. You'll probably get fired for being that lucky." I leaned against him, both of us trembling. "Does it matter what people think?"

"A lot of journalists in the unemployment line probably ask themselves that question too."

I squeezed his hand. "Why does anyone have to know?"

"They'll know. I'm a terrible actor. And everyone can already tell I'm crazy about you."

Crazy about you.

My heart took a tumble. My gaze drifted over his face, and his eyes caressed mine. I had fallen under his spell.

"And then, there are all my questions about him."

I wanted to pretend I didn't know what he meant by *him*.

"Firefighter. Rescuer. Google you, and you'll see a lot of photos of him with you. Everywhere. Your father was expecting him at the opera instead of me."

I drew a deep breath. I should've said that Eric and I had broken up. But something held me back. "And there are all my questions about her."

"Paige."

"Anyone with eyes can see her feelings for you."

He let go of my hands. "We both have a lot to figure out."

∽

Maybe it was a flaw of the human heart. Or just a flaw in me.

Feelings were supposed to happen on a measured path. You waited a long amount of time after your breakup, and then you eventually met someone—who was available—and maybe sparks flew. Or maybe they didn't at first. And then you liked them, they liked you, and over time, you might fall in love.

That was the way it was supposed to happen.

But what if attraction didn't come when you thought the timing was right? Maybe it didn't always wait until you were ready. What if it didn't follow a series of predictable steps?

I brought my fingers to my lips, remembering his kiss, the way his hands felt in my hair.

I tried to explain the feelings away: It was simply a reaction to being a fish out of water in Manhattan. It was a short-lived office romance, an intensity that would inevitably sizzle.

I was lying to my heart.

As much as I was trying to resist him, our kiss, his words, had cracked open something inside me. Feelings were flooding in. Possibilities floated to the surface.

Maybe it wasn't entirely a flaw falling for him. Maybe it was out of my control.

∼୨

I don't know what woke me up at two thirty that morning. I thought I heard a click, a creak, from the apartment settling. Felt a dip in the temperature.

I pulled the covers close. Listening. Other than the hum of the old refrigerator, the apartment was quiet. But I had the feeling I wasn't alone.

I listened for a long while, my breathing shallow, and realized I was simply spooking myself on my first night back in my apartment. Would I ever feel safe here again?

I left the bed, my body heavy and cold but my mind on high alert. My former news director, David Dyal, called late-night awakenings like this "pay-attention moments" and urged all his reporters not to fight them because they often brought insight into whatever you were wrestling with in your waking hours.

I headed into the living room to find a notebook. Maybe it *was* a pay-attention moment, but it felt like panic.

I'd left the shades partially open, letting the blue-white light of the streetlights peek in. When I went to pull on the cord to close them, I saw someone standing at the bottom of the front steps. He was holding something smooth and metallic in his gloved right hand.

I crouched down to peek through the bottom of the window, careful not to move too quickly or risk him noticing me at the window. In the dim light, I couldn't see much of his face, but he was wearing a brown sweatshirt, a couple of sizes too large. Whatever he was holding glinted in the light, and when he turned his hand slightly, I could see a can of spray paint.

I crept from the window and found my cell phone. With trembling hands I dialed 911, but the call went to a recording asking me to hold for an operator. My breath high in my throat, I returned to the window and saw him crouched down now, his hand inches from the bottom step, spraying.

The next thing I knew, I was running. Out of my apartment door. Yanking open the heavy front door of the building. Standing on the landing.

The words in red paint glared at me:

STOP KATE.

With adrenaline pumping through my veins, I acted on fearless instinct. "Stop!" I shouted, trying to sound in control, but my voice sounded like a squeak.

His head snapped up, and I saw recognition sweep across his brown eyes, sunken and angry.

His mouth moved, but no words came out. Then suddenly: "You'd better stop looking for Marie."

Whatever I thought he would sound like, I was wrong. I heard a melancholy tone in his voice. Worry.

My chest heaving, I breathed out a single word: "Why?"

"She doesn't want to be found."

"She sent you to warn me?" My body was shaking. Hard. "To threaten me?"

His hands were clenched in tight fists. "I don't have to tell you nothing. Just stop looking for her. Or you'll regret it."

He started to rush away. He was easily 250 pounds and taller than me, so I wasn't going to chase after him. "You care about her. That's why you're doing this."

He kept walking. "What's it matter to you?"

"You're Jordan, aren't you? Marie's nephew." It was a wild hunch, but it got him to stop walking. "I know your name. A description. Won't take police long to find you."

With his back to me, I didn't know if he was going to turn around and assault me or race away. I glanced at the front door, and suddenly it seemed farther away than six feet.

"Don't," he said.

"Don't what?"

He drew a deep breath. "Don't call the police. She wouldn't like it if I got into more trouble."

"More trouble?"

"If you want all she's doing to continue, stop looking for her. There's a reason she doesn't want to be found."

I took a step toward him, even though my body was vibrating with fear. "What reason?"

He sighed. "It might kill her," he said, then started running.

I ran. Gravel and debris on the rough sidewalk cut into my bare feet. He was fast, but it didn't take long to gain on him.

What would I do if I caught him?

Across the street, I spotted a guy walking his dog, and I waved my arms at him.

"Stop him!" I shouted, but it sounded like a grunt. Uncontrolled.

Jordan rounded the corner. Then stopped. He placed his hands on his thighs, chest heaving.

I slowed, gaining control of my breath, deciding what to do.

"You really want to find her this bad?" he shouted at me.

I blew out a breath. "Yes."

I walked slowly toward him, steadying my wobbly legs. His entire figure was shrouded in shadow. If he attacked me, I had nothing. Not even my phone.

"Why will it kill her if we find her?" I asked.

"She's sick. It's serious."

"What is it?"

"I don't know. But I can tell by everyone's voices it's not good."

"So that's why she doesn't want to be found?"

He looked up at me. "That's what I think."

"But you don't know."

"No."

I stopped ten feet away from him. From here, I could see he was much younger than I'd originally thought. Late teens. "You could've misunderstood."

He turned toward me then, and I could see fear in his eyes. "Don't think so."

"Do you know what she's doing? Who she's working with?"

His voice was strained. "I don't know anything."

"Then how do you know she's even the Marie we're all looking for?"

He rubbed his jaw. "I found a lot of cash in her kitchen. Took some of it, you know, planning to pay her back. But then she caught me with it. Explained to me that it had a purpose. That she was part of everything I was seeing all over the news."

I stepped close enough that he could have grabbed me if he'd wanted to. "Does she know you're here?"

"No. This is me taking care of her, for a change. She's bailed me out a lot."

"For?"

I looked into his eyes and saw the weight of shame there, dark-purple streaks from what I assumed were sleepless nights. "Stealing stuff. Cutting school."

"I'll bet she's been bailing you out like that because she cares about you. But I don't think she'd like to hear that you've been writing threatening letters to me."

His voice shook. "You gonna call the police?"

I thought about it for a moment, fear rising. "Not if you stop the threatening notes. Stop following me."

He took a long moment to respond. "Will you stop looking for her then?"

I shook my head.

"I can't let you do that to her." He walked away. Something in the way he said it pulled on my heart. I let him go.

⁓

Our video from Marie's concert went viral. Seven million views in less than twenty-four hours, giving us hundreds more leads to follow—people who claimed they'd seen her, a few who thought they had talked with her, and even one woman with fifty thousand Twitter followers who claimed she'd met Marie at the concert and, after she returned home, discovered her rosacea had suddenly cleared up.

Of the five thousand concertgoers, Scott and I turned out to be the only journalists invited, so our reports carried the banner "Exclusive to ANC." Otherwise, thousands of concertgoers posted their own videos, sending Marie's message ricocheting through social media, reaching tens of millions more.

As I headed into the newsroom that morning, I thought about what Jordan had told me. Marie was sick. If that was true, I had the feeling he'd keep trying to stop me from finding her. But after talking with him, I wasn't afraid of him like I'd been before, and his story made me want to soften my approach to finding her.

At the same time, her illness was an essential clue that none of the other networks had. Not only did it give us insight into why she might be doing all this, but it also helped explain why she was upset when she found the note on her airline seat.

At my desk in the newsroom, I dug into the lead that Jeff the concert producer had given us: the construction company that Marie had insisted they hire to work at Floyd Bennett Field. I googled Hagerty Construction in Kentucky, the company Jeff's coworker mentioned, and scrolled through a dozen or so photos and bios of the team—from the bright-smiled CEO through the red-bearded CFO through a slew of young project managers. Was one of these people related to Marie? I thought about calling the company, asking them why they'd been chosen to do the work for the concert, then nixed the idea. If one of them was related to Marie, I doubted they'd admit it.

I mulled over the idea that Hagerty Construction had worked on another project connected to Marie. But what? On their Projects page, I scrolled through endless photos of construction sites— scaffolding, wood framing, cranes, and backhoes—and completed stores, banks, and warehouses. Nothing stood out. Until I found a group photo of a construction team finishing up a Dollar Tree store. It was a playful shot, a row of guys in white hard hats and mud-stained work pants clowning around for the camera, big grins on their faces.

My eye fell on the guy on the end. With his tall, slim build, he stood out among the other, more sturdily built construction workers.

Logan.

Minutes later, I was dialing Hagerty Construction in Kentucky, based in Hawesville, a small town on the banks of the Ohio River.

I worked to sound calm. "I'm looking for one of your employees. His name is Logan," I said to the woman who answered the phone.

"Logan Wilson or Mattingly?"

"Blue eyes. In his twenties."

"You mean Logan Wilson. May I ask who's calling?" she asked with a soft Kentucky lilt.

"I'm Kate Bradley from ANC."

"ANC?" She sounded impressed. "Usually wouldn't find him here in the office. But you're in luck. He was here just a minute ago. Let me see if he's still here."

I waited a few minutes before we heard shuffling on the other end of the line.

"Hello?" a young man's voice said.

"Logan, this is Kate from ANC. We met the morning you—"

"Look, this isn't a good time. My car just got slammed in a hit-and-run."

He sounded so calm that it felt like he was making it up. But if he didn't want to talk to me, he could've asked the receptionist to say he wasn't available. That meant he was probably curious to find out what I wanted. And maybe he had actually been in a hit-and-run?

"I'm sorry. Are you okay?"

"Yeah. The car was parked. But the whole thing sucks. My deductible is steep, so I've got no way to get it out of the body shop."

"My timing is crummy. But I'd like to talk to you about Marie."

He was silent for so long I thought he'd hung up. "I don't know who you're talking about."

"We have witnesses who saw you with her in the Dallas airport," I said.

"Give me a sec," he said slowly. Then the noise around him quieted, as if he had gone into another room. "I was there, okay? But you have to stop looking for us. For Marie."

"Why?"

"It's not for me to say."

"Can you at least tell me how you met her? I know she helped you when you couldn't rent a car in Dallas."

His voice was distant. "Yeah, I don't know."

"This is off the record, of course," I said, trying my best to sound like someone he could trust. "I'm . . . just curious."

"I'll just say that was a really low time for me."

"What was going on?"

He sighed. "I'd been unemployed for almost nine months after making a big mistake at my last job. Then I lost my license because of another really dumb move. I had debt collectors chasing me day and night, and money was so tight I had to pawn my guitar to pay for the plane ticket to get to my cousin's graduation."

"You didn't know Marie before Dallas?"

"No. I met her at the rental-car place. She invited me into the car, listened to my story, and told me she thought I had an important purpose in the world. She was one of the few people who didn't think I was a loser."

"She believed in you."

"Yeah," he said, his voice trembling.

"Did you know the others?"

"No."

"Why did she choose Hagerty to do the work at the concert at Floyd Bennett Field? Was it because you work there?"

"I think you already know the answer."

"Then at least tell me what happened on the car ride through the storm."

He hesitated. "She asked me to take a leap. And that's all I'm gonna say."

"A leap? What kind of leap?"

His voice was tense. "I'm hanging up now. But before I do, I'm going to ask you again to stop looking for us. Stop looking for Marie."

CHAPTER TWENTY-FOUR

What was a leap, anyway? I knew Logan wasn't talking about a physical leap, like jumping off the Brooklyn Bridge. Maybe a leap of faith? But even that had many meanings. It might involve doing something you weren't sure would succeed. Or accepting something that wasn't easily believed. It could even mean doing something that was beyond the bounds of reason.

Whatever it was, why was this leap a secret?

Lost in thought, I returned to the newsroom, dodging frantic producers and editors working on the Category Four–hurricane story on the way back to my desk.

Stephanie rushed up, her face flushed with excitement. "Look what I got," she said, waving two tickets in front of my face. "One of the producers just gave me these. They're for *Perfect Crime* tonight, one of the longest-running shows Off Broadway. And Scott's girlfriend stars in it."

She held up her phone and showed me a poster for the play.

I felt a pang of jealousy. Dressed in a slinky black dress and four-inch heels and holding a gun, Paige was luminous, slender, and, by all evidence, flawless. I could see why she and Scott were together.

"I was hoping the show would take your mind off the robbery for a few hours," Stephanie said. "Can you go?"

"It sounds great, but I can't. I'm meeting the owner of the party-supply store who saw the guy buying grosses of balloons a while back. Thinking I missed something when I talked to him the first time."

She looked surprised. "Wait. Are you still working on that story?"

I nodded. "Of course. Why?"

"I overheard Mark telling Andrew he was taking you and Scott off it."

My voice rose. "Are you kidding me? Again? Even after the viral concert video?"

"Mark pitched the idea of giving it to Jason Berman."

I stared at her. Jason was one of the network's best-known anchors, a nightly fixture on ANC with his signature black glasses and anchor-perfect salt-and-pepper hair.

"Mark and Jason go way back. Worked together at a station in Philadelphia before coming here."

"Why would Jason want this story?"

"For the obvious reasons, of course. And I heard Jason's mom was one of the people whose hospital bills were paid off by that Marie person. This is personal for him."

My reaction was instant and physical. I winced. Like someone had just punched me in the gut.

It took me a moment to realize why. The story was personal for me too.

There is a peculiar smell in a party-supply store. A musty, grandma's-attic-y scent mixed with latex balloons, plastic of every species, and the sweet smell of cheap candy. Village Party Store was no exception. Lit by long fluorescent-tube lights that looked like they'd been installed fifty years ago, the store aisles were so narrow I had to walk sideways to squeeze past the masks, plush animals, bulk-size containers of candy, and party favors bursting from the shelves.

Most of the employees seemed like they were recent high school graduates, but the owner, Burkley McCarthy, was well into his sixties, trim and fit with silver-gray hair and trendy Warby Parker glasses. He was the one who'd called me to report that he'd seen a guy in a hoodie leaving with bags of purple and white balloons.

I found him in the back of the store trying to balance a Book of the Dead in the spindly hands of a wraithlike witch in a Halloween display.

"He had to be carrying, what, like ten thousand balloons in all those bags," he told me.

"Did he rent some helium tanks too?"

He shook his head. "For that kind of volume, not from here. There are dozens of places he could've gone that do tanks for commercial use."

"What made you notice him?"

"The purple and white balloons. My first thought was he hadn't paid for any of it. We get a lot of theft here. People come in with shopping bags and just take stuff off the shelves. But he had a receipt."

"You have security cameras?"

"Of course. But I already told you where he went. What more do you need?"

"Problem is, I talked to the woman in the apartment you saw him enter, and she hadn't seen anyone like that. Nor did anyone in the building."

He frowned. "I know what I saw."

"Maybe we can find the guy on your security footage and run a photo of him in my next report. Find him that way."

Burkley seemed to like that idea and showed me to his office, where we could access the recordings. The technology was surprisingly sophisticated, allowing us to zip to specific dates and times and, with striking clarity, view what each camera saw. It took us a few minutes to figure out what date he had seen the balloon guy in his store, but once we did, we quickly spotted him.

Unlike the other shoppers whom we'd seen wandering through the aisles, browsing through the novelty items, this guy, his hoodie pulled tight to his face, hurried to the balloon aisle, scooped up the entire shelf of bulk-size bags of purple and white balloons into a couple of shopping baskets, and rushed to the cashier. He knew what he was doing.

As we watched him do this from several camera angles, Burkley pressed the stop button. "You know, I don't like watching him like he's some kind of criminal. Ever since he started doing all this, things in this city have gotten better. People are friendlier. Happier. If you find him, you think he might get in some kind of trouble?"

"Trouble?"

"No good deed goes unpunished," he said grimly. "Maybe police will slap him with fines for littering the city with balloons. Or someone will claim his balloons damaged their property—"

"I've got to believe that people will see the good in this. And not try to crush it."

He sighed. "You're an optimist."

No one had ever called me an optimist. *Skeptic. Cynic.* Those were words people used to describe me. How could I be an optimist after covering thousands of violent, brutal, and cruel stories for TV news?

Was it possible I was becoming one?

He pressed play again. "Crazy stuff happens all the time in this city. And when I first saw them putting balloons everywhere, I thought, *Well, this takes the cake.* But then I noticed how everyone reacted to all of this—smiling and talking about the balloons with people they don't know—and I realized I was wrong about the balloons. It's a simple but genius way to connect all of us."

As he continued talking, I watched the footage as the balloon guy handed a stack of cash, bound in a purple currency band, to the clerk. Twenty-dollar bills. When the clerk took the cash from him, the balloon guy's fingers peeked out from the oversize hoodie. They were long and slender, topped off with light-blue nail polish. Then he reached up to tighten the strings on his hood. But before he could, a long lock of blonde hair had escaped.

The balloon guy was a girl.

The guy who answered the apartment door at 828 East Thirtieth Street twenty minutes later looked like Josh Groban, the famous singer-song-writer, only a decade younger. Same wavy brown hair, a scruffy beard, and big brown eyes.

It wasn't, of course.

"Brad Darnell," he told me after I introduced myself.

"This is going to sound strange, but did you get married a few weeks ago?"

He shot me a skeptical look. "Yeah. How'd you know?"

"I met your wife's maid of honor here. Blonde hair. Lives in Dallas."

"Alexia?" He shifted his weight to his other foot. "What do you want to talk to her for?"

"She and I were discussing a story, but I forgot to get her phone number. Would you happen to have it?"

"Is this about her kidney?"

My mouth fell open, trying to make sense of what he was asking. "Actually, it's—"

"Is this about the donor? Did he die or something?"

"Donor?" I repeated, trying to put it all together. "Sorry, does Alexia have a kidney donor?"

"Yes, I thought . . ."

"I'm here about the balloons."

He looked at me like I was crazy. "What balloons?"

"The ones she brought here," I said. "She'd bought grosses of them. We think she's part of the group that's been leaving them all around Manhattan."

He shook his head. "You sure you got the right Alexia? She doesn't have money to buy balloons. And why would she be part of that when she doesn't even live here?"

"You never saw them?"

"No. But I wasn't in this apartment when she was. I stayed with a friend when all the bridesmaids were in town."

"I'd like to talk with Alexia. How can I find her?"

He shook his head. "She's gone back to Dallas."

"Can you give me her number?"

"She wouldn't like that." He pulled his phone out of his pocket. "Let's call her together."

❦

Alexia hung up on me. Twice.

"What's going on?" Brad said, frowning. "This isn't like her. She's probably one of the nicest people I know."

I could see my plan was faltering, but I pleaded with him to try once more. "If she hangs up again, I'll leave her alone."

On the third try, the phone rang and rang until she finally answered. "I don't want to talk with you. Please stop calling."

"Wait," I said. "I've talked with Logan."

She was silent for a moment. "About what?"

I was grasping at straws. "About why the four of you were in the Dallas airport."

She sighed. "I'm hanging up now."

Sweat broke out on the back of my neck. In order to crack this story, I needed to keep her talking. "Wait, would you tell me about your kidney? Your donor."

"Did Logan tell you about that too?"

"Actually, Brad did."

She sighed. "I wish you hadn't, Brad."

I softened my tone. "I'd like to hear about it. Not for air."

She blew out a breath. "Okay. This isn't for you to share or anything, but I had kidney disease and spent a few months on the transplant list. Then, four months ago, the hospital called to say that some anonymous person was donating one to me. I couldn't believe it. They wouldn't tell me his name. But I managed to find out he's a principal at a high school somewhere in Idaho. The hospital says he doesn't want to meet me."

"Do you want to meet him?"

"Sometimes it's all I can think about," she said, her voice pitching higher. "Wondering why he did it. Why he doesn't want to meet the person whose life he saved. If I'm being honest, the balloons gave me a way to celebrate what he did for me." She was quiet for a moment. "I've said more than I should. I'm ending this call now."

"Wait," I said, desperately. "Before you go. Can you tell me where I can find Marie?"

"She could be anyone," she said, then hung up.

Maybe I'd never find her. Perhaps she was like so many things we sought but could never grasp. Like chasing rainbows. We'd captured moments, instances, snapshots of her: descriptions of those who'd encountered her, stories from people who'd worked beside her.

But not her.

Finding Marie was a wild-goose chase. She was always ten steps ahead of me, and each time I caught up a step or two, she slipped through my fingers.

I wondered if I should continue to chase her or if Andrew was right about this story damaging my prospects at ANC. Making me look like a failure. Time had marched on, and the stories I'd missed out on were big, newsworthy, important. Why pursue something so elusive?

Maybe I should let Jason Berman take over the story.

The story. It started out being about that. About proving that I had what it took to deliver ratings. First and exclusive. That I deserved to be here at ANC. But the goal had morphed into something I was still trying to grasp.

I'd tracked down murderers, rapists, and white-collar criminals. To bring them to justice. To help the victims get closure. To drive ratings. But this—finding Marie—was about something else: I wanted to understand why she did it.

I wanted to be like her.

~9~

Back in my apartment building that night, the Andersons were playing ABBA's greatest hits at high volumes, and someone, I thought it might be Raymond, was cooking a dish that smelled like dog food. Oddly, it didn't bother me all that much. In a way, it felt comforting and familiar, yet another reminder of the tapestry of the city around me. My new friends.

Cora wasn't back from Ukraine yet, so I used the key she'd left me to feed a pair of red-eared slider turtles she kept in a small tank in her living room.

Outside my apartment door, I discovered that Artie had left a glass container of one of his food creations with a note:

This is Chicken Bog. Let me know what you think.

In the days since the neighbors surprised me in the apartment upstairs, Artie had slowly warmed up to me, lifting his head and saying hello when we passed on the doorsteps but not much more than that. I felt like cooking was his way of communicating, reaching out.

Some people expressed themselves in words or music. Others, like Artie, through food.

As I stood by the window enjoying the creamy dish, my eyes fell on the lamp in the window across the street. For weeks the woman had been a nightly fixture, her nimble fingers fashioning beautiful things out of sumptuous fabrics. But for the past several days, the lamp had languished there alone, its yellow beam constant through morning and night, with no sign of her or any movement in the apartment. Maybe she'd finished her masterpieces and taken a holiday. Or she'd won the lottery and moved to someplace exotic.

There were a hundred good reasons to tear my eyes from the window and get back to my work. Maybe a thousand.

But I was worried about her.

Before I could consider all the reasons it was a bad idea, I made my way across the street to her apartment building and up a set of faded red steps to an ornate steel door. Although the wind had picked up and the temperature had dropped, a room air conditioner was humming in her window. I was trying to figure out whether I should press the button for apartment 1A or 1B when a man wearing gray sweatpants and a tank top buzzed out of the door, carrying a French bulldog.

I stepped inside and knocked on her door. I could see light beaming through the peephole, but then it suddenly shut off. The apartment was silent.

I knocked again.

Finally, shuffling noises, and then the woman answered. She was younger than I expected, maybe fifty, slightly sleepy eyed, with smooth porcelain skin.

That's when I realized I'd made a mistake knocking on a stranger's door. "I'm Kate Bradley. I live across the street and—"

"What is it you want?"

"I'm just here to introduce myself," I said, trying to find a way out.

"I've seen you in the window too. Across the street." She fixed a pair of pale-blue eyes on me. "What really brings you here?"

"To be honest, I was worried about you."

"Why? We don't even know each other."

"I'm sorry, I—"

She waved a hand at me. "Looks like you work all hours into the night. What do you do?"

"I'm a reporter. For ANC."

She must have been expecting a different answer, because she looked at me, puzzled. "Come in already. It's hot out here."

She ushered me inside and led me to the living room, where she turned on a lamp by the couch. I glanced at the familiar sewing table by the window, the lamp off, the fabrics gone. Up close it somehow seemed smaller, ordinary.

"You want a glass of wine? Something stronger?"

"Nothing. I'm fine."

I took in the old cracked walls, a hall closet overstuffed with heavy coats, a coffee table covered with medicine bottles.

"I need to throw all this away," she said, noticing my gaze. "What made you worry about me?"

"I noticed you weren't sewing for the last several days . . ."

"And you came all the way over here to check on that?" she said, heading into the kitchen.

"I hope that doesn't seem strange."

She returned with a can of ginger ale and a plate of store-bought cookies. "It does, actually."

"I'm sorry, I didn't mean to—"

She thrust the can in my hand. "I don't like strangers. But since you're here, why don't you tell me what you want."

"I already told you."

She motioned for me to sit on the couch. "Are you a friend of Karen's?"

"No," I said, settling beside her. "I don't know anyone by that name."

She crossed her arms on her chest. "Then why are you here? You watched too much *Rear Window* or something?"

"I've been working on the story about all the good things happening around the city. And trying to find who's behind it. And then I noticed you weren't in the window." I stopped for a moment when I realized I was rambling. "I worried about you. Well, I guess I'm a little lost."

"If it's any consolation, we all are. Lost."

"Maybe, but I—"

"Maybe you've been going about it the wrong way. Maybe we both have."

I smiled, trying not to look surprised that a complete stranger was giving me reporting advice. "How so?"

She shrugged. "I'm just saying that if you want some kind of proof of who they are, you might never find it."

"That's not exactly encouraging."

Her voice broke. "Maybe it's okay not to know."

I wasn't sure what she was getting at. "I think a lot of people would like to know who they are and what inspired them to do this."

"Maybe we have to be okay with not understanding. To let go of our need to find answers for every question. Maybe some questions don't have answers."

I wondered if we were talking about the same thing. She looked away, a faraway expression on her face.

"I've taken enough of your time," I said. "It's great to meet you. I'm glad you're okay."

I started to stand.

"You were right to be worried about me," she said quietly.

I turned. "I was?"

She drummed her bony fingers on the armrest, silent for a moment. "My husband died a few weeks ago," she said, and for the first time, her voice was gentle. She waved her hand toward the medicine bottles. "Those were his. But I can't bring myself to throw them away. I haven't known what to do since then. I go to my bookkeeping job during the day, then throw myself into making dresses until I'm so exhausted I fall asleep. Every day the same."

I sat beside her. A light rain streaked the windows. "What are the dresses for?"

She sighed. "I don't know yet. But sewing, working with fabric, has always been something I've loved to do. Only the dresses aren't enough to distract me anymore."

I felt her pain moving and breathing between us. "I'm so sorry."

A softness settled in her eyes. "My friends, they ask me what they can do for me. I can't make a list of what I need because I don't know what that is."

In the long silence, I felt my own heart crack open. Tears welled in my eyes. Suddenly our separateness, our aloneness, faded away, and I felt connected to her, fused with her in a way that at once seemed strange and undeniable.

She spoke finally, her voice trembling. "You coming over like this . . . you listening to me . . . even though we didn't know each other . . . this is good."

CHAPTER TWENTY-FIVE

I didn't wait for Andrew and Mark to take me off the story. Instead, the next morning I rushed straight past Andrew's assistant and through his open door, where I found him sitting at his desk talking on the phone.

He looked at me with surprise but then waved me in. As he continued his call, I felt my heart pounding. I'd never used the "Senator Bradley's daughter" card on a story before, but that was my plan. But even as I rehearsed in my mind what I was going to say, I began to have second thoughts.

Andrew finished his call and hung up. "Did we have a meeting on the books?"

"I heard that you and Mark are going to take me off the secret-good story and—"

Anger flashed in his eyes. "Take that up with Mark. I don't interfere with his assignments."

"But you can stop him from giving it to Jason Berman."

He frowned, then motioned for me to sit in the chair opposite his desk. "I see the ANC rumor mill is hard at work." He clasped his hands together. "I've said this before, but this time you need to listen. Let this one go. I have bigger things in mind for you."

I was about to remind him of his friendship with my father. Talk about the reasons I'd agreed to come to ANC. Instead, I told him about meeting a stranger I'd only seen in the window. As he listened, I watched his shoulders relax. Andrew had been a journalist for decades before ascending to the executive suite, and I could see he understood where this was heading.

"After she told me her husband had died, I spent another hour with her, listening to her story. A complete stranger. And that's when I realized what these people are doing. They're connecting us. Everything that's happened, all of it is changing the city. But it's also changing me. I mean, I knocked on a neighbor's door, a stranger, because . . . I was worried about her."

He blew out a breath, and his expression made me think I'd convinced him. I was surprised when he said, "Jason feels the same way. These people paid off his mother's medical debts, bills that she'd been hiding from him because she didn't want him to worry. This is personal for him too."

I shrugged. "Okay then. Let him have the story . . ."

"Good, I appreciate—"

"I'm kidding, Andrew. There's no way I'm giving up that easily."

He leveled a hard gaze at me. "You're not expecting me to tell Jason—"

"No, I'm saying let him cover it. But keep Scott and me on this story too."

He scratched his head. "Having all three of you on this story is like driving a Porsche forty miles an hour . . . I can't remember a time when a soft story like this had so much star power."

"Is that such a bad thing?"

He fiddled with a pen on his desk, thinking. "Look, if I'm being honest, it inspired me to help too. There's a woman in accounting who just took on two foster sons. They came to her without shoes, extra clothes, school supplies. Anything. I knew she wouldn't accept any help from me, so I secretly left a gift card on her desk loaded with enough money to get them everything they need."

"It's changing you too . . ."

He leaned forward. "Don't let that get around the newsroom. I don't want anyone thinking I'm growing a heart or anything."

"I'll keep your 'heartless' reputation intact. You want me to tell Mark that I'm staying on the story?"

He stood. "You better let me handle Mark. And don't think I'm going soft on you. I want answers—closure—fast."

❦

The Kindness Busters finally caught someone on tape. Not a rat with pizza or a guy walking his white rabbit, like I'd seen in previous clips they'd sent.

Instead, they captured a man in a tan jacket and white hat staggering through the crosswalk at a busy Eighty-Eighth Street intersection. The time stamp was 7:32 p.m.

I wondered why Kindness Busters founder Peter Venkman sent it to me, but then, in a recording shot from the vantage point of a GoPro strapped to a street sign, the man had only made it to the middle of the street when the light changed. As cars streamed past him, his body trembled, and he lurched sideways. He was about to fall when a teen girl in a bright-blue puffer vest appeared. Her presence surprised him, and he flailed his arms, almost careening into a passing car. Then a woman with a ponytail raced into the street to stop traffic and prop him up. Seconds later, two burly men with their backs to the camera, one in a blue T-shirt and another in flannel, ran up to guide him across the busy street as the teen in the vest made a call, perhaps to 911. When they reached the sidewalk, a guy in a Red Sox sweatshirt and black sandals helped the group lift the man over the curb.

It was a beautiful sight. Five strangers working together to help a man they didn't know who was probably drunk or strung out on drugs.

The guy was recovering from a stroke, Peter texted. *Good example of how this city is changing. Thought it might help your story.*

I watched the recording continue, and the man in the blue T-shirt turned toward the camera and flagged down a police car. The light from a passing truck blinded the camera for a moment, but then I could see his face.

Joe Raley. Or at least it looked like him.

When did you record this? I texted Peter.

Last night.

Are you sure?

100%

I rewound the recording to the point where the man looked toward the camera. Even without the army fatigues, I recognized his face from the city hall footage: deep-set brown eyes beneath thick eyebrows. I snapped a screenshot.

Joe Raley was not in White Sands. He was in New York.

I waited. Focused on the door to the Raleys' apartment building. Without the cocoon of a car to sit in, I did what everyone else did in Manhattan: I put in my earbuds and scrolled through my phone, pretending to listen to some awesome music while waiting for someone.

My pulse was pounding as though I were doing something wrong. A guy eating from a cardboard tray of nachos passed by me and glanced at me briefly, but otherwise, everyone else ignored me. This was one time that feeling anonymous in Manhattan was working for me.

I didn't like to think I was doing ambush reporting, a technique employed by paparazzi or investigative reporters looking for dirt. This was a form of it, but I didn't see any alternative.

Either Joe's parents thought he was stationed at White Sands Missile Range or they were lying on his behalf, and the only way I was going to get to talk to them was to confront them with the photo.

As rush hour came and went and the number of people on the street dwindled to just a few, I weighed and reweighed the pros and cons of simply ringing their doorbell. Kevin had already told me, "Do not come back," so I was sure that once they saw me in the peephole, they wouldn't answer.

Then twilight shifted into evening, and no one had entered or left the Raley apartment. Just as the streetlights flickered on, I saw him.

Joe Raley. Dressed in a T-shirt and jeans, he rushed up the street carrying a large box, but he made it look easy. My mouth went dry, and suddenly I wondered if I could go through with this.

From here, he looked to be over six feet tall. And strong. With military training. And in the dark, he might have thought I was trying to attack him and react accordingly. My stomach twisted in a knot.

"Joe?" I heard the words come out of my mouth, sweet and friendly. "Joe Raley?" He turned to look at me, and I started to cross the street. "It is you," I said, buying time.

He towered over me. "Do I know you?"

"Not yet." While my stomach quaked, my voice sounded surprisingly calm. "I'm Kate Bradley."

A look of recognition swept across his face. "I'm not . . . this isn't gonna—"

"Please don't go. I've spoken to Alexia and Logan. I know about the plane tickets you gave to the tow truck driver."

His breath quickened. "Then why are you chasing me when my family has asked you to leave me alone?"

I didn't have a sound bite. Or an answer that might persuade him. So I landed on the truth. "I get why you'd want to help people you care about. Your friends. Family. I also understand why you'd want to help the poor. But why are you helping people you don't know? Complete strangers?"

He set down his box. "That's what you want to know?"

I smiled. "Well, that and a few other things. What happened in that car ride from Dallas to Manhattan?"

He stiffened. "I can't talk about that."

"At least tell me how I can find Marie."

He drew a deep breath, thinking. "She could be anyone."

Alexia had said the same thing. Was this their party line? My frustration mounted. "Why won't you tell me?"

His anger flashed. "You got a lot of nerve badgering me like this. You wanna know how I spent my day? My day was about being turned down for job after job. Did a tour of duty in a war zone, did over four hundred debriefings of Taliban members. But I'm not qualified to track inventory for an aircraft-parts supplier here. Or work the warehouse at the dollar store. Even the frame store won't hire me. And now you're stalking me to find Marie."

I softened my tone. "I'm sorry for what you're going through. I didn't mean for it to feel like that." I saw his body tense and decided to take another approach. "Everyone I've talked to says she's special. Is that your experience too?"

He relaxed his shoulders. "Marie, she's not like everybody. When I met her, I was so weighed down by my sister's death that it took all my energy just to breathe. I didn't talk. But Marie saw past all that. She invited me into the car without even a question. A big guy like me can be scary to a lot of people. But not her." He lifted his box. "She has reasons she doesn't want to be found. Honor that."

It was time to give up.

Time to admit that I wasn't going to find Marie and the other three were never going to agree to be interviewed.

Time to move on.

But even as I reached that frustrating conclusion, a new idea was forming. A sense that there was another way through this, even if I didn't know yet what it was.

In the newsroom the next morning, I focused on a report about the Supreme Court's ruling on unconstitutional gerrymandering in two states, working the phones to get reactions from federal judges and other advocacy groups. But my heart wasn't in it.

Instead, another idea was percolating in my mind. Maybe I would never get the Secret Four story I had desperately wanted, but what if I could make something of my failure? What if I used what I knew to do something important?

I was headed to the assignment desk to talk through the idea with Mark when I caught a glimpse of Scott entering the newsroom. I had thought a few days away from him would give my feelings a chance to scatter and weaken, but it'd had the opposite effect. My cheeks warmed.

This had to stop.

Anyone with good observational skills—meaning most of the reporters here—would notice that my face was flushed when I was around him.

The next thing I knew, he was heading toward me. "What have I missed on this story while I've been buried in *Wonders* prep?"

My heart sped up as I walked him through the discoveries I'd made. The dead ends. Marie's illness. All of it. Even though we talked through every story point with complete professionalism, a flicker of a flirty smile crossed his face, and he laughed at one of my lame attempts at humor. The charge was still there. Stronger even. But it was clear neither of us was going to do anything about it.

He glanced at his watch and frowned. "I'm late for a meeting upstairs. Can I join you for your morning run tomorrow?"

His question caught me by surprise. My face heated again. "I start at five. Are you sure you want to run with me that early?"

"I can't think of anything I'd rather do."

The sunlight was making the sidewalks sparkle. In a few hours, they would be bustling with activity, but in the hushed early-morning light, they glittered, beckoning Scott and me to follow them into areas of the city neither of us had been before. Along the three-mile route, I told him the crazy idea that had been bubbling up over the past day.

"I'm probably never going to find Marie," I said. "Never going to get the four of them on camera."

He turned to look at me. "Wait, you're giving up?"

"I'd say I'm 'pivoting.' If I've learned anything about adapting to this city, it's that when something isn't working, you've got to try a different approach. I may not ever be able to find them or convince them to let me interview them. I'm probably going to fail on this story. But there's something I can do. Something we both can do. We can help them."

"Help them? How?"

"Alexia received a kidney transplant from an anonymous donor. She wants to know who it is. All she knows is that he's a high school principal in Idaho. Let's help her find him."

He brightened. And instead of telling me all the reasons it wouldn't work or why we shouldn't do it, he said, "It'll take a bunch of phone calls and digging, but I bet we can track him down."

"That's step one. Because even if we find him, he still may not want to meet her. We'd have to come up with a compelling reason."

His gaze was intimate. "I don't know if you're aware of this, Kate, but you're very persuasive. I think you can use those powers to talk him into it."

"You're putting a lot of faith in these supposed powers of mine."

He smiled, not taking his eyes off me. "I've seen them up close."

His words distracted me. Made my thoughts evaporate. I tried to get the conversation back on track. "We wouldn't stop there. We'd help all three of them. Joe Raley told me he's been having a tough time getting a job after his tour of duty in Afghanistan. Maybe we can help him find a job?"

We slowed to a stop at a restaurant with a red awning and ginormous sign that read: Most Fabulous Restaurant.

"That might be tougher," he said, taking a swig from his water bottle. "But I have an idea. Remember that story we did about the Wall Street guys who gave a job to the homeless veteran in the wheelchair? What if we reached out to them and asked them to meet with Joe?"

"We could at least help him get an interview."

"Problem is, we don't know anything about him. We'd need a résumé or something to convince them to recruit him for an interview."

"We know he's a veteran," I said. "And we've got another secret device. You."

"Me?"

"You say I'm persuasive, but I'm pretty sure you can charm those Wall Street boys into taking the meeting. Just flash that smile of yours. Charm them with a story or two. They'll set the interview."

He arched a skeptical eyebrow. "This 'charm' thing you're talking about. Does it work on everyone?"

I met his gaze and felt my pulse jump. Could he see the effect he was having on me? "It works on *some* people," I teased.

"You guys coming in?" A stout, bald guy appeared at the restaurant door and called out to us. "Or are you just gonna stand there staring at each other?"

"Give us a minute," Scott answered.

"New York rule number thirty-two," I said. "No standing on the sidewalk and staring."

"Were we staring?"

I shook my head. "We weren't staring," I said. Even though we had been. "We were figuring out a way to help Logan."

"How will we do that when we know so little about him?"

"He told me someone wrecked his car in a hit-and-run. Said he couldn't scrape together the deductible. So maybe we can—"

"We'd have to find the body shop."

"How many body shops could be in a town of a thousand people?"

"I'll split the cost with you."

"Deal," I said. Then a strange feeling came over me. Warmth. Like the way sunshine felt. I was so excited about what we were going to do for them that for the first time, I glimpsed what it must feel like to *be* them, knowing that you had made someone's life easier. Better.

"You know what I'm thinking we should do to celebrate our plan?"

"Let me guess. Waffles," I said, motioning toward the restaurant door.

He grinned. "Your mind-reading skills are on the fritz this morning."

"They're broken, are they?"

"I was thinking eggs and a bowl of oatmeal."

"Sure you were," I teased.

His eyes met mine. "There's something I want to tell you, first. Before I lose my nerve."

My stomach twisted. Ideas flashed in my head, none of them good. I wondered if he was going to tell me he couldn't work with me on this story anymore. Or maybe, like my dad, he was going to tell me that he just got engaged. But he was taking so long to say anything that I rushed to fill the silence.

"You're going to finally admit that you left me the *Harriet the Spy* book on my desk?"

A warm look spread across his face, and I knew it wasn't that. His voice was low. "I didn't want you to hear it first from the ANC rumor mill . . ."

My breath hitched. Was he going to tell me he was engaged? If so, I would have to make sure to hide my disappointment and act, through the awkwardness of it all, as though I were happy for him. Wouldn't I be happy for him?

And then, as he stood before me, crushing words about to fall from his mouth, I suddenly realized what I was losing. Someone who understood me, my range of moods. Who shared my love for journalism. Who made me laugh.

Who was smart and sexy as hell. I was about to lose all of it.

I held on to the moment, the two of us standing there in diamond light while the city awakened. Until he uttered the bruising words, everything could remain as it had been between us.

"Paige and I have broken up," he said. Or I thought he had. But a van wheezed by in the last part of his sentence, and I wasn't entirely sure.

"Say that again?"

He repeated the words, and this time, the door to the diner opened, and a sweet wave of waffles and pancakes perfumed the air, swirling around us.

"I'm so sorry," I said, but my voice sounded dreamy, confused. The mixture of surprise and relief made me speechless.

His eyes said more than his words. "Don't be."

My heart felt wild, untethered.

"We'd only been dating for a few months. But she wanted something more. And I couldn't."

He let that hang in the air. The reporter in me wanted to know why. I couldn't imagine what was stopping him from taking the next steps with her. But even though I made a living asking questions, I couldn't ask this one.

He seemed to be reading my mind. "Because she's not you, Kate."

CHAPTER
TWENTY-SIX

My heart raced through the entire breakfast. Once we'd slipped into a mint-green vinyl booth in the diner, I was so afraid—of what he'd said, of what I may have misunderstood, and of what was yet to be explored—that I made sure we talked about everything except what he had just told me.

"What do you have going on today?" I asked, but even as he answered, my mind kept playing over and over what he'd said.

"First, I'm heading to the doctor to get a typhoid booster. Then I'm meeting with a cinematographer we're thinking about hiring for the Alaska episode."

Like a reflex, I kept asking questions. "What do you hope to find in Alaska?"

His gaze locked on mine. "We're looking for billions of pounds of copper hidden deep in the ground near Bristol Bay," he said, but the way he was looking at me was making me breathless. "Hoping we can also capture the world's greatest sockeye salmon run."

The waiter, the same bald guy who had shouted at us, ambled up to our table. "Know what you want?"

Know what I want? Yes. I wanted this. All of this. But my pulse was racing so fast that I wasn't sure how to respond. How to get back to what he'd said.

I managed to blurt out an order. Waffles, of course. Scott ordered the same.

When the waiter left, Scott kept up the casual banter, but his eyes were questioning. "I saw your father on the news last night," he said, taking a slug of coffee. "He was talking about the bill he and another senator are sponsoring. Wanting to close down the tunnels at the border. He's smart, very intense. Is he like that in real life?"

"He can be," I said, trying to focus. "When we debate about the news, the discussions can get very heated. But he's also pretty normal other times, running with me or playing wicked games of chess and backgammon. He's the kind of dad that would let me stay up past my bedtime to watch *60 Minutes* with him. What was your dad like?"

"He died when I was little, so all I know about him is from photos. There's one of my parents at their wedding. And then, when I was leafing through one of the family albums, a clump of loose prints fell out. Photos of my parents at, I think, Niagara Falls a few months before I was born. They're about the age I am now. Which seems strange. My mother is so happy, posing and showing off her bump. My father has this mop of hair, and he's smiling like he's on top of the world. He was only around a fraction of my life, but I still miss him."

"Sometimes I miss my mother, even though she died when I was five. She'd been an adviser to the mayor of San Francisco, so my parents' career lives were extensively photographed. But what's missing from any of the photos I've seen were the nights she must have tucked me into bed or celebrated my birthdays or walked with me around the neighborhood. I've always wondered what it was like when I was her daughter."

I paused, worried that I'd shared too much, crossed the line. Most conversations stopped whenever I talked about my mother, as if my friends and lovers had been afraid of speaking about loss. Acknowledging its existence. But Scott was still with me.

"I wonder what they'd think of us if they met us now," he said quietly.

Sometimes moments passed by without you realizing their importance. But not then. I felt the shift to something deeper, his full attention on me, me wholly attuned to him. I knew I was experiencing something solid. Rare. Real.

He reached across the table and rested his hand on mine. I felt the weight of his gaze, and my pulse accelerated. "I like this. You and me," he said softly.

I could feel his unspoken question floating between us. *How do you feel about me?*

I trembled. Running into a burning warehouse or chasing a robbery suspect down a dark alley was easier than saying my feelings aloud. Those required a different type of fearlessness. An easier kind of bravery.

"I do too."

In that gauzy moment in the diner, it didn't seem to matter that a romance between two journalists at the same network was an HR nightmare and big trouble for our careers. As we dove into a shared mountain of waffles, I was stunned by how happy it made me to hear him laugh.

CHAPTER
TWENTY-SEVEN

That afternoon, one of the conference rooms became the "war room" for helping the Secret Four. The fabric walls were plastered with everything we knew: photos, maps, and anything we could glean online about them, studded with colorful Post-its.

A production intern, Robbie, who was built like he played Texas football—and it turned out he had—posted photos of Joe and Logan and a placeholder photo of a blonde girl for Alexia.

"Joe now has an interview with Russell Bransfield," Scott said. "He's the exec who's in charge of the veterans initiative at Goldman Sachs."

"You think there's any chance he'll get the job?" I asked.

"The interview's tomorrow. They'll let us know."

"And get this: we found Alexia's donor," Isabelle said, rising from her chair. She pinned a photo on the wall. "His name is Derek Nielson." The man was tall, with closely cropped brown hair and a neatly trimmed goatee. "He's a high school principal in Westfield, Idaho. Problem is, he doesn't want to meet Alexia."

"Did he say why?" I pressed.

"Hard to pin him down about why. But it was a definite no."

"You sense there's any chance he'd consider a reunion?"

She shook her head. "Doubt it. But I told him you'd call him." She handed me a Post-it. "Maybe you can change his mind."

"Robbie has news," Scott said.

Robbie's face flushed. "I called the only body shop in Hawesville, Kentucky, and found out that Logan's 2011 Toyota Corolla was there. I used your credit cards to pay his deductible. And made them swear not to tell him it was from you."

I smiled. As I looked around the room, I realized we were all doing the same thing. Beaming. We weren't likely to find Marie or get any of them to talk with us, but it felt insanely good knowing we had found a way to make something good out of our failure.

The letter was on top of the day's mail when I returned home that night. Addressed to me. No return address. I stared at it, wondering if I should open it. The postmark read "New York, NY," but I knew few people here, and none of them were likely to mail me a letter.

Was it from Jordan? Was this proof that he was going to continue to threaten me about Marie? I wondered if I should show it to the police before opening. On a mail fraud story I'd worked on back in LA a few years ago, I learned that only about half the fingerprints on paper could be made sufficiently visible, even with the latest forensic techniques. Still, 50 percent was better than nothing.

But the longer I stared at the envelope, the more I wanted to know what was inside. How long might it take to get the police to investigate a note that, from the outside anyway, didn't appear remotely menacing?

Using a plastic bag to keep the oil on my hands away from the envelope, I opened the back flap, careful to make as little contact with the paper as possible. I unfolded the note inside and scanned to the bottom, looking for a signature.

Julia.

My blood pressure settled a notch as I read:

> *Dear Kate,*
> *I know how hard this must be for you. But I want you*
> *to know that I love your dad and I will do anything to*
> *make him happy. You and I don't know each other well*
> *and perhaps because of that, this all feels so sudden. It*
> *did for me too.*
> *Please let's grab some time to get to know each other*
> *better. I will devote my life to making him happy.*
> *Yours, Julia*

∽

The walls of Julia's newly remodeled Upper West Side kitchen were filled with cubist, modernist, and other -ist art, and her dining room completed the look with bronze sculptures, luscious red and white peonies, and porcelain dinnerware in shades of matte gray and gold. Sporting a shiny blowout and a powder-blue cashmere sweater, Julia made it all look effortless, yet I had no doubt she had worked hard to achieve all the exquisiteness.

She put me to work making guacamole. I think she figured that since I was from California, I must know a thing or two about avocados. But while I infused my recipe with the secret for all great guacamole—fresh corn kernels—it paled in comparison with the feast she was preparing.

As we dug into baked salmon, pasta with arugula, and honey-balsamic-glazed brussels sprouts, all recipes of her own creation, I sensed her nervousness. Her voice was unsteady as she told a story about how the cast of the Met's *Aida* thought ghosts were guilty of making a towering column on the set topple over in the middle of a performance.

Once we had exhausted the chitchat, I dug into the truth. "I've been looking into your ex-husband. The money laundering."

Her eyes widened with shock. "Your father said you had concerns, but . . ."

"I looked for connections back to you," I said, then heard how combative that must have sounded. I realized then that I wasn't all that different from Jordan, who had also taken an impulsive and aggressive approach to protecting someone he loved. "But I didn't find any."

She sighed. "I know how it looks. And I don't blame you for looking into all that. I'd do it, too, if I were in your shoes. But I promise you, Kate, I wasn't involved in any of it."

I'd had a lot of experience interviewing liars, so I knew the obvious tells. Sweating. Lack of eye contact. Fidgeting. But the measured way she spoke made me believe her.

I softened my tone. "How did you and my dad meet?"

She relaxed into her answer. "I was in DC and heading into a concert in Washington Cathedral. Outside the front doors, I noticed a woman who was going on quite loudly, ranting actually, about some political issue to a very handsome and patient man."

"My father?"

"Yes. The woman was angry and grabbed his arm, shouting something like, 'You have to do something!' I could tell he didn't know her and was having a hard time finding a way to politely leave."

"That happens a lot to my father."

"Everyone else was ignoring the woman. Or at least pretending to. Then I did something I'd never done. I pretended to know him. I ran up to him, put my arm through his, and said, 'I've been looking everywhere for you.' Then I kissed him on the cheek. Which surprised me. And him too. And I turned to the woman and said, 'Would you excuse us?'"

I laughed. "I'll bet my dad was speechless."

She poured some wine into my glass. "He was. But then he played along. The look on the woman's face was priceless. We got a good laugh

out of it, then ended up talking during intermission and into the night."
A small smile spread across her face. "And we became inseparable after
that."

"And now you're getting married next month . . ."

She looked at me in surprise. I think she hoped we would ease into
this question instead of diving right in. "I know this seems sudden to
you. It does to me too. I used to think that falling in love was a process.
You like someone, and maybe you even go through a checklist to see if
he might be the right one for you. Then maybe it turns into something
more, and maybe it doesn't. But what I learned was . . . sometimes love
floats in . . ."

As she told a few stories about my father, she left no doubt that her
love for him was genuine. She had an easy laugh, the kind that drew me
into it, and I smiled, even though I hadn't expected to.

By the time we'd settled into coffee and dessert, I'd begun to warm
up to her. Begun to trust her. Then she brought up a fundraiser she had
attended with my dad in Southampton. "They held it on a horse-farm
estate owned by a former ambassador to Spain. Your dad's speech was
very inspiring."

The mention of the fundraiser sent a sharp warning through my
nervous system, surprising me. Maybe it was a sign that I had been right
all along to be skeptical about her.

Or maybe it was because I could see that my father was moving on
without me. For as long as I could remember, I'd always been the one
my dad had asked to go to these events. The first time I attended, I was
seven and wore a pink-and-white polka-dot dress with kitten heels, feeling very grown up with my hand clasped in my father's. The heels got
higher as I got older, but even though I sometimes grew weary of the
routine, I was always proud to be there with my dad and liked hearing
him speak about issues that mattered to him, soothed by the measured
cadence of his voice, especially in tumultuous times. And when the
rhetoric inevitably got a little heated, my dad would often change the

subject by turning the attention to me, talking about some accomplishment of mine he was proud of. As a teen, I'd been embarrassed that my father was talking about me, but once I entered my twenties, I began to see these moments for what they were: my dad was letting everyone know that no matter what the political crisis du jour was, I was always the center of his universe.

Was that going to change?

Julia seemed to be reading my mind. Or maybe she saw my eyes shining with moisture.

She smoothed a wrinkle in the tablecloth. "You're everything to him, Kate. I'm only going to attend a few of these events with him. I know he hopes you're going to keep going with him when you can."

"I think he probably told you that I can't stand political fundraisers," I said, eyes clouded with tears. "But I've always loved going with my dad."

She looked down at her hands. "I know it feels like everything is about to change. But I'm not here to take your dad away. I want things to be the way they always have been between you two."

I'd been wrong about her. About their wedding. On my way home from her apartment, I called my dad. "I'm sorry about the way I've been acting."

"I said some harsh things too," he answered. "Forgiven and forgotten?"

"Forgiven and forgotten."

And although I don't remember the words either of us said after that, I could actually feel the current of forgiveness, strong and deep, circulating between us.

CHAPTER
TWENTY-EIGHT

At six foot two, Alexia's kidney donor, Derek Nielson, towered over her. From twenty feet away in one of the ANC studios, I waited as she listened, listened, listened to something he was telling her. Then her face burst into a smile, and she threw her arms around him in a giant hug.

After a discussion with me in which I'd persuaded—and, yes, pleaded with—him to reconsider his decision, Derek had agreed to meet Alexia, and I told them both that ANC would fly them to Manhattan so we could capture their reunion on camera.

After their embrace, the two of them broke down in tears. I let them have a moment, then walked over to talk with them on camera, stepping into the emotional veil that cloaked them.

"You've made my whole life new," Alexia said.

He wiped his eyes. "This feeling I have inside. It doesn't get much better than this."

"Tell me how all this came about," I asked.

"A friend of mine needed a kidney transplant. I went in to see if I was a match, but I wasn't. Still, I couldn't shake the idea that it was something I was supposed to do. Could do. So I decided to donate to a stranger."

"You didn't know it would be going to Alexia?"

He shook his head. "I didn't know her name or her hobbies. I had no idea who her favorite sports team was or what music she liked or who she voted for in the last election. I didn't know anything except that we were a match."

"What made you do this then? Why did you choose to have an important part of yourself cut out to give it to someone you've never met?"

"I've got good health, a job, a little bit of savings. I thought this was a way to share my good fortune with someone else."

I turned to Alexia. "I know you've wanted to meet Derek for a long time. How does it feel?"

"There aren't words, really," she said, her voice trembling. "I'm still trying to process that I'm only alive because of a stranger's gift."

Derek put his arm around her shoulder. "If this isn't the greatest moment of my life, it's in the top three." Alexia looked up at him. "Okay, it *is* the greatest."

All three of us became teary then, ending the interview. Their moving story ended up airing throughout the day on ANC, with one specific caveat. Although Derek and I knew Alexia's identity as one of the Secret Four, we were not allowed to tell anyone or mention it on air.

After the reunion interview, I asked Alexia for some time to talk about what happened in Dallas, off the record, but she turned me down. "We talked about this, Kate. I've made a promise, and I'm going to keep it."

I drew a deep breath, reining in my frustration. I made sure my expression looked calm, but inside my mind was racing to come up with an approach that would change her mind. But I was coming up empty. "I respect the promise you made. It's just that—"

My phone chimed, and Logan Wilson's name flashed up.

I showed her the phone. "Want to listen in?"

I tensed, hoping she'd say yes. The more time I could spend with her, gaining her trust, the more chances I'd have to convince her to tell me her story.

"Okay," she said, seemingly as surprised as I was that Logan was calling me.

"Kate Bradley," I answered.

"I know it was you," Logan said. "The body shop guy wouldn't say who paid off the deductible, but it had to be you."

I tried to sound confused. "I don't know what you're talking about."

"You're the only one I told about my money troubles with the car."

"Alexia is here with me," I said. "We're doing a story about her kidney donor."

His voice rose a notch. "You finally found him, Lexi?"

Alexia blushed. Were there sparks flying between these two? "ANC did. Just spent a couple of hours with him. Remember how I told you what I hoped it'd be like? It was all that. And more."

They were both quiet for a moment, which gave me an idea for keeping the conversation going. "Logan, what would you say if I brought you to Manhattan? You and Alexia could get some time together, and the two of you could tell me the parts of your story you're comfortable telling."

He was silent for a long moment. Then: "You wouldn't ask us about Marie? Or about the leap?"

I drew a deep breath. "We'd only talk about whatever you want to share."

"I'd like to see you again, Lexi," he said. "I've been thinking a lot about what we all did."

Alexia did the persuading for me. "You should come, Logan. We have a lot of catching up to do."

I was finishing up with Alexia when Scott found me. He was hiding something behind his back and said four words I never had expected to hear: "Joe Raley is here."

"How? Why?"

"No idea. Showed up and asked the receptionist to see you and me. When she told him he needed an appointment for that, he left. Then he came back and asked her to deliver this to us."

He brought a bouquet of purple coneflowers from behind his back and presented them to me.

"He sure knows how to get our attention."

He grinned. "He's waiting for us downstairs."

We raced together to the lobby, giddy with excitement.

Dressed in a slate-gray suit and garnet-red tie, dimpled in just the right spot, Joe looked like he'd been a Wall Street analyst for years.

"They told me," he said, eyes glistening. "They told me what you did."

"I don't—" Scott tried.

His tone was serious. "They said you guys got me the interview. Guess they can't keep that stuff a secret from job applicants."

Scott and I were both speechless, looking at each other helplessly, hoping the other would know what to say.

Joe broke into a smile. "I got the job. I'm going to be in the trainee program starting next week." His voice wobbled a bit. "Thank you for making this happen."

"You're welcome," Scott said.

"I just want to say that Alexia is here," I said quietly. "And Logan is on his way. They've agreed to talk with us about whatever parts of this story they're comfortable with. You want to join them?"

It took him a moment to process what I was saying. Then his expression brightened.

"Damn, I miss those guys," he said. "You won't tell anyone it's us behind it all? We're just going to talk?"

I nodded.

He rubbed his jaw. "I'm in."

⌒୭

"It was the riskiest thing I'd ever done," Alexia was saying the next afternoon in one of the ANC conference rooms. "I got this brand-new kidney four months earlier, and my doctor said to stay away from stress and the possibility of infection. So, getting in a car driven by a woman I didn't know with a bunch of people I didn't know, either, in the middle of a storm? That was . . . crazy."

"I was just lucky she invited me in the car," Joe said. Sitting next to the petite Alexia, he looked even larger and more muscled. "There were lots of beautiful, outgoing people vying for a space in her car, and there was me, exhausted and pretty much unable to hold a conversation. One guy offered Marie this expensive bottle of wine—he was in the business or something—but she picked me instead."

"Yeah, I don't know why she chose me either." Logan clutched the arm of his chair, clearly nervous. "I'd given the rental-car guy a fake driver's license because I'd lost mine in a DUI five months before. The photo didn't look remotely like me. He had brought his supervisor over when Marie walked up. I know she saw I was trying to run a scam, but she still invited me into her car."

My eyes took in the three of them, and the moment still felt unreal. I'd given up hope of ever getting this interview, but here they were. "Weren't any of you worried about getting into a car with strangers?"

"That's what our moms always warn us about, right?" Alexia said, smoothing the sleeve of her blue-striped dress. "I texted my mom, and she said that I should not get in that car. But I didn't want to miss everything my friend and I had planned in Manhattan: shopping, tea at the Plaza. I guess I was desperate."

"I thought Marie was scamming me," Logan said, unzipping his black hoodie. "I mean, a nicely dressed older woman walks up and asks if you want to join her in her car on a daylong trip to Manhattan? I figured some bad-ass dude would be waiting for me in the parking lot and beat me up or something. But yeah, I got in."

Joe sighed. "I was fine until we all got in the car, and then I thought: *We don't know this lady, and we're letting her drive us in this storm?* I grabbed onto the oh-shit handle, put on my headphones to drown out my nerves, and figured this was the stupidest decision of my life. I'd made it back safely from a tour of duty in Afghanistan, but I was gonna die in a storm in the middle of nowhere."

"But you all still got in a car with strangers in the middle of a storm anyway," I said.

"I needed the ride," Logan said. "Then, once we got away from the airport, it was pitch black and raining so hard that Marie couldn't hear what the navigation app was saying to do. She asked me to help out. I was so freaked out I just kind of stared at it. Like I couldn't wrap my head around what I—what we all were doing."

"It just got worse as we went on," Joe added. "The wipers couldn't keep up with the downpour, and we could barely see the taillights of the cars in front of us. Marie—she seemed really anxious and had a death grip on the steering wheel. I offered to take over the driving, but she insisted. She wanted to do this. And she asked me to tell her my story."

"Your story?"

He drew a deep breath. "I told her about my sister." His voice broke. "How proud she was when I completed basic training. How she looked up to me. She was only nine when she died from cancer while I was in Afghanistan. We talked about all of it. Everyone else had fallen asleep or was on their phones, but Marie, she listened for hours. It's wild. I was talking to a complete stranger, but it was like I knew her."

"I was drifting in and out of sleep, but I remember you guys talking," Alexia offered. "It did sound like people who'd known each other for a long time. Then she asked about me, and I told her about my kidney. The whole time we were talking, I remember thinking that something about her was different. I couldn't put my finger on it, but then I realized she actually cared about what I was saying to her. You could feel it. Then she asked about your story, Logan."

Logan frowned. "I didn't want to talk. I kept wondering what she thought about my fake driver's license and how I'd been trying to scam the rental-car company. But eventually I told her about my DUI, trying to explain it away. Then the next thing I knew, I was telling her everything: about losing my job, getting behind on my payments and having debt collectors chasing me all the time, getting kicked out of my apartment. And instead of giving me a lecture or telling me what I needed to do to straighten out, she listened."

"The whole time she was talking to you was very comforting," Alexia said. "Until we popped that tire."

Logan stood. "That's when I was sure we were totally dead. No cell service. None of us had any. And the only lights we could see were way in the distance. Miles."

Joe shifted in his seat. "And the rain was like we'd driven into a waterfall or something. I got out to check in the trunk, and there wasn't a spare. And no other cars on the road."

Alexia's voice shook. "Then the wind picked up, rocking the car. And I . . . started crying. I thought you guys might hate me for that, but Logan, you told me everything was going to be okay."

Logan smiled and touched her arm gently. "I said that. But I was terrified too. I was kicking myself for making yet another stupid decision getting in that car."

"Me too," Alexia added. "And that's when Marie said something that changed everything."

Every journalist learns by trial and error that there are times when you press for answers and other times when your silence, your listening ear, is the best way to keep an interview subject talking. This was one of those times. Of course I wanted to know what Marie said, but I knew the only way to find out was to let them tell their story.

The three of them looked at each other, and then Joe continued. "She said: 'We have to figure out where the light is.' I had no idea what she meant by that. Light? I mean, the only light was coming from the dashboard and our phones. What light was she talking about?"

"I kinda knew. I thought she was going to give us some kind of religious lesson or something. Make us pray," Logan said. "I figured then that was her whole reason for getting us in the car. I wasn't having any of that."

"You put your head back and closed your eyes," Alexia said to him. "I knew what she was trying to tell us. But I couldn't see any hope in where we were. We all sat there completely quiet in the dark for what, like, fifteen minutes?"

Logan nodded. "And that's when he showed up."

"He?" I asked.

"The tow truck driver," Logan said. "He had his brights on—they blasted through the rear window, practically blinding us."

"It's like he came out of nowhere," Joe said.

"We were literally looking at where the light was," Alexia added.

"I was pretty nervous," Logan admitted. "I mean, we're disabled in the middle of nowhere. Times like that are when people get robbed."

"Or worse," Alexia said.

"I mean, the guy sat in his truck for a long time before he got out," Joe said. "And the light in the car was so bright we really couldn't see who or how many people were in that truck. Everyone voted for me to get out of the car so that they'd think not to mess with us."

"He was wearing fatigues and all . . . ," Alexia offered.

"Still, I was pretty tense when I got out," Joe said, running his finger along the rim of his Coke can. "But then the driver came out and asked me if he could help. Changed the tire. Not with just some spare but with a new tire he said would get us where we needed to go."

"What are the chances . . . ," Alexia whispered. "Four months earlier a stranger had saved my life by giving me a kidney. And here was a stranger saving my life a second time."

Joe pointed at her. "That's when you said we should all pitch in to do something for him."

Alexia nodded. "And that's when Marie said we should take a bigger leap than that."

CHAPTER
TWENTY-NINE

A bigger leap.

I knew the question was off limits, but at this point, I had to ask it. Sometimes that's the only way to get to the truth. To understand why they did it. None of them had any real reason to keep talking with me, so I worried they'd bolt. But I'd rather have failed by asking the right questions than failed by playing it too safe.

"What was the leap she asked you to take?" I heard the desperation in my voice.

Logan sighed. "We all promised not to talk to anyone about the leap."

"And you promised not to ask," Joe said, glaring at me.

"Okay, then let's not talk about the leap. Just help me understand why—whatever it is—it's a secret?"

None of them spoke. Then Alexia smoothed her hair back and broke the silence. "We never imagined that it would spread like it did."

"That's all we're gonna say," Joe said, standing. He nodded to the others. "Let's go."

"Wait," I said. "I'll stop asking about the leap. Promise. But there's something else I don't understand."

Joe sat back down slowly, crossed his arms. "Go on."

I leaned forward. "When Marie asked you to help all these strangers, each of you was struggling with your own problems. Logan, you had money trouble. Joe, you needed a job. Alexia, you wanted to find your donor. Why didn't Marie help you?"

Joe's eyes narrowed. "You mean, like, why didn't she give us money?"

"She tried to, actually," Alexia said quietly. "At the end, right before we all had to go back home."

"But we all said no," Logan added.

"We weren't looking to be rewarded for what we'd done," Joe said. "That didn't even cross our minds, I don't think." Then he cracked a smile. "But, Marie. She doesn't take orders from us. Or anyone. She ended up helping us anyway. I found out she paid my family's funeral expenses."

I nodded, remembering hearing from a man named Hector that the funeral home he worked for had received cash to pay burial expenses. "I guess that way you couldn't say no to the gift."

He rubbed his jaw. "Marie's clever that way."

I turned to Logan. "What about you, Logan? Did Marie help you?"

"After the construction company where I work was hired for the concert gig, Marie sent my boss a note. She told him she only chose them because I worked there. I mean, I have the lowest-level grunt job you can get there, but now the top boss knows my name. Talks to me all the time. I feel like I might get to keep this job for a while."

"The thing you have to understand about Marie," Alexia said, her fingers toying with her necklace. "She doesn't wait for you to tell her what you need. She just acts. I never told her about my medical expenses for the kidney transplant. Ever. But she paid them off."

"But the biggest thing she did for us was to make us realize we had the power to change things," Joe said. "Not just for others. Ourselves too."

I let his words float. Allowed the silence to envelop them and give them weight. Looking at them, I realized there wasn't an altruism gene that some were born with and others weren't. These three were proof that we all had it in us, waiting for the right experience to spark it into action.

"We should go," Joe said.

I wanted them to keep talking with me, but I knew I'd worn out my welcome. "One more question?" I pleaded. "Do you even know Marie's full name? Where she lives?"

"You promised not to ask about Marie," Logan said. "But the truth is, we don't know her last name or address. We don't know how to find her."

I shot them a skeptical look.

"Really, we don't," Alexia said.

I sat back in the chair. Crossed my arms. "I don't get it. You're all keeping some big secret for a complete stranger. Why?"

In contrast to my sharp tone, Alexia's voice was gentle. "Because in the car that night, she also told us her story."

Isabelle narrowed it down to two Marie Riveras. We went back to the short list of all the Marie Riveras, discarding the former pageant queen and the convicted felon, and searched for anything she could find— news stories, social media posts, YouTube videos—that might give us a glimpse of why Marie Rivera had started all this. She tacked photos of the top two contenders on the fabric walls of the war room.

The first Marie Rivera had a bottle-blonde mane and a straight-up Ralph Lauren catalog look. She was wealthy, the fortysomething CEO of an on-demand booking service for all things beauty, which apparently made her a staple on the fashion week front rows and at every notable party, because the photos Isabelle posted all seemed to have been taken at some club or high-end event.

"Seriously?" I asked. "I get that she's wealthy, but—"

"I know how it looks." She turned her laptop toward Scott and me. "But get this. A few months ago, she was driving her car in Queens when she hit a pole and flipped onto the parkway, and the car caught fire. She was trapped inside until some sixty-four-year-old guy walking his dog rushed to the scene and pulled her out. She's quoted in the *New York Post* as saying she was so grateful and would 'go to the ends of the earth to do kindness for a lot of other people, the silent heroes of New York.'"

"You think she's doing all this to repay a kindness?" Scott said.

Isabelle nodded. "One that saved her life."

"But why start that 'repayment' at a car-rental counter in Dallas?" I folded my arms across my chest. "I'm not buying it. She may have the means and the motive, but—"

"And she's known for having her company throw branded concerts like the one you both attended," she said.

I gazed at Marie's photo and rubbed my jaw. "If she were a killer, we'd have a list a mile long of all the reasons she might have done it," I said. "Jealousy. Anger. Revenge. Looking for respect. But we think people only do good things if they've had something good happen to them first."

Isabelle pointed to the second photo. "That, or maybe they're only motivated to do good after *bad* things happen to them. Like this Marie Rivera."

Dressed in a tweed blazer with thick brown hair pulled back into an elegant chignon, this Marie was a successful Manhattan realtor.

"Her father was killed by a stray bullet while sitting in a town car last month after attending a concert at the National Jazz Museum in Harlem. He got caught in the middle of a gunfight between two rival gangs. After that, she became a big activist, donating a lot of money to several social organizations, speaking out about how she wants to heal the city and 'bring us together.'"

Scott and I looked at each other. Could this be the Marie we'd been searching for?

"Let's track her down," I said. "See if we can get an interview."

But even as Isabelle set off to try to find Marie, something was gnawing at me. I flipped through the master list of all the Marie Riveras and glanced at the two- or three-word summaries Isabelle had written about each of them. Then I scrolled through their bright-smile photos on the laptop.

"I know that look," Scott said, glancing up from his laptop.

"What look?"

He leaned back in his chair. "The look that says, *I'm not convinced.*"

I sat beside him. "You're becoming an excellent face reader. These Maries feel too . . . easy. Obvious."

"Yeah, but sometimes the correct answer is the simplest. Or so says Occam's razor."

"Or . . . my dad often says that we could be searching in the branches for what appears in the roots."

"Botany lesson?"

"I think he means we're looking in the most obvious places for what's actually hidden from sight. Deep in the roots."

"Smart, your dad is."

My hands flew across the keyboard after that, searching for Marie Riveras in New York City who didn't have big headlines or tragic stories or thought-provoking rhetoric. Who didn't appear in well-known magazines or Getty Images. Deep into the Google search, I stumbled upon an online bulletin for a high school on 129th Street.

A retired special education teacher named Marie Rivera had donated $25,000 to a scholarship to help a special education student with the cost of going to college. The article didn't show a photo of

Marie or say anything about her wealth or where she got the money—only that she was known for helping former students find jobs in the community years after they left high school.

Could this be Marie?

Scott called Logan, Joe, and Alexia and asked them to stay one more day in Manhattan.

CHAPTER THIRTY

Retired teacher Marie was difficult to track down. A phone call to the high school where she had worked was a bust, because they wouldn't give out personal information. But a much-loved teacher like her had lots of grateful students and parents, so it didn't take me long to find a few of them who knew her. Johanna Olvera, whose daughter had been in Marie's class the year she'd retired, had organized a retirement party for Marie and was eager to tell me story after story about her.

"She helped some of the high school science kids to build electric carts from scratch, then give them to the kids who use wheelchairs, for free. You should've seen the eyes of the first boy who got one. Like, total disbelief that he could move around like that. And those teens who made the carts? They were just as happy."

"She sounds amazing."

"She is. You know how you can sometimes tell if someone is faking that they care? Marie is not like that. Something about her is different. You can feel it, even if you don't know exactly what it is."

"I'd like to do a story about her on ANC. Do you have an address? Phone number? Anything you can share?"

She bit her lip, thinking, then scrolled through her phone. "I don't have her number, or I'd call her first to see if it's okay. But here's her email address. It's about time someone special like her was on the news instead of just all the people wreaking havoc out there." She pulled a pad of blue Post-it notes from her purse and started to jot something down.

I knew that the Marie we were looking for wouldn't respond to an email from me, so I pressed for more. "Any chance you'd also have a street address?"

She glanced at her phone, then back at me, as if gauging whether she could trust me. I had the feeling that she hadn't made the connection between the Marie everyone was talking about on TV and social media and the teacher Marie who had helped her daughter who was on the autism spectrum.

"She just moved six months ago. Here's her new address." Then she started copying information from her phone. She handed me the note. "Give her a hug for me."

The address looked familiar, but it was not until Scott, Chris, and I had pulled up in front of the house with faded yellow vinyl siding and a front yard fortressed by a white iron fence that I realized we'd been here before.

"Are you kidding me?" Chris groaned as the three of us peered through the windshield.

I wasn't sure what to make of the discovery. It felt like we were back where we started, covering the same ground all over again. Hadn't the woman offered us a ton of proof that she wasn't the Marie we were looking for?

"I mean, she had that orthopedic boot on her foot," I said.

"And told us she hadn't ever been to Dallas," Scott added.

I sighed. "Or city hall."

Scott rubbed his forehead. "She's going to try again to convince us we've got the wrong Marie."

"True. But we have three people that might change her mind."

Chris, Scott, and I jumped out of the van. But when we got to her door, we froze, all of us staring at the door, giddy and nervous and keyed up about what we'd find on the other side.

"Ready?" Scott whispered, straightening his jacket.

With a shaky hand, I knocked.

Even though I'd met her before, I'd been looking for Marie so long that I half expected her to have transformed into some kind of ethereal creature, gliding to the door on a cushion of air. The other half of me expected—no, was actually worried—that this was yet another dead end.

But the first thing I noticed when she opened the door this time was how ordinary she looked. Yes, she was beautiful, with a flame of red hair and deep-blue eyes, but if I'd passed her on the street, I would never have thought she'd be behind an event of this magnitude.

And another thing. Even though she hadn't yet uttered a single word, I felt like I knew her. I'd heard so many stories about her from people whose lives she'd touched and changed, people she'd never know, that it seemed as though I'd always known her. Somehow, she'd reached into my heart and made me feel a sense of wonder, just standing there on the doorstep.

"How can I help you?" she asked.

Good question.

"I've found Logan, Joe, and Alexia," I said quickly. "They're here in Manhattan. They want to see you again."

Her hand moved to the door as if to shut it.

"And I want to talk to you about 8:28," I continued, which stopped her hand in midair. "'All things work together for good.'"

"I don't know what you're talking about."

I had her attention. Even if she was going to keep pretending. Now I just had to keep her from shutting the door. "I want to know why you were so upset when you found a note with those words on your airline seat."

I thought she was going to deny everything and tell me, again, that I'd come to the wrong address. Instead, she spoke softly. "I wasn't upset."

I smiled. It was the closest thing to a confession that I'd gotten yet. "Then what were you?"

"I was relieved. Hopeful. I had just come from the doctor, where I'd learned some scary news about my health. Finding that note gave me hope that maybe, even in times of great sadness, good will prevail if given the chance. I had no idea how true those words would end up being. I cried because I realized I could have a hand in making them be true."

I tipped my chin toward the camera. "Could we talk some more on camera?"

"No." She fixed her gaze on me. "But I would like to see the others again."

⚬

To my complete surprise, Mark gave me the set of *ANC Tonight* to do an interview with the Secret Four. This was the studio that anchor Jason Berman would occupy in a few more hours, and it was stunning—a total 360-degree set with high-resolution images of the New York City skyline and a white staircase that led to a balcony emblazoned with the ANC logo and bathed in pools of soft lights that cast beautiful shadows on the back walls.

Even Logan, Joe, and Alexia couldn't resist the studio's charms— their eyes widened in astonishment as they filed in. The studio was lit for broadcast, but no one was running the cameras because the group had demanded that we not record the interview.

That didn't mean the studio was empty. At least fifty staff had gathered in the back, and so many others wanted to watch the interview that security was instructed to send everyone else back to work. A violent protest had erupted in Tehran, sending the news team scrambling to arrange coverage, but even that wasn't enough to keep staff from trying to catch a glimpse of the Secret Four.

Still, I was troubled. The interview met none of the requirements of network TV news: no sound bites, no names or identities, no visuals, and no video. That would set off alarms with the top brass. They wouldn't care that I'd achieved something I cared about if it didn't translate somehow to viewers and ad revenues. I worried that Mark might even leverage my lack of on-air assets to edge me out.

I was restless as we waited for Marie to show, pacing around the studio and trying to burn off the nervous tension in my arms and legs. After what seemed like a long time, Marie stepped into the studio. Dressed in a sapphire-blue blazer, her red hair pulled back in a sleek low bun, she was escorted by a security guard who guided her past the throng of journalists and producers like she was a celebrity or a movie star.

"I'm glad you came," I said, crossing the studio with Scott.

"We've been looking for you for a long time," he added.

As I shook her hand, I noticed the red scarf tucked into her blouse. "Beautiful scarf," I said.

Her blue eyes lit up. "A gift from my mother long ago. She'd be happy about how I've put it to use." Then her eyes fell on Logan, Joe, and Alexia, and her lips curved into a smile. "This is a clever way to get me to come out of hiding." She drew them into a long embrace, as though they'd been separated for years, not just a few weeks. "I'm so happy to see you three again."

She sat in the chair next to me and started talking before I had a chance to ask any questions. "My guess is that you're hoping for some story where I tell you how someone did something kind or lifesaving for me, and this whole thing is just me returning the favor," Marie said. "But that's not what this is about."

"Okay. Then what is it about?"

"If I'm honest, it started out as bargaining. Thinking I could bribe my way into good health. I'd gotten a tough health diagnosis. Colon cancer. I was willing to do anything to buy more time. I thought if I did some good things, I could change the outcome." She cleared her throat. "And then I realized how wrong that was."

"Wrong?"

"Kindness is not some kind of exchange: *I'll help you, but then you have to help someone else. And maybe I'll be rewarded for my kindness.* That's not how it works."

I leaned forward. "How what works?"

"Connecting with others," she said, softly. "It's not transactional. It starts with understanding that everybody is struggling, even people who don't appear to be suffering on the outside. Loss. Grief. Brokenness. Hurt. Worry. Everyone around you, the people you share the grocery line with, sit next to at work, meet on social media, and see across the kitchen table. They're all wrestling with something. And we all have the power to help."

Scott shook his head. "Most of us don't think we can change things like that."

"But you can. We all can. I did a small thing. Invited these people into the car with me. And look what happened. It grew into something . . . far bigger than any of us ever imagined."

I glanced over at some of the staff watching the interview and saw that they were, like me, transfixed by her. In an industry where everyone's gaze was always locked to their phones during waking hours, no one was looking at anything except what was unfurling in front of us.

"Some, like the *New York Times*, are calling you a miracle worker," I said.

"I don't believe in miracles." Her tone was sharp. "Not the things we hope will happen magically. But we can create miracles for each other, person to person."

"Then you are a person who spreads miracles," I said.

"Perhaps. But I'm not special. When my flight was canceled in that storm, I was bitter. Resentful. Angry. Just like everybody else. I looked around at the crowd of people who wanted to rent cars and get away from the storm. I thought, *Well, everyone here has it better than me. Everyone got dealt a better hand. That girl over there is young, healthy, and very beautiful. She probably doesn't have a care in the world.* That turned out to be Alexia, who'd almost died before she got a last-minute kidney transplant a few months before. And then I saw this big guy, Joe, in army fatigues, listening to music on his headphones, and thought, *Look how strong his body is. Decades of good health ahead of him.* From the looks of him, I couldn't have known that he was grieving the loss of his sister. And when I met Logan, I kind of assumed he was just a handsome con artist. Young, carefree, charming. But it turned out he was running from a lot of mistakes and was trying to find his way back. Everyone's struggling with something."

"But getting in a car with strangers," I said. "I can tell you a lot of stories of how something like that can go terribly wrong."

"I think I've heard all of them," she said, with a small laugh. "But these strangers changed me. When I told them my story, they didn't see a frail, angry woman battling a terrible disease. They saw me as . . ." Her voice drifted off, and she was silent for a long moment. "They saw me as something more. So I became more."

Out of the corner of my eye, I noticed Mark had entered the back of the studio. Although he had slowly warmed to the story over time, I knew he continued to have his doubts about the people behind it. The fact that they had refused to allow us to record or broadcast the interview had both frustrated and intrigued him. It was proof they weren't in it for the attention, but it also meant we had nothing to show for all the work we'd done.

I leaned forward. "What made you decide to work together this way?"

She took a long swig of water from the bottle the security guard had given her. "After we'd told our stories in that car late into the night, I realized that I'd made a connection with each of them, even though we had seemingly nothing in common. It made me wonder if maybe we're all just fooling ourselves with the idea that we're strangers. Maybe we're all connected by some kind of thread that's invisible to us."

"But what you decided to do. That's a huge undertaking."

She inhaled a shaky breath. "Everything good that has happened to me in my life was a direct result of helping someone else. Everything. I knew this is what I wanted to do. What I was meant to do."

"The whole thing was only supposed to be for twenty-four hours," Joe said, leaning forward, elbows on knees.

"Then we got inspired to do more," she said. "You have to understand that all of it became quite addicting. The high, the joy—it's not like anything I've ever experienced. The more we did it, the more beautiful the world became."

"The happier we all became," Alexia chimed in, "the more we wanted to do."

I let my gaze fall on each of them, realizing their story had cast a spell on me. And I was terrified about asking the next question. Afraid that after all this searching, I'd never know.

"What is the leap?"

Marie took a long moment to answer. So long I expected her to answer vaguely, like the others had done.

Instead, her face lit up. "A leap is something you do without knowing what the outcome will be. It's just as likely that something good will come out of it as something bad. But you do it anyway. That's what I asked these three to do. To go from being strangers to doing these big things together. To take a leap into a larger life."

Joe smiled. "It sounded crazy at first. A leap to a larger life? Then she started talking about balloons, gift cards, flowers. I thought: *This lady is completely off her rocker. There's no way we could do all of that.*"

"And no reason we should," Alexia said, pulling her hair back. "We all had things to do. A wedding. Graduation. Funeral. How could anyone expect us to do anything like what she was imagining?"

"I figured we'd get caught," Logan added. "Maybe the police would think we were up to no good. Or we'd meet up with some people who wanted to make trouble for us. My grandpa always said, 'No good deed goes unpunished,' and in this case, I thought he would be proved right."

"And then I started doing the math and realized we were going to need a lot of money," Alexia said, straightening the collar on her light-blue blouse. "None of us had any. And this woman didn't look rich or anything. I mean, she told us she was a retired schoolteacher. So I was out."

"Me too," Logan said, cracking his knuckles. "I just didn't think we could do it. It's not like any of us had any special skills."

"Except we actually did," Joe said with an infectious laugh. "I grew up here and knew where to go. Where to find things. Alexia had all the creative ideas. Logan, no offense, but you knew how to sneak around, avoid cameras and nosy people, so no one would see us."

"I've had a lot of practice," he said sheepishly.

Alexia leaned back in her chair. "Still, we all thought it was a crazy idea."

"Impossible," Joe added. "But she was right. We did take a leap into a larger life."

Marie's expression softened. "But the leap did have one rule. And we've broken it." She glanced at the three others. I waited for her to continue. "We agreed we would never tell anyone—not even the people closest to us—what we were doing."

"We didn't even know each other's last names," Logan chimed in.

"Why was it a secret?" I pressed.

She twisted the bracelet on her wrist. "By staying a secret, there's no chance for us to be admired or for people to think they had to repay or reward us for what we did."

"We wanted people to focus on what we were doing, not on who we were," Logan said. "Because it was never supposed to be about us."

I glanced over at Scott, wondering what he was thinking. His expression said everything: a mixture of curiosity and wonder, because, like me, he'd never experienced a story like this. Then I looked at Marie, and a figurative light bulb went off, brighter than any of the studio lights, which suddenly felt hot on my face. I realized then why it had been so important to find these people, even though they'd worked hard to stay hidden.

They were proof that a small group of ordinary people could change the world.

"Where did you get the money to do it all?" Scott asked Marie, bringing me back to the moment.

Her face crinkled, registering her discomfort with the question. "I'm not rich, but I've been saving—investing—since I started working," Marie answered. "By some people's standards, I hadn't amassed a fortune, but I never once doubted what we did was *exactly* what I wanted to spend it on."

"Even when she told us about the money she had, we weren't sure," Alexia said.

"We had a lot of doubts. But Marie wasn't having any of that. She told us to put aside everything," Joe said, "and take a leap with her. Trust that it would all work out."

Logan shook his head. "Which was ridiculous, when you think about it. I mean, four strangers surviving a near apocalypse of a storm, then hatching up a plan to connect strangers in Manhattan."

"And keeping it a secret . . ."

"But how?" I asked. "How did you figure out how to do it? In the beginning, it seemed like you were giving to some of the people featured in my news stories here on ANC."

She nodded. "At first I thought that was the easiest way to find people to help. I mean, where do you start? But then I realized that most people won't ever make it on the news unless something really terrible has happened to them. Many people come forward to help in situations like that. But I wanted to help those with everyday troubles. Those that are struggling silently. So instead, I stood in grocery store lines, coffee shops, pharmacies, doctors' offices. And I listened."

"Eavesdropping?"

She laughed. "I guess you could say that. I heard what they were worried about, what was weighing on them. And that's when I figured out what to do."

I drew a deep breath. Leveled my voice so I wouldn't sound anxious. But their answer to my next question was crucial. "Everyone is going to want to know who you are. What can we tell them?"

Marie looked at Logan; then her eyes drifted to Joe and Alexia. "Let them think it could be anyone. It could be the stranger they pass by every night on their way into work. Or the woman behind the counter at their favorite store. Or the taxi driver who's driving them home. Don't tell them it's us."

I leaned forward, meeting her gaze. "Don't you think it would be better if they knew?"

Her voice was soft. "They're not looking for us, Kate. They're looking for each other."

CHAPTER
THIRTY-ONE

Scott and I recorded our stand-ups on busy Fifth Avenue during rush hour. Which drove Chris crazy, because commuters kept jostling him and his camera, and a couple of takes were interrupted by taxi horns and people shouting in the streets.

As excited as I was to finally crack the story, I was on the verge of tears. I was so proud of what we'd done to find the Secret Four but also struck by the realization that it was all coming to an end. The search for Marie. Working with Scott. In two weeks, he'd begin a twenty-seven-mile hike at ten thousand feet in Peru for the season's first episode of *Wonders of the World*.

My voice shook as I started the report. "Four strangers survived a near apocalypse of a storm thousands of miles away and turned that nightmare into an extraordinary gift that transformed New York City. After their harrowing trip through a deadly storm, they dreamed up a plan and took a leap, transforming themselves from strangers into friends."

"And changing us too," Scott continued. "For weeks now, these four strangers have been hiding a secret. What started as small acts—purple balloons, gift cards, bouquets of fresh flowers—bloomed into something far bigger."

"Anyone who's been in Manhattan for the last few weeks can see that there's a different feel when you walk down the streets," I said. "And that feeling has spread around the country, inspired by what people are seeing happen here. We promised the Secret Four that we'd keep their identities anonymous. So we won't tell you their names or where they come from. But we will say that they are the richest people in the world. Not because they have unimaginable wealth or are heirs to fortunes. Not because they are executives in Fortune 500 companies or lottery winners. They aren't. They are the richest people in the world because every day they reap the benefit of knowing that the world is a better place because of what they've done."

A hipster with a man bun had been watching us record the report and approached us afterward. "They're not even going to tell us who they are? Or collect the reward? That makes no sense. Why?"

"They really want to be anonymous," I told him. "And they don't want anything for doing it."

He raised his eyebrows in astonishment. "Not even followers?"

Our report aired throughout the day on ANC. The story even rocketed to the top of newscasts on every network, and the next day, Andrew summoned me to his office.

When I arrived, he was sitting on his couch, flipping through the channels on his monitor. He seemed on edge, his fingers rubbing repetitively along the handle of his coffee mug. My stomach clenched. Was this going to be more than a lecture about delivering a story without video assets, names, or sound bites? Was he letting me go?

"Have a seat," he said, motioning to the couch.

The room suddenly felt hot. Prickly heat rushed up my neck as I settled next to him. I smoothed the fabric of my skirt and looked down at the floor, waiting for him to speak.

"Ken and I have been talking . . . ," he said, his eyes still on the monitor. Ken was the president of ANC. The top boss. "And we aren't happy that what was a huge story culminated without us being able to reveal their identity or show any images."

"I know. But we couldn't—"

He turned to look at me. "Until the emails and messages started coming in. Viewers *thanking* us for not identifying the group. A lot of them writing things like, 'Thanks for leaving them alone.' And lots of people saying they're glad we 'let them be.' So our thinking has evolved. We don't need to know who they are. Your story of how they came together, why they did this, was powerful enough."

My mouth fell open. I had been expecting a warning. A reassignment. My anxiety inched down a notch, but I was still so on edge that the only words I could say were: "Thank you."

"I also shared with him what you said to me the other day. How our focus on negative news makes viewers think that's primarily what's happening in the world. And that led us to another decision. We want to give you your own show."

That's what I thought he said, but he couldn't have. My voice broke. "A show about?"

"We'd like to call it *Good Things*," he continued. "You'll be doing stories that highlight the best of what's happening around the world. Weekends for now."

My entire body was abuzz. Surprise. Disbelief. His offer felt like it had fallen out of the sky. From nowhere. But it hadn't really. Marie and the Secret Four had stopped us all in our tracks. Reoriented our thinking about what was important.

I tried to look composed, like I was used to hearing news like this. But I couldn't hide my own grin. "No politics?"

He shook his head. "No campaign stories. No scandals. No crime. When there's a crisis, you'll look for the positive aspects: the rescuers, the people making it better. Show viewers how they can help." He leaned forward. "I think you'll figure out the rest, Kate."

ᏉᎧ

I'm pretty sure my feet didn't touch the ground the whole way through the newsroom, down the hallways, past countless reporters and producers, looking for Scott. I found him in his office, drenched in yellow sunshine. Outside his windows, the deep-blue skies were dotted with puffy white clouds. A perfect Manhattan morning.

As I told him the news, I'm certain I sounded like a kid who'd just found out she had gotten a pony for her birthday. My voice was breathy, high pitched. Not like me at all. Except it was.

"That's fantastic," he said, folding me in his arms. The door to his office was open, so I knew we shouldn't stay there very long, even though I wanted to.

He handed me an envelope with the words *Kate and Scott* on the outside.

"What's this?"

"It just arrived. It's from Marie," he said, pointing to her signature on the back flap.

I ripped it open, and Scott read it aloud:

> *Dear Kate and Scott,*
>
> *Thank you for keeping our names and identities a secret. And for bringing the four of us back together. We'll never forget what you did to reunite us.*
>
> *I just learned what you did for the others and we are all deeply moved.*
>
> *All things work for good. You've just proved again that it's true.*

Yours,

Marie

PS: It wasn't just a lucky break that you were the only journalists invited to the concert at Floyd Bennett Field. I saw the two of you reporting on what we were doing and thought I might have a hand in bringing you together. Hope it worked.

Scott's eyes gleamed with emotion. "I had no idea we were being set up. I actually thought this was our own doing."

"Wasn't it?" I said, my heart racing. "But seriously, what kind of journalists are we that we weren't suspicious about being the only reporters there that night?"

He stroked my cheek. "We might have been a little preoccupied."

"And distracted." Then suddenly I was overcome with emotion. I wasn't sure if I wanted to cry or laugh, or a little bit of both. I only knew I wanted to stop time at that exact moment. "I'm going to miss you," I said, my voice cracking. "I know you're leaving soon for Peru . . ."

His eyes traveled over my face. "You know, there are these new inventions called airplanes. They have wings and can fly you anywhere. And they can even get you back in time to do your show. You could take one of these newfangled inventions and meet me in Madagascar."

"Madagascar . . . ," I said, and I felt like I was already flying.

He pressed a kiss to my forehead. "Promise you'll meet me there."

My pulse raced, like I'd been running. "I think I need waffles."

He grinned. "You need waffles. Right now?"

The door was open, and I could hear laughter in the hallway.

"So I don't lose my nerve."

He held my hands and waited for me to find my words.

"I'm always nervous around you."

His voice was liquid and warm. "Why do I make you nervous?"

My eyes met his, and all my self-consciousness faded away. "Because I'm falling for you. Even though it seems too fast, too soon. Too everything." I'd never been so honest about my feelings. But I wanted him to know how I felt, even if saying it aloud was terrifying to me. "I want something more with you."

He leaned in to kiss me, and his lips were a whisper away from mine when a peal of laughter down the hallway drew our attention.

He kicked the door shut. "The ANC rumor mill is going to have a field day," he said, softly. His fingertips trailed the curve of my mouth. "Want to take a leap with me?"

His lips were still moving when I kissed them. He tasted like coffee and adventure. Like possibility.

CHAPTER
THIRTY-TWO

My stomach was alight with butterflies as I stood in the doorway and gazed out at all the people who had gathered on the beautiful outdoor patio at Pier 26. Instead of the music you usually heard at weddings, the band was playing a mash-up of artsy yet funky tunes—a little bit of Bach, Coldplay, and Satie, with some Rascal Flatts mixed in.

The patio was capped with a staggering wall of white blooms: roses, peonies, and hydrangeas. Beyond that backdrop was an unrivaled view of the Hudson River and the New York City skyline.

My eyes fell on the skyscrapers in the distance, and a warm feeling came over me. Home. The city that was once filled with strangers was suddenly populated with people who looked out for me. People I loved.

"Ready to give your old man away?" my father whispered from behind me. I whirled around to see his eyes glistening.

"Wait, I'm not walking you up the—"

He embraced me in a hug. "I'm kidding. I think I'm old enough to do this myself. But it means a lot to me that you're happy. About Julia coming into our lives."

He held my hands in his, and I could see his happiness. Suddenly I was flooded with joy, realizing how fortunate I was to witness it. I had been too young to see the love he and my mother shared, but now I knew what it looked like when he was truly happy.

"I am. Dad, I want to say again that I'm sorry—"

"Forgiven and forgotten," he said, pressing a kiss to my cheek. "Now, you'd better go find your seat before there aren't any left."

He was right. The outdoor pavilion was filling up. There were plenty of faces I recognized—aides in my dad's office who'd flown in from LA and DC, a few senators, and many government officials whose titles and job duties I wasn't sure about. There were also many people I didn't know—likely Julia's friends, who were a mix of arts luminaries and New York State government types.

I hugged my dad once more and straightened his tie. "You've got this."

Then I headed down the aisle to find a seat and was surprised to see Scott's mother, Virginia Biltmore, standing near the front, talking with some guests who were already seated. She was a vision in a stunning yellow satin dress, her coal-black hair falling to her shoulders in thick waves. Why was she here?

The next thing I knew, she'd spotted me and was headed in my direction. Or I thought she was. Was she actually looking at someone behind me? I turned around, but no one seemed to be paying attention to her.

"You're Kate, aren't you?" she asked, grasping my hands.

"It's great to meet you," I said.

"I've been hearing about you in both ears. Scott, of course. And then I get it in the other ear from Julia. I've been friends with her mother for a very long time. I probably don't have to tell you she's over the moon about your father. And she very much admires you as well. This is a wonderful new beginning for all of you."

The idea of new beginnings made me feel light inside. When I'd arrived in Manhattan, I'd never imagined that life would lead me here to this moment. I'd thought my miserable beginning would be my forever life.

But time . . . and love . . . floated in.

Her blue eyes took me in, and she smiled. "And then there's Scott. No matter what he starts telling me about, it always comes back to talking about you."

"I hope you aren't telling her embarrassing stories about my childhood," I heard Scott say. And when I turned around to see him, he literally took my breath away in his dark suit and lavender tie.

"I haven't gotten to that yet," she said with a laugh. "Did he tell you how, when he was seven, he was a catalog model?"

He laughed and hugged her briefly. "We're going to find our seats before you tell her any more stories."

As we headed to our chairs in the front row, he took my hand in his, then interlaced his fingers with mine.

"I can't wait to see what happens," he said softly, his eyes meeting mine.

As the ceremony began, his fingers moved slowly over my skin; smooth, warm, sensual.

A simple gesture. Small, intimate, yet it felt a little bit like magic.

I had the feeling it was the beginning of something good.

ACKNOWLEDGMENTS

"Kate never does find a Good Samaritan," he was saying. I was interviewing directors for the motion picture version of *Good Sam* (a Netflix Original film), the first in the Kate Bradley Mystery series, and his comment was a part of his proposed approach to the film. I wondered what he meant. *Of course Kate finds good people,* I thought.

His observation stayed with me for many weeks, and I began to realize its meaning. Without giving away any spoilers, in the first two books in the series, Kate investigates people doing good things for others, and both times she learns the reasons why they chose specific people to help.

I began to think about the concept of a Good Samaritan. Perhaps he/she is someone who helps complete strangers, without knowing who they are or judging their needs or their worthiness. Could people like that actually exist, or is a Good Samaritan in the fantasy realm of superheroes?

I wondered: Is it possible that we all have a little of this Good Samaritan superpower within us, waiting for the right experience to spark it into action?

That question became the catalyst for *The Good Stranger.*

While I was developing the idea, I was on set producing and writing the screenplay for *Good Sam* in Montreal, and although the days were long, the ideas floated in. The story swirled around me as, week after week, everyone around me spoke about Kate, Eric, and Jack as though they were real people, and each day brought discussions about Kate's wardrobe or what the newsroom looked like.

As we got closer to filming, the story for *The Good Stranger* grew more insistent. We were fortunate to cast Tiya Sircar (*The Good Place*) as Kate Bradley, and when I heard her speak in the first read through of the script, I had an almost out-of-body experience. Tiya so embodied Kate's fearlessness, with the perfect balance of curiosity and vulnerability, that it felt as if I'd suddenly and irrevocably fallen into the world of Kate Bradley and that everything I'd once imagined had become real.

At one point during filming, director Kate Melville asked if I would read Kate Bradley's father's lines in a scene. The real actor's voice would be inserted later, but this would allow Tiya to act with someone saying her dad's lines on the other end of a phone call. As Tiya/Kate spoke to me on the phone, I was overcome with emotion: *I'm actually talking to Kate Bradley. She is real.*

That brought up many questions for me. If Kate Bradley is real, then what is she wrestling with? Who is she trying to become? What is she trying to figure out?

That's when I truly began to understand her next journey.

I'm forever grateful to Lake Union Publishing editors Christopher Werner and Danielle Marshall for giving me the opportunity to write this novel and for their tireless work to bring it to readers. Their belief in me and in Kate's world is truly an extraordinary gift of a lifetime. Thank you also to the stellar team at Lake Union—editor Krista Stroever, copy editor Bill Siever, proofreader Riam Griswold, author-relations manager Gabrielle Dumpit, and production manager Nicole Pomeroy—for their unwavering commitment to making my work stronger.

To all my readers, thank you for embracing Kate Bradley's world and for being ever present in my life. I'm truly fortunate to know you on social media (and, when I'm lucky, in person!), whether you're sharing stories about the beautiful, good things people do in real life or telling me how Kate's stories have inspired you or lifted your spirits. Your notes, your messages, your videos where you're holding my books and cheering me on, and your stories about your "book hangovers" from one of my novels—all of you have buoyed and inspired me. Thank you for reading. You are truly the Good Samaritans in my life.

Many pages of this novel were written at my friend (and author) Kes Trester's beach home in Southern California, so if you've felt the optimism and hope in this story, some of that comes from me writing while gazing at the diamond light and ocean waves at her magical home. Thank you, Kes, for our brainstorming sessions under the stars.

Thanks also to my friend, the journalist and documentary filmmaker Barbara Schroeder, for sharing her insights on what it's like for a reporter to move from local news to a national news network.

I'm also thankful for everyone who worked on the *Good Sam* film with me, from my producing partners in "good crime" Jesse Prupas, David McFadzean, and Matt Williams to the stellar cast members Tiya Sircar and Chad Connell (as Eric Hayes) to the outstanding Netflix team of Christina Rogers, Harry Lacheen, and Vivian Lin. Thank you for your inspired work in sharing a story of human goodness with millions.

If you're wondering how I can write so many stories about human kindness, you need look no further than my family. In the early-morning hours while I wrote this story before work, my husband, Paul, would often bring me chai lattes and slip plates of fresh avocado toast on the desk beside me. My daughter, Lauren, heard me read aloud sequences of the book and patiently listened as I rambled on about what I was trying to accomplish in those scenes. Thank you to all of my family—Paul, Ben, Jake, Lauren, and Alex—who put up with me and embraced the quirky rhythms of my writing periods.

BOOK CLUB QUESTIONS

1. When Kate discovers the balloons, flowers, and gift cards all around Manhattan, her colleagues suspect a scam or a marketing gimmick. Kate thinks people are afraid of seeming naive if they lean toward the positive. What do you think of Kate's belief?

2. When people in New York start fighting over the gift cards that have been left all around the city, the news media grabs hold of the story and makes it seem as though there is an "epidemic of bad people everywhere." In general, how does the media's portrayal of the bad things people do affect how you perceive others?

3. When Kate confronts Raymond about his shouting in the hallway, she wonders, "Beneath his shark persona, might there be a goldfish?" Do you think it's true that some people are "reeling in pain, disappointment, and loss and hiding that behind a tough exterior"?

4. When someone breaks into and trashes Kate's apartment, the event tests her belief that people are inherently good. Have you ever experienced a negative event that made you more suspicious and less trusting of others?

5. After Kate hears Jordan's concern for Marie, she lets him go and doesn't call the police, even though he has been

stalking her and sending her threatening notes. Do you think she was right to have compassion for him here?

6. The Secret Four all talk about a leap they took with Marie. Marie defines the leap as "something you do without knowing" whether the outcome will be bad or good. Have you ever taken a leap in your life? What happened? Were you surprised by the outcome?

7. When Marie's flight is canceled and she looks at the stranded passengers, she thinks that "everyone here has it better than me," but she learns that she was wrong about that. Have you ever assumed someone is better off than you are, only to realize they're also struggling?

8. Marie asks the others to "take a leap into a larger life." What do you think she means by "a larger life"?

9. Marie doesn't want anyone to know who's been behind all the good things happening around the city. She tells Kate, "Let them think it could be anyone. It could be the stranger they pass by every night on their way into work. Or the woman behind the counter at their favorite store. Or the taxi driver who's driving them home." Why do you think Marie gives these examples instead of letting people know she and the others are behind the good deeds?

10. Why do you think Kate calls the Secret Four "the richest people in the world"?

ABOUT THE AUTHOR

Like her heroine Kate Bradley, award-winning and bestselling author Dete Meserve is always looking for people who are doing extraordinary good for others. Instead of tracking a killer or kidnapper, Meserve's Kate Bradley Mysteries seek to uncover the helpers, the rescuers, and the people who inspire us with selfless acts of kindness. *Good Sam* is the first Kate Bradley Mystery, followed by *Perfectly Good Crime*. Kate also plays a pivotal role in Meserve's stand-alone novel *The Space Between*, helping protagonist Sarah Mayfield solve the mystery behind her husband's disappearance. The film adaptation of *Good Sam* premiered on Netflix in May 2019.

When she's not writing, Meserve is a film and television producer and a partner in Wind Dancer Films. She lives in Los Angeles with her husband and three children—and two very good cats that rule them all. For more on the author and her work, visit www.detemeserve.com, or connect with her on Twitter @DeteMeserve and on Facebook at Facebook.com/GoodSamBook.